Copyright © 2020 by Sola Odemuyiwa

First paperback edition April 2020

ISBN 9798623842565

www.solaodemuyiwa.com

Cover design by Genentech

Wale, I miss you.

One

It was danger week, and Ade hoped to tuck his balls safe in bed long before his wife got home. He glanced at his fake Rolex. Nine seconds to ten minutes past eight. Half an hour to spare but Lagos *go-slow* in his way.

The mega-city roiled in its daily ferment - as if struck by a natural disaster, and another imminent. Horns blared. Tempers rose and fenders fell. Stray cats and dogs and harried chickens, eager street hawkers, sharp hustlers, Aladuras in white cassocks and the ragged queues for take-aways spilled on to the road. Just as the passing seconds gnawed through the last few fibres of Ade's taut nerves a woman hopped on to the moped beside him, and as if to a conductor's baton, the tempo changed. Tepid air from the hoary air conditioner tickled Ade's greasy face as Rashidi hunched over the steering wheel to shoot the car forward, feet tapping from pedal to pedal in defence of the lane against a white van. Keep going please do not stop, have a home to get to before madam or she will not take no for a response. Should he have worn three not two underpants to piss off the balls? Sweat cools them you mumu. Is that not why Allah made them dangle outside? Google it, under sperm or underwear or spermal underwear? The car gathered speed, to ambling pace. Ade puffed his cheeks and sat back in anguished hope, but seconds later, the brake lights flickered on the bus in front and he smacked his knee in frustration as his car rocked to yet another stop.

Two cars ahead, a lofty cow had strayed on to the middle of Bar Beach Road to assert its bovine privileges to stand and defecate. Ade stewed. His head, shaved again that morning, streamed with sweat. Self-important cow, bound soon for saucepans, could be the end of him. A motorcyclist wearing a red plastic potty instead of a proper helmet weaved through the traffic to prod the cow with a sandaled foot. The cow shook its head, swung its tail into the night sky and manured. Then from the dark roadside came the promise of relief. A blessed herdsman

1

swaggered with arrogant and belligerent perplexity into the headlights. The motorcyclist withdrew. Ade pictured the languid salutations between cow and man. 'Been waiting long, how are you, Moo, darling? Sorry, I couldn't find any toilet grass, shortage from panic buying,' said shepherd. 'Never mind. I'm ultra-orthodox cowslam, we don't wipe our shitholes with grass. And it will soon rain.' The cow swung its bulging eyes at Ade. 'Haba, look at your southern friends fuming and cursing as if they are the only ones with deaths to go to?' it said. 'That is why I carry this rifle. Licensed to help them along. Let's go,' said shepherd and tapped the cow on the neck. Chewing this stimulant or the other, the herdsman, rifle slung over shoulder, sauntered across the striped green and white central reservation with his bovine accomplice to block the traffic going the other way.

'Oga Julius, this Lagos go slow is something oh,' said Rashidi, shaking his head into the rear-view mirror. He asked if this happened in Harare. Ade sucked back an angry retort because he was sure he told Rashidi he came from Bulawayo. 'Roof right over our heads,' sang Rashidi along to the car radio and tapping the steering wheel. 'Roof rack over our heads,' said Ade.

'Oga Julius, you are too funny, but that is not the right way to sing it,' said Rashidi. Ade's hearing had not been the same since those corrective taps from Madam Superbad's stilettoes. He was going to pretend to pull rank and insist on his version of the song when a siren went off behind them. For minutes not one car or push-bike dared move, but the throngs still surged from shops, bars and offices, to fight for the bulging buses and the narrow streets filled with the same sweaty, sooty, willing people that they had to turn round before daybreak. Lagos State centre of excellence read the licence plate in front. Excellence in wahala more like.

The car's struggling air conditioner sputtered and died. Ade groaned, opened the window and fanned his face with a brittle official envelope. The open ditches croaked with toads and youthful women hurrying past brushed against his elbow. Their firm bodies, the whiff of their coconut oil aroma and the strenuous quivering and rotation of their buttocks as they faded into the night crowds brought a tingle to his penis. No, not now, no, wait until you get home you bastard thing. I will sack you if you do not take your time. Ade clamped his thunderous thighs together and tried to burst his swelling desire by thinking of his last shift at Kakirikiri Maximum Security prison where yet another inmate died of dysentery that morning. But summoning those horrors failed, and with the traffic sizzling on the same spot, the pleasant vibrations in his pelvis rose to a credible threat to his mental health. Haba, this body part you just could not reason with. Ade checked his watch. Nine oh five and twelve seconds. He was late. Drumming the driver's seat he said, 'Rashidi, find place to park and wait. I want to check something. Your phone get credit?' Ade did not wait for a reply. Pushing his glasses back up his nose, he clambered over the massive boulders and marched to the dip in the beach where a dozen women sat roasting plantains. Beyond them his favourite raffia booths swayed and creaked in the wind.

A woman in a red top called out, Marcus, Marcus, and smacked her lips, but a man whispered in her ear and they lolled downhill. Ade's eyes narrowed in envy. He marched past the grasping hands, the sibilant hisses, clicks and clucks until he reached Cordelia. She was wearing silvery glasses and a yellow, off the left shoulder, crop top, and Ade his official khaki uniform.

'What have you got for me?' he said in the strong Southern African accent he reserved for this place.

'Your money will find your level,' said Cordelia, with peeving nonchalance, but when Ade wafted the scruffy five-dollar bill he won at Ayo under her nose she

3

whipped off her glasses. 'Very sorry, Marcus. I didn't see you well.'

Five dollars in his pocket and he got to swap his sheepdog life for the exhilaration of command. 'If you don't take time I will bring my boys to clear this place.' For emphasis, he puffed his chest and pointed in the direction of Kakirikiri prison.

'Please, no vex Marcus.' She slipped a phone out of her blouse, made a quick call and turned to Ade. 'You will trek small but dem be fresh girls, college girls,' she said after a drag on her cigarette.

Ade found three hostesses sitting on a bench, backs to the sea, huge waves from the Atlantic Ocean racing up to die, foaming, at their feet. Attracted by the artless way she held her cigarette, flipped her head away from its tendrils of smoke, Ade tapped the middle one's shoulder. She swung around, her pupils widened, whether from fear, hope, resignation or duty, Ade did not care, because, without a word, she handed her cigarette to the girl on her right and led him back uphill. The imagined sway of her hips under her gown, the heavy panting from the punters through the raffia walls pumped Ade near bursting point - so horny was he now that he could fuck a rotten pear. 'What do you call yourself?' he said. He snatched the snagged plastic blind out of her clumsy fingers and yanked it over a bamboo rail.

'My name? Cordelia,' she said.

Cordelia. Ophelia, Cleopatra etcetera, they rhyme with liar or Shakespeare. How for do. Had he, Lagos boy, not had a few names himself?

Cordelia clasped her hands together. 'Oga, help me? If only five hundred naira make I take chop my sister dey for house,' she said. Anything he could afford.

Ade groaned and tried to steel himself against stabs of empathy. He'd come for someone to pour his balls out to not his wretched soul. 'I give you bonus, two thousand? Yes? And next time I will ask for you.'

Business took place under the stars, on crates, she in the busby wig lapping at her eyes, he in shoes with his glasses strapped on and his fluorescent dial glowing through his sleeve. When Ade tugged his belt off, a hostess raised the alarm. 'Quick run oh, police dey come.' Ade's girl jack-knifed him on to the sand. 'Go, go. Didn't you hear? Run, go before you cause me big trouble,' said the young Cordelia, her eyes on stalks of fear.

'What's the problem?' Ade tugged his trousers up and grabbed Cordelia by the wrist for a refund. Ade meant the cash for Controller until the temptation stuck its nose in.

Cordelia jerked her wrist out of Ade's grip. 'I don quench oh, dem don seen us, oh,' she said but slipped as she took to her heels. Two police officers waddled downhill towards them, handcuffs and huge keys dangling from their belts. Ade ducked under the torch beams, leapt over a rusting dustbin and sprinted across the rocky beach. Keep on, keeping on, round that log, jump that bag, that box and scooter. Where did Rashidi park the car? Panic whipped Ade on, lactate tore at his calves. The pitch of the wind's hum told him that he was not far off his old hurdling speed. He galloped in a wide arc around the raffia booths and doubled back to find Rashidi smoking a cigarette. 'Where were you?' said

Ade, in confected rage as he tried to suppress his panting breaths. He felt guilty for leaving Cordelia in the lurch but consoled himself by promising to make it up to her if the Roadsweepers brought her to Kakirikiri. He must get a brain transplant one of these days. This factory issue model he got from mum and dad made him leap from one mess to the next like a scavenging marsupial.

**

Lekki Peninsula lies to the south-east of Lagos State, its multibillion naira mansions built on reclaimed land. Ade and Yeni's gated estate boasted more SUVs per head than anywhere in the world, except Surrey? You saw no stray cattle, dogs, goats, toads or poor people here, and so quiet was it at night that you could hear your neighbour's tinnitus. Nor did the estate lack its share of swimming pools, manicured tennis courts, and eccentric neighbours. Rumour had it that Chief Moyo, the rotund retail tycoon, had a boy just to clean his collection of slippers and make sure they sat facing Mecca, as did his fleet of sports cars. Reports that another boy tasted the man's urine for sugar, diabetes, and salt for hypertension, most attributed to Lagosian hyperbole.

Stiffening from his exertions, Ade hobbled from the car under a sky smeared by worn-out clouds. Like Ade, the moon seemed to have ingested a gigantic bag of worms. He trudged up the drive. Through the mist, five forbidding first-floor windows frowned at him on either side of the glazed pediment from which red electric bulbs spelled M for Martins. Ade turned the key in the front door with the graveness of a mauled zookeeper. Other than the oak grandfather clock's reproachful clucking on the landing, a timorous ambiance greeted him in the high-vaulted marble hall. A glossy frieze of the history of the Martins family and other heirlooms, bronze busts, an oak secretariat, glittering in the brilliant glow of a tiered chandelier, lined the left wall. From his family nothing, and he might as well be invisible, but for the jewels dangling between his legs and by which she, they, had him.

Twelve-year-old Zaki, the youngest of the houseboys, skipped up the hall, past the ornate corkscrew staircase on the right, his vest straps dangling over his left shoulder and his eyes wagging for approval.

'Welcome. Your pyjamas is upstairs, sir, and I wramp your moinmoin in dat your leaf you like, sir.'

Ade smiled. 'Who cooked?' He hoped it was not his wife. Yeni's anaemic and watery moinmoin ran off the plate. Not to put too fine a point on it, Yeni did not cook - she assembled food. Every dish except boiled egg, tasted and sounded, as it landed on the plate, the mess it looked. Banned from the kitchen, when Ade complimented a cook for her egusi stew Yeni sacked the woman at once.

'Madam gone upstairs,' said Zaki, miming sleep with his hands.

Ade stretched out a hand to ruffle the orphan's thick hair but Zaki pulled back. A wheal the size of a slug peeped from the side of the boy's neck. 'Who?' Ade said, fuming, but he knew the answer to his question. 'You don chop?'

The boy hesitated for a beat and slung up his baggy shorts. It was obvious from the boy's dry lips and hungry eyes that Zaki had not had supper, punishment from Yeni for some grave error - a table fork out of position, perhaps. Ade winced. He'd been there himself as a little boy with Madam Superbad. Simmering with empathetic anger, he led Zaki through the pantry to a cupboard in a dark recess. 'Take,' he said, pressing a tin of evaporated milk, a packet of cashew nuts, and a small loaf of bread into the boy's hands. 'Go, quick, quick before madam hear,' he said, hustling the little boy out of the back door then he stripped his boots off his damp feet and crept up the marble staircase, a burglar on eggshells, taking the steps three at a time.

The bedroom door roared over the thick-pile rug. Ade leaned it back closed inch by inch. Was she snoring or was that a fan? Don't let her wake. How had he come to this? How to get out of this? He snuck past the foot of their king-sized bed, slid into the pyjamas and under the sheets with his socks on so that his feet did not wake her. Nothing happened. To chugging in his heart he straightened his right leg a degree at a time, but when he thought his foot reached safety 'where were you?' she said. Yeni reached under the sheets, probing through the long gap in the front of the silk pyjamas she'd bought him especially for this singular item on her agenda and pulled him by the one member he hoped would abstain. 'Zaki's neck is bleeding. What happened?' Ade said, in the desperate hope of provoking a sperm-saving row. He grabbed his phone. Nothing. No messages. No texts. That snuff addict Kunle had forgotten to call. While he squirmed and turned Yeni's busy fingers had cajoled his member into nodding its head, desperate to cast its vote, always the same way. She squealed with delightful intent, dragged the covers back over and rolled on top of him. 'We are in our tent, Julius.' She giggled. 'I, Cleopatra come to bury Caesar and will be internally happy if you give me belle.' She spoke dirty market woman demotic, tossing in the classical reference to Caesar to please him.

'It's not your big fried plantain today, only tired banana,' he said and tried to push her away. But his nostrils flared to the smell of her sweat and wetness and his treacherous member nodded harder and was not going to take no for an answer, not twice in one night. Needing without admitting it the consolation this passionate chief's daughter gave him, Ade let himself go, sinking and swimming, fucking blind again. After, he stared at the ceiling in the dark, wet in his eye, berating himself once again. Lagos boy, the pet dog, go, come, bark, sit, stand, salute, take this name, change your face, cover your eyes, shut up, don't bark, stand in the corner, fuck off, fuck up. This briefest of fusions can produce an explosive nuclear family, Allah, please send the sperms up the wrong tube, blunt and wrinkle them, ambush them in some cul-de-sac, kill them with woman acid. Did sperms last long in a double under-pants strategy? Heaven forbid he had long-lasting sperms, like those energy-saving light bulbs they sell at the Palms Shopping Mall. Oh, how he wished that men had only one sperm each month. But such creatures probably went extinct millions of years ago.

Two

It was a muggy Saturday night and Ade would rather have his teeth flossed by a rabid wolf than Chief's "small together." He hated the humblebragging and backslapping. Having to hold his tongue because they thought him a foreigner, in a city to which he had at least as strong a claim as anyone, gave his brain a hernia.

Peering between two giant waiters for Ranti, his ex and the famous star of the TV show, "Punchline and Juicy," Ade squeezed his hand up to scratch his nose, but stopped to rub his shaved head instead. That nose, his mother's, used to dominate his face like a giant wedding album on a tiny coffee table, but not after plastic surgery in Cape Town. They say the trick to public camouflage is not to stand out, and he'd learned to resist his urge to knead his nose or thrust his chest at doors, as was his wont in his days as a champion hurdler.

He'd dreamt again of Ranti sitting at dinner with a baby between them. How he yearned to see her in the flesh for the first time in months, instead of gawking at her on the internet. Pretending an urgent need he pushed through the throng in search of Ranti, telling himself not to overwhelm her. Ranti hated surprises. If she had her way no mosquito should bite her without an export licence for the red cells. She sounded as if she was single. Crackling brilliant. Who cared what happened to that Bambo man? The crew member beside a water dispenser shrugged and pointed in the vague direction of the glass veranda. 'Madam Shogun, go small, soon return,' he said and went back to chomping on the turkey leg. They called her Shogun, after her motto that the "show must go on." Where was she? Shit of no nation, finding her was proving more difficult than washing your ears with your elbows.

He ducked under a huge photo of Chief and Princess A, the cover version of Chic's "Freak Out" faded and Yeni strutted on stage to an appreciative hum, her hair braided into intricate whorls that met in a tall midline ridge with thick extensions. She was wearing an electric blue ankle-length skirt. A sleeveless black silk blouse showed her well-toned shoulders. Statuesque, she had the classic oval Martins head and bronze-red skin, and eyes which looked up to no one. From her father she inherited her height, six feet if an inch, as tall as her younger brother, Bola, and two inches taller than her thick-set husband, Ade. Jaws dropped, but none wider than that of the rampant Dr Opa the gynaecologist, Lickpockets, in his trademark shiny suit, green for fertility. Wives, girlfriends and concubines clenched fists behind tense buttocks, ground their teeth or frowned at their rubbernecking husbands. It could have been worse. Fucking blind after his accident, he could have ended up with a penurious gargoyle. Ade's neck tightened to Yeni's proprietorial wag of finger at him, and, sneaking another look round the hall for Ranti, he gathered his maroon agbada in his hands in front of him and stepped back into the crowd with a platinum smile dragged to face.

'Where is your watch?' Yeni said, pointing at Ade's wrist. Ade lifted his sleeve to show her the fake designer watch. He'd pawned the other to a Frenchman at the Club. She clucked, signalling grudging content, with the admonitory cast of the face that was never far behind her default pout. She reminded him of a prison warder.

"The "Percussive Mosquitoes" broke into one of Yeni's favourites "fingers are not equal but the hand likes it like that." Ade glimpsed a Nefertiti haircut to his left. It was Ranti, but Yeni saw her and jerked ramrod straight. 'Hunh. Julius, you think you are clever?' she said, her tone waspish. 'Don't insult my intellectuals, oh. You are more stupid than toilet paper. You like the way she walks like a duck?' Ranti was born with dislocations of the hips and hid her residual limp under a swagger. 'I know why you are shaking like egg inside frying pan. If you and cunts 'r' us are messing behind my back, hunh, you know what will happen.'

Ade prodded Yeni on to the balcony and shooed away an eavesdropping steward. 'Yeni you are jealous of even the keyboard on my laptop. If you don't cool it you will end up in the emergency room one of these days.' He tried to lower his angry voice and keep his accent foreign. 'I'll meet you later,' he said to another glimpse of Ranti but as he set off in pursuit, the wide body of Dr Opa blocked his way.

Squat and barrel-chested, the doctor had a lumpy head suggestive of a Buddha, with dark close-cropped hair and thick grey sideboards. The doctor rubbed his hands together. His eyes laughed to Yeni, dimmed at Ade. 'Mr Julius. How is life in Kakirikiri, sorry, *at* Kakirikiri?'

Dr Lickpockets thinks he is funny. Ade's hand went up to knead his nose, but he stopped and scratched his chin. 'I told you that I am mainly based at KIYO, the youth offenders' centre.'

Yeni nudged Ade in pointed rebuke. 'Don't mind him doctor. Julius is too modest. He is a security consultant. Recommended by Chief,' she said.

'But for sake of clarity are you not a prison warder all under the same directorate?' said the doctor, putting a stress on Ade's actual title.

Ade's toes flexed at the put-down. 'We also have a few doctors in service.' He could not resist adding, 'some as inmates.'

Dr Opa turned to Yeni. 'What some of those officers know about prison welfare can fit inside the eye of a needle,' he said with an expansive mien. 'Why did they send only pretty waterfalls, Bach and Beethoven on the Voyager probe to represent life on this planet when they could have sent pictures of our constipated prisons and garrulous city? Don't they know that if they attract ET it is Africans they will take first? Plus our mineral wealth? Madam I hope you don't mind me asking? Mr Julius, which Afediyabamba are you? You resemble one I know but maybe not so fair in the face.'

'It is a rare and ancient Zimbabwe name. Sailors and traders came and stayed here and I result from these accidents of trade and history,' said Ade, affecting a wistful air.

The doctor beamed at Yeni. 'Ah, such is love, such is love.'

Ade ground his teeth. Wrong diagnosis sir, not even close. Dr Lickpockets, haven't you licked enough? Weeks earlier the doctor confirmed that after treatment in Italy Yeni should have as large a family as she wanted. On the morning before she got the results, in her haste or anxiety, Yeni had painted her nails in unique colours: equivalent to Queen Elizabeth II turning up in Parliament with frizzy black hair extensions from Lewisham hanging from her Koh-i-Noor. Ranti left the clinic ecstatic, Ade's feelings mixed. He was happy for her but dreaded a child with her; and should their offspring inherit its dad's wide nose, any half decent police officer aware of the case of the fugitive Flying Paintbrush would soon come knocking on the massive Lekki door, Chief or no Chief. Why can't Dr Opa and his Italian friend keep their hands off a man's fucking conditions? A vasectomy was out. Someone might recognise identify him by his wizened foot and there was the fear of permanent sterility. What then to tell Ranti?

'Fantastico, my Paulo always does a grand job. Madam you must take Mr Julius to Milan one day. Milan in May, take him one day, get my lyrics, say? Better than that rap stuff - nursery rhymes.' The doctor grinned. 'Forget any talk of surrogates. The words should not even have reached my teeth. 'One day you too will have a bouncing baby. No, not one, but two. What do they call two babies in a cot? Dicotyledon,' said the doctor and laughed with calibrated servility. 'But madam you need to be patient. Not five minutes since you returned from overseas.'

14

'Doctor, you can take your time with patience. I don't have time for her.' Yeni dismissed the doctor with an abrupt silence. As he backed away and Ade prepared to escape, Yeni's demeanour softened. 'Good evening, sir,' she said, over Ade's shoulder. Ade turned and his mood sank to the occasion.

***

Ade's boss, Comptroller Sheki Gbagba, otherwise known as Controller, ran Kakirikiri Maximum Security Prison and the adjoining KIYO young offenders' unit where Ade worked. A man as devious as the alimentary canal, he led the Roadsweepers, the team that interrupted Ade and Cordelia on Bar Beach. Formed to arrest vagrants during one obscure state visit, their remit now oozed much wider and, according to Moji at work, deeper into the underworld. Spindly, with skin the colour of terracotta, cruel, pig-tiny eyes and a hairline that reached his bulging eyebrows, Controller had a first-class degree in the theology of the pursuit of money, the organised religion known as Economics. 'That is a fake. Is it Bulgari?' he said, lifting Ade's wrist. 'No, don't answer, Rolex. Fake for sure. Dissociation between a label and the internal workings,' he said and chuckle-cleared his throat.

Ade shrank back, fished around in the folds of his garments for an antacid but found none.

'I have a simple request,' said Controller, leading Ade to a dark corner in a recess between the limbs of the M-shaped (for Martins), mansion. Below the Georgian glass veranda a stream twinkled in the floodlights on its way to the Atlantic. Controller's voice was a rasping insinuating whisper, rumoured to result from Diphtheria.

15

Only he, out of hundreds, survived, an account that added to the myth of his indestructibility. He leaned over the veranda wall with his white lace *agbada* bunched, reminiscent of a slimy comb.

'Is it to do with work?' said Ade, tremulous with foreboding.

Controller lit a cigarette. 'After everything I have done that sleepy saturated fatty bastard DIG Kafu and the others want to destroy me. Yet when they caught that noisy Alhaji yen-handed he showed not an iota of remorse. In his village they danced in the streets because he built them a borehole. The thing was dry, and since been landfilled with his cast-offs. But they chase me from pillar to post, from Lagos to Abuja and back because I fight for Lagos people. Now they want to retire me.'

'I am only a foreigner sir, know nothing,' said Ade, having to repeat what he said over the clang of pots and pans in the kitchen.

'You don't have to pretend with me,' he said in his faux conspiratorial tone. 'I backed the villagers in their land case against the Martins. I am a great-great-grandson of the White Cap Chiefs that ran this place before British and Akitoye came with their boats and ammunition. But sadly the villagers lost the case, and I lost my emotional investment. And as a matter of fact who do you think has been floating Vv and the other officers to keep the service going and Lagos people safe? My very self, using the careful and innovative husbandry of our meagre resources supplemented by donations from people like you. Do I not deserve something for my efforts? Should a man die and leave his children drowning in poverty because he made patriotic mistakes?'

'I heard of Iya's case,' said Ade. Poor Iya. Another lost court case. Devastated no doubt. Ade sent her a message the other day to tell her he was alright. He stifled a nervous yawn. 'Eeh, you are too young for that negative talk, leaving your children and so on, sir.'

Controller's smile rode up his left cheek. 'May your river of flattery never run dry.' He dragged on his cigarette. 'You know Dangote?'

'Not personally.' Where was this going?

'Dangote is our homemade oligarch. Born of a woman. Same age as me. Fingers in everything, from biro to cement to generators to bags of rice. Transport of course.'

'The rich are our warders in this prison we call life,' said Ade.

'That is a good one. And no escaping them except through death or madness. But in all seriousness, what do I have to show for my hard endeavour but scratchings from the wilful and unfortunate, ernh?' Cigarette smoke billowed from his mouth. 'So I said to myself Sheki, this job of yours, a job that you could only dream of when you were a naked little boy running around Isale Eko, is a ladder for your children to climb. He dragged on his cigarette. 'As you know your Zaria show, re the Olabo girl, signatures are in that file in my office.'

'But sir, you know that I am innocent.'

'And is it not a shame that the records speak clearer than your words?' Controller took a last drag and tossed the cigarette away. 'Next month, July, you get an upgrade. I need from you ten thousand dollars cash in hand and I tell you now that before I retire, I will give

17

you your files. Then you can keep your lifestyle, cars, Lekki mansion, low profile and watches, and your top of the range suspension bridge wife. Why should I leave the fruits of all my endeavour to some placeholder successor, ernh?'

Was this happening? If, as Dr Opa joked, ET did land here in error, Controller, the hypocrite who dresses pure greed as a public duty would trade in slaves. 'Sir, but that is way above me, as you know they have not paid us for months and that's way beyond what I have or can find in this time.'

'Borrow from your pretty wife. Nothing wrong with that, considering what they owe you.' Controller screwed his nose up, as though put out by foul breath. 'They will soon call us in to eat, but if it is any help let me reframe my proposition in a positive light. Are there many serious problems in life that you can solve with only a few thousand dollars? So go beg, borrow, steal or print it.'

***

The bell rang and everyone, including a smattering of chirruping and grandstanding Indians, Pakistanis, English, French, Lebanese, in well-cut *agbadas* fanned out to search for their seats, tripping over each other, as the police did during a well-funded witch-hunt. Scented air-conditioned opulence greeted them in the hall. When the enormous crimson curtains behind the band opened to show Chief and Princess A thrones decked in peacock feathers, the wild cheers must have warped the earth's orbit. Yeni jabbed Ade in the ribs and he tapped his fingertips together, like a man at a detested rival's wedding.

18

A nosey woman sat next to Ade at dinner. Did he know a man called Nkolo on Mugabe Avenue? Did his father fight against Rhodesia? Do they have television? What of the internet? Would he be going back? Yoruba, English or Zimbabwean names for the children? Ade could not tell if she was serious or just winding him up because her breezy air alternating with earnest inquiry amused the other guests. That his *agbada* sleeves kept rolling down his arm, once, to Bola's glee, dipping into his side-dish, did not help his mood. He's very quiet said the woman when she tired of his curt and anodyne replies. Maybe he is listening to the hairs growing on his cap said a friend of hers, hinting at a foreigner's unfamiliarity with such finery. Ade sweltered under an agbada that had the manoeuvrability of a sheet of tiles. Oh, the irony, Lagos boy. You owe a police officer a bribe for a crime you did not commit and you wanted fame but live disguised in public exile.

The feast ended. 'I have an announcement,' Bola said. The hand-sewn jewels on his *agbada* sparkled and he skipped on to the stage as even the most ungainly politicians did for the cameras.

Ade craned his neck. Was Ranti avoiding him? Lagos boy, engage your higher faculties for a change, how can she avoid a man she does not know is present? Yeni nudged him, a glow of childlike anticipation in her eyes. This must be the grand announcement she talked about all week, as often as the torment of her empty womb. One thing for sure, according to Ade's law of relativity, good for Yeni meant worse for him. QED.

A Law student at Oxford, until sent down for trying to flog a fake Hawkeye line judge software to a betting syndicate, Bola, had his mother's long neck, but a mild

19

stoop and tiny folds under his eyes. His small chin and dimpled nose gave him the look of a giant foetus. 'See what Chief bought from China,' said Bola, in his deep and incongruous baritone, with an extravagant gesture at the glittering waist-high porcelain vases lining the walls. The ear-splitting cheers that followed might be mistaken for those greeting the eradication of Malaria, Cancer and TB. 'Ladies and gentlemen, I present to you, Chief and Chief Mrs Martins,' said Bola. An eager hush fell as waiters swivelled around and snapped to attention. A heartbeat later Chief Martins, and his wife, her orange skin, *soyoyo* they used to call that shade, sauntered in through a side door. Dressed in the same scalloped pattern of chatoyant gold lace as his son, Chief, in his early 70s, lean of limb, light of tread, face unlined, only a fleck of grey over one temple, could have passed for a man twenty years younger. As decorum or tradition or vanity demanded, he ambled a couple of funereal paces behind his wife, allowing his head vague sways of acknowledgment on his ringed neck, from which a gold pendant hung to his waist by a blue satin band. The Percussive Mosquitoes, in red stood to attention, guitars, saxophones, by their sides. The tall drummer looked forlorn because he did not know what to do with drumsticks that did not reach the floor. Chief sat on the throne next to his queen and Niari, the diminutive queen of folk and praise songs, danced up to the podium. Ade shoved a waiter aside to see her. Was this the same Niari, the daughter of Iya's friend who was going to record his Oriki, praise song?

As Niari whooped into the second verse of a paean she composed for the Martins family, Bola cut her short, "sprayed" her forehead with a dozen ten dollar notes and bustled her off the stage.

Hey, that's rude, but how for do, Martins get away with everything.

Chief cleared his throat. 'As you know, my daughter Yeni Martins is an international trader of world-wide repute,' he said in that deep voice unique to plutocrats. Yeni winked at Ade and nudged him to pay attention. Was this the grand announcement? He hoped for a damp squib. Then she might sulk and ignore him for a day or two during danger week. Unlikely, but so was the Crazy Gang's defeat of mighty Liverpool in the FA Cup in 1988.

'Yemartins group of companies won the WABOTY award. West African businesswoman of the year 2013/2014,' said Chief. He cleared his august throat again. 'For excellent customer service and relations and philanthropism. Reliability, prompt settlement, integrity. You have no light? Anything from bicycle dynamo to hydroelectric dams, she is the woman for you. Our brightest beacon to the spirit of free enterprise.'

Ade grimaced. If you can stand the stench, you can apply free enterprise anywhere, hoard spades during an earthquake, make fake drugs, or jack up the price of hand wash during a pandemic, poison locals with your blind punt for-profit, gaslight the quick and quickly bury the dead. Eyes turned to Yeni. Ade wedged his glasses back up and tried to look the awe-struck foreign consort. Chief smiled at his daughter. 'It was her thirtieth birthday last week, but it has not yet pleased his Almighty to bless her, and for you God's blessing too, oh.' Loud amens rang out. 'Julius, up to you,' said Chief.

The crowd tittered. Ade grinned but his toes curled up inside the tight boots. Who gave Chief the right to poke his nose into their bedroom? The man even chose the names of their unborn, Mowe, short for Eniaoleomoweju (you cannot be too learned) or Gaju, for Wakoletogaju (you will build the tallest skyscrapers). These people think everything is for sale. Well, *e pele*, this one that Yeni found is from Zimbabwe, not what we had in mind but for the luck that has left her on the shelf again, thirty, her eggs like overripe mangoes splattering to ground and wasting, the least and best we can do is get her young fool to squirt and obey, squirt and obey for no other way for him but to reproduce for his betters and squirt and obey. Ade wished he could tell everyone that behind the thick glasses and bleached skin, a dark man called Ade Bioseyi was dying to get out, that he kept a closer watch on his wife's follicular cycles than the balding Berlusconi of Italy did on his. That he onanised his potential progeny in the prison toilets or popped round on occasion to dispose of them or, in financial terminology, invest them in Bar Beach. That if he found the ten thousand dollars and retrieved his false statement from Controller they'd not see him for scorched earth. The titters to Chief's punchline faded into an excited buzz. Bola kneeled before Chief.

Chief tapped the microphone. 'As you know Yeni is my first daughter but as I said she has other matters on her plate at this crucial time. My first son here before me, Bola, is a patriot. He is a warrior in the courts.' Bola won an injunction against a company for encroaching on farming land, a popular victory in Lagos because the same organisation, claiming links with Apple and through a complicit headman, passed blackened mirrors off to gullible villagers as the latest I-pads. 'As you know by the grace of God, he will win another and ultimate victory in the High Court in the land case of all land cases. Today I am putting him forward as our PDP senatorial candidate for Lagos State.'

Yeni dug her nails into Ade's wrist. 'Hun. Why can I not be senator ernh? Is it because I am a woman? Is that what he is saying? So because I do not have a child they cannot respect me?'

Yeni, playing the injured innocent? A woman who thought hunger an idea dreamt up by anarchists and troublemakers? Yet, Ade felt a tiny twinge of sympathy for her because it must have been such a shock for Yeni not to get her way and because he'd been there too, as a boy, passed over and ignored, his mind flooded with sharp words, putdowns and insults. 'Maybe Chief decided to give it to Bola because of your condition.'

Yeni smacked her lips. 'Which condition? Balloon with no air condition? You wait and see. Bola will drive the villagers from the land and use the money to buy votes for his campaign.'

Ade, steeped in guilt for dropping out of Law School, recoiled in horror at Iya's plight. Yet he did not dare show his face in her village until he got those files from Controller.

Ade and Yeni left soon after the speeches. His ears ringing from the loud music and disappointed for not seeing Ranti, Ade started the engine and joined one of the ragged queues of cars chugging out of the dark on to the floodlit drive. Ahead, roadside stood a long white van. On its side the words "The Extra Mile Television Company" stood in bold blue letters a foot high. The "Mile" swung open and when Ranti appeared at the top of the stairs Ade's belly turned a somersault. Shaking, he fumbled for the gearstick, put the car in reverse by accident first then eased it nearer the silver cabriolet in front and tried to keep Ranti in view.

Yeni jerked ramrod straight, the scratchy clinks of her clasp setting Ade's ears on edge. But she ignored his hostile look and set off again, singeing him with her satanic flamethrower of a mouth. Yakkity, ngbati, yakkity, sebi this sebi that, yakkity, yakkata, on she went, the provenance of the tears that arrowed to her cheeks impossible to define because she turned them on and off at the drop of an eyelash. 'If I catch you with cunts 'r' us I will show you bitter pepper, do you hear, bitter pepper.' Seething, Ade gripped the steering, his left foot digging harder and harder into the floor of the car. How did he end up with a woman who'd pick a quarrel with her dying breath if it went on too long, whose mouth petrified toothpaste, who beat the house-help to within inches of their lives, locked the kitchen and pantry to spite his visitors, cursed neighbours' children till they cried and poisoned the farmer's sheep with weed-killer for a perceived slight? In Cape Town, he'd made excuses for her volcanic temper tantrums - the poor thing was missing Lagos, her friends, Chief and the rest of her family, but she crossed the line when, because the girl did not curtsey fast and low enough, she accused the hotel cleaner of taking the complimentary box of chocolate. 'If we are not careful, these people will spoil South Africa for us,' said Yeni. Cape Town's yours as well? He still whinnied with shame for not standing up for the chambermaid.

As he reached the primary gates, he stole another desperate look into the mirror for a sight of Ranti, but the

24

rain flowed down the rear window as thick as molten steel.

Days after the party, Bola and his army of lawyers defeated the Oremi villagers in the "land case to end all land cases." The result was never in doubt claimed Bola. Never one to pass on a chance to show off and rub noses in it, he let Ade come along on a "weeding expedition." Beg, borrow, steal or print the police thief said. With the right flattery Bola might help get the escape fund started with a loan. Not the whole ten thousand dollars - the man was no fool, neither was Yeni - but a modest sum, then scrape the rest, stealth funding without a crowd, and get out of this tenacious mess.

Three

He needed the loan but Ade's priority that Sunday morning was to protect Iya from Bola's thugs. The car's air conditioner howled in its battle with the mind-boggling heat of a July afternoon - the gauge read 38 degrees. Bola's driver, dressed in fatigues, ran out from behind a tree and round the topless men lazing in the shade. 'I go piss sir, sorry, sir,' he said, clambering back into the brand new red SUV Bola bought to celebrate his recent victory. 'This man is flipping incontinent,' said Bola, turning to Ade beside him.

They set off under the fuzzy glare of an ovoid sun, the throngs in bright headscarves, hymn books tucked under their arms, swayed to silent rhythms roadside. Bola gestured through the tinted window. 'Doesn't the sun shine brighter on Sundays? Is it so God can see them bear witness? Think how much better off we'd be without two days off each week. I cannot wait for elections next year. Proper reforms to this economy are sorely overdue to get these lazy godstabbers off their knees.'

'Money can never do enough for you, that is why you never have enough of it,' said Ade.

'Vladimir Julius Lenin, is it not the lack of the very lucre that you so despise that toddles you after me? You remind me of nappy rash,' he said and to Ade's bum-squeezing alarm, they took the second exit and set off in the direction of Iya's village, Oremi.

'Did that carpenter back in Gorimo village deserve to lose his front teeth?' said Ade.

Bola turned the pink pages of the Financial Times. 'You mean that nonentity? He was lucky he only lost two. Gave them back, didn't we? But that's what you get for hiding. I know just what you are going to say but don't tell me that it was out of fear. Everyone hides something and as a proportion of their lives these village people harbour more secrets than normal people,' Bola said with a grin. 'But you can talk, if it was your family land, and your great grandparents broke their back for it, shed blood and tears and blistered their hands for it, you'd just give it away?' He raised his newspaper again.

'That you won the case does not make it right,' said Ade. 'Why not let the older ones stay? They have lived there for generations.' He wished he'd been there in court with Iya.

'Generations of lice can live in your hair. You should accept it?' said Bola.

A bitter taste soared to Ade's mouth. Iya was no louse, and he owed Bola serious damage, starting with that leaky mouth. He sucked on his bitterness, shoved his palms under his thighs and fixed his angry gaze on a cruciate wrinkle on the back of the driver's seat.

Soon they turned off the busy outside lane of Ikorodu Road and onto a dirt track, past a stack of old car engines and stopped under a bunioned breadfruit tree. Ade smelt burning rubber.

'Great, let's go and weed,' said Bola, his sparkling eyes darting about, like a bird's. Ade dropped out of the car, disturbing the flies swarming over a dog's rotting carcass. On the left, they passed small groups of men kneeling in circles, their heads dusty, sweaty and bowed, hands tied behind them. A dozen strides further on a passel of women and children quaked, prayed and wept

27

before a ragged row of adobe huts whilst a thunderous bonfire consumed wooden stools and tables, schoolbooks, precious photographs. Plastic packets of noodles, dried nuts, cereals and crisps warped in the heat. Soot and smoke darted this way and that as if in search for more prey.

Bola clapped his hands. 'Good. Omo Bugude has prepared the ground well. All I want is respect plus my land back in my aggrieved pockets,' he said and pointed to an old woman who was wearing a striking necklace of orange and black beads. 'You. Come here.'

'You are talking to me?' She snatched her arm from the grip of a Bola thug. 'Is that how they teach you to talk to your elders?'

Bola flinched. 'Just answer me my question. I get enough attitude from this Roman Julius beside me here.'

'If you touch me none of you will wake well tomorrow.' She swung her arm. One thug ducked.

'Mama, your mumbo jumbo juju may impress and confuse these fools. Not I. Where is the headman?'

She looked over her shoulder at the other women. 'Do we know?' They shook their heads.

'Leave mama alone,' said Ade.

'Mr Bola me I don't want your trouble oh, sir,' said a youthful woman in a green top, scurrying out of a hut to kneel in the dust at Bola's feet. With an angry glance at the older woman, she turned round to point at the forest. 'He dey there. Inside bush, that tree with a blue flower.' From the group behind her came a chorus of indignant sucks of teeth.

'She has more brains than the rest of them put together,' said Bola. With Ade in anxious tow, Bola strode into the long grass at the forest edge ahead of a

28

dozen of his men. They dragged the old woman behind them. 'There,' said Bola. He pointed at a clump of thick shrubs twenty feet away. 'See that plant there, pointy leaves.' He picked up a pebble, took careful aim and let fly. 'Come out or my men will shoot.' A dog yelped and scampered out of the undergrowth followed by a balding man, his thick grey beard heavy with soil and blood. Two thugs dragged the man back in front of the crowd. 'All of you. If you don't pay arrears and leave this place by next week, something red will come out of this man's neck. Understand?' said Bola.

A thug seized the old woman and shook her. 'You hear?'

Ade jumped in front of the frail woman. 'Leave her alone. Enough is enough. Mama *pele*, I will talk to my brother Bola.'

The woman huffed, jack-knifed away from Ade, her scornful frown flinging back in his face his desperate bid to atone for his craven role in a capricious coalition.

'Hah, nearly three o'clock. Where is this driver? Let us go to the next village, not too far. I can see it from here, I think,' said Bola, scratching his long neck.

The driver appeared from behind a tree, fastening his baggy army fatigue trousers as he ran.

'What is wrong with you this man? How many times do you piss in a day?' said Bola.

'Only three time today, sir. Doctor say I should count it, sir.' He squirmed and rubbed his thigh. 'I didn't finish to piss, sir.'

'Either we go now you piss later, or you piss now and piss off.'

The driver bent over, rolling his knees, crossing and uncrossing his legs, in obvious distress.

Bola puffed his cheeks and muttered to himself. 'These plebs and their precious perineums.'

'Why don't you connect a tube to his bladder for efficiency and advertise your law firm on his urinary bag? Naked lawyer has no briefs. You can even charge the man rent. That will be sick,' said Ade.

'Don't push me Julius.' Bola turned again to the driver. 'Ok, piss quickly and get ready for Oremi now. Time is going.'

'Hey Bola,' said Ade, in desperation, shouting for the benefit of the watching thugs. 'Wait. The other villages will pay I am sure when they hear what happened here today. Why not give them a few weeks and avoid all this trouble? Think of the good publicity for your campaign instead of having to buy rice for voters.'

Bola brushed a speck of soot off his sleeve. 'Who told you that I am buying rice? Marcellus? The only reason that man's tongue is still in his head is that if you cut it out, its pieces will go on spreading lies.' Bola spluttered, cleared his throat. 'Let's go.'

Apprehension wobbled Ade's legs. He stood a better chance of finding the Crown jewels in a dog's dinner than stopping Bola going to Iya's village. 'Hey, Bola do we have enough fuel to get there and back?' He tripped over a tree root. How for do. Should he throw a Yeni fit? He scoured his mind for other ruses and diversions.

'Surely you cannot be drunk at this hour?' said Bola.

'But to Oremi and back when the direct route is blocked? And what of Aja and Henry? Are they coming with us or in their vehicle when they have not eaten?' He teetered on the edge of panic. Should he say he heard gunfire?

'Excuse, sir,' said the driver.

'Driver wait, can't you see that we are talking?' said Bola. He flipped open a shirt pocket. 'Julius, I can give you a taxi fare home. The rest of us have work to do. The matter of the cash you want to borrow we can discuss later.' Bola harrumphed and gave him a searching look. 'But if you are coming keep your mouth shut and stay on your wretched feet.'

'Excuse me, sir,' said the driver, shuffling up another inch.

Bola snarled. 'Look, don't disturb me. If piss you want to piss, go now and don't piss in my car.'

The driver stood with his knees clenched, the pain from his recalcitrant bladder raising the pitch of his voice. 'Oga Julius is a hundred percent correct, sir. Fuel no dey for de moto to reach the place and, and, and, Henry say you never pay dem, sir.' He crept back and dropped his head as though trying to shave his chest with his chin.

Bola's voice boomed over the burr of a passing trailer. 'What of the fuel we bought on Friday? Wait.' Bola ransacked the pockets of his safari suit but his hands came out empty, to Ade's relief. 'Ok, tell them we adjourn for the day,' Bola said. The driver ran into the bush.

'What of the loan?' said Ade.

Bola shook his head and turned his palms. 'My hands are willing but my pockets say fuck off.'

Four

But for his games of Ayo with Baba Lawyers, Tailor and the rest of the gang, Ade lived in disorientating and claustrophobic loneliness, yearning for his old ways and connections but terrified of exposure, desperate for legitimacy but afraid of new allegiances, and increasingly doubting his abilities and prospects. He lived like an illegal immigrant in his fatherland, but in lightened skin.

It was six minutes to six o'clock, and the streets roared with commuter traffic when Ade, head shaved, bespectacled and dressed in his usual simple blue *Buba and Sokoto,* arrived at the "Ayo University" on Old Yaba Road. He needed a loan from Baba Lawyers, but he did not know how to pay it back. As they say on the molue buses, God will provide, or God's time is the best, or God sees all. You choose the slogans most appropriate to your world views.

Baba Lawyers sat hunched astride the senior Ayo bench outside Tailor's single-storeyed house, next to the sign of "this property is not for sale" scrawled in bold black letters on the wall.

'Cufffingers, you wanted to see me?' said Baba Lawyers, juggling with the game seeds. They called Ade Cufffingers because he worked in a prison. 'I'll wait,' said Ade and sat on the bench. Above him a clothesline sagged with dripping laundry. From the mosque nearby echoed a muezzin's call, which reminded Ade that he owed arrears in prayers. To the left, behind Baba Lawyers, Haruna Ishola's Arabic inflected Apala music brayed from the TV set mounted in a cage outside the beer parlour.

Jeri, a man in a white shirt, ran up to ask Ade to thank Baba Lawyers for getting a wholesaler to settle his bill. What had taken him eighteen months of struggle, Baba Lawyers had solved in ten days. Did Baba Lawyers and his "son" Ade want a drink?

'Ah, Jeri, it was nothing,' said Baba Lawyers. Baba Lawyers, Tony Ware, a retired English officer in the Nigeria Police Force, was an immense man, round-shouldered, without a hint of the usual lobster sunburn his compatriots suffered in the tropics because he strived hard to keep out of the sun. He stood three inches taller than Ade, had unnerving greyish green eyes, a fleshy nose, and a marked overbite. The man could get a juicy mouse off in a case judged by feral cats. Before and after every problem is its solution, he said, or *Kemikals ni,* he said in his perfect Yoruba accent, pointing to his head. Life boiled down to what went on inside your bonce.

'I have a small cash flow problem,' Ade said as the game ended.

Baba Lawyers got off the game bench. 'How can a Lekki man be short of cash?' he said, tapping his cap. He had slender fingers, except the knobby right ring finger that he could bend back to his wrist, poked from hands as wide as tennis bats. He said he kept goal in Essex. Or was it Sussex?

'I did not say that I was short of cash? I said I was short of flow,' said Ade, at once regretting his sharp tone.

Baba Lawyers picked up his cap and led Ade a few yards away from the loud benches to sit at his regular table under the limp row of pennons advertising Guinness. *Think black drink black.* 'Can your brother-in-law not help?' said Baba Lawyers, wiping the sweating plastic tabletop with his elbow.

'Bola?' said Ade, with a shake of the head. 'If that man lends you a pencil he will ask for a complete library in return. You know that plot Chief gave me?'

'A welcome to my family thing,' said Baba Lawyers with that dismissive air that irked Ade on occasions.

'I can use it as my collateral. Banks will extend my facility when I reach the decking stage, which will be in two, three weeks?'

Baba Lawyers took his cap off and scratched his head. 'Cufffingers, what are you building there? Tower of Babel? Ok, say I launch my money on this rescue mission when will it re-enter my back pocket?'

Ade's hand went to his nose. 'Er, six weeks, plus or minus not long,' he said, an interval he chose as a compromise between the elasticity of his conscience and Baba Lawyers' trust and generosity.

'Six weeks enh?' Baba Lawyers stared at his cap and put it back on again. He did that when puzzled, as when in trouble during a game of Ayo or when he could not decipher a drafted document. 'Ok, how much are we talking?'

Ade scribbled on a piece of paper and handed it to Baba Lawyers. 'That is my target, but I will gratefully receive anything.' He coughed out the tension in his throat. Shaving so near outright lies took so much effort.

'Cufffingers, wow, not peanuts. I hope this cash thing is not for a woman because I can tell you for the price of raging whitlow that if it is a woman pray for luck.'

'And if a sheep pray that it is dumb,' said Ade. Someone behind him laughed.

Baba Lawyers grinned, wedged his green cap back on, and smoothed the thick inky hair on the back of his head. 'Well, since you asked nicely. Take this.' He thrust his hand deep into the pocket of his agbada and handed Ade a white envelope. 'From work I did for Mrs Alubonye,' he said, in prosody so good that when locals anglicised their names for his friend, it brought a leathery twist to Ade's guts. *Kemikals ni.*

'I will repay you on the dot, even before the b of the bang,' Ade said, reproaching himself for the careless reference to his days as a hurdler. Propriety and caution stopped him counting the money there but after the last advance from Baba Lawyer he got home to find that his friend had short-changed him by fifteen dollars. Was it the retired policeman's discrete way of earning interest? Can you claim to know anyone until money passes between you?

Baba Lawyers downed his can of beer, grimaced and belched. 'No don't get up on account of me, finish your drink. Tailor, our esteemed master of stitch-ups,

35

will look after you. I'm going to watch the match,' he said. Baba Lawyers also supported AFC Wimbledon, not the usual Premiership clubs, one reason amongst many why people said they got on. Baba Lawyers waved at the main Ayo bench, hopped over the gutter and disappeared in a dark alleyway with a minder, or another eager petitioner.

Tailor stroked Ade's shoulder. 'Cufffingers, your overseas godfather has gone oh. Now show us whether you are a man or a boy. Where have you been these past days, ernh?' He turned round to the house. 'Lati, Lati, bring light and I will show this Bulawayo man how we play this game in Lagos.' The same age as Baba Lawyers, 60, but only five and a half feet tall, dapper in shiny grey shirt and trousers, Tailor had bushy dark brown hair, flecked with grey, a short frown line halfway between his eyes so neat he could have pencilled it in himself. 'How much you will bet today? Last time you got lucky.'

'I am not sure that I want to play tonight,' said Ade, eager to get into bed before Yeni got home.

But Tailor wasn't having any of it. 'How can Cufffingers man work for Kakirikiri when he fears to play ordinary Ayo? Look at his eyes, shining brighter than this squashed beer can,' said Tailor, bouncing on the bench and juggling the pebbles into the twelve carved wooden pockets for the start of a new game. 'Come on, Lagos versus Bulawayo, man to man.'

'I have work tomorrow and have to go,' said Ade, to disapproving looks and sounds from the watching benches. On second thought Tailor was one of the worst players. Tempted by the lure of doubling his war chest, Ade opened the envelope Baba Lawyers gave him and counted out two hundred dollars. A "better pass my neighbour" generator fired up next to the beer parlour and a fluorescent bulb tied to the nearby banana tree and the TV in the cage flickered back on for a minute, then died. They decided to play by the light of mobile phones. A dozen men sat on the benches to watch.

The game started in a flurry of hands and seeds, Ade swinging each game piece, the smooth moss-green seeds the size of a pebble, anticlockwise around the board with flamboyance born of years of practice with Iya. Iya, his grandmother, taught him the game. In Ayo you aim to capture seeds in your opponent's half of the board when your turn ends in a cup containing one or two seeds. The first to gain twenty-five seeds wins. Soon, a pebble for one-nil dropped in front of Tailor. 'Lucky,' said The Tailor.

'Lucky?' said Ade. 'Did I hear right? Lucky is the name of a dog,' said Ade, turning to the spectators. 'Have you seen a dog play Ayo? Anybody see performance-enhancing bone in my head or jaw or inside my trouser leg? You want test my first and second samples under this banana tree?' said Ade, keeping the banter just on the right side of respectful, but you don't play Ayo if you can't take stick.

'I have fever,' said Tailor.

'Fever. Excuse me Tailor, sir, but you always get tailor-made excuses. Malaria, diarrhoea, yellow fever, losing fever, never winning fever? Russian radioactive fever. I hope I will not catch it oh, I beg.' He put his hand to Tailor's forehead and yanked it away in affectation of terror. 'Who sewed this shirt? Yourself? Go retake your measurements because the collar is blocking blood to your brain. Find me a fireman and shears to cut his shirt from his neck, oh ah beg,' said Ade. From the watching benches came roars of laughter. If life is not fun, poke fun at it.

Taylor lost the second game, and another pebble landed on his side of the bench. Needing only the next game to win the set and the money, Ade paused to buy a round of popcorn and peanuts for the gang. As he looked up over Tailor's shoulder, a callow thick-haired and dark-skinned student version of himself came up on the TV. Ade wedged his glasses up his nose and tried to concentrate but a familiar roar for "Punchline and Juicy" went up from the TV. To the jaunty signature tune for the popular investigative and light entertainment show, Ranti flounced in to view, in a burgundy and grey top. She had her hair in a Nefertiti hi-top and her face glowed with her self-regarding smile.

A man tapped Ade on the knee. *'Oya*, Cufffingers your turn *o jare.*' Did he come to watch TV or play Ayo? Tailor feigned a grab at Ade's glasses. 'Make I clean them for you?' Ade wrenched his eyes from the TV, his hand frozen in mid-air. 'Sorry, it's the smoke from that big lorry in my eyes.' He affected a sniffle, stared at the board, his hand hovering over one pocket then the next and back again, until, on another tap from Tailor, unable to think straight, he took a punt and moved from the fourth cup. 'I know what I'm doing,' Ade said in response to a loud gasp of rebuke from the bench.

'Welcome to Punchline and Juicy,' Ranti said, her honey face glowing under the studio lights. 'Yes it can be done, even in Lagos. We exposed the Probate department. Mister and Madam Miliki are behind bars for selling bogus letters of authority, exploiting the bereaved when they are most vulnerable. Tonight we launch an investigation.'

'Come on Cufffingers play now. Or are you waiting for manna from Bulawayo?' said Tailor.

Ade counted his *odu,* the store of twelve seeds he built up in the second pocket. He thought he had Tailor on the run but miscalculated and left his seeds exposed.

It was Tailor's turn now to take the mickey. 'You know why Putin took Crimea? Because he knows how to play Ayo. We sent people to teach Obama how to play Ayo but boastful Barack said do you know who I am? I am a lawyer who went to Harvard you know. I was editor of Law Review you know. Why do I need to hear how to play West African village games such as dominoes or Ayo? Until Putin takes Latvia, Ukrainia, Estonia, any Nia near him still Obama will not hear. And you and he are just the same. You lied to us, maybe, sef, you are not from Bulawayo but Kenya. That is why you and Barack share the same big and deaf ears and lighter skin than us. When you meet please tell him loud from us in the father continent that if only he could play Ayo he and the USA will not have a care in the world. Abi?' said Tailor.

'No care? What of Obamacare?' said a grey-bearded man in a Sunderland replica shirt. Cruel laughter cannoned from a dozen throats and Tailor rolled another pebble between Ade's thighs. Ade needed to win three consecutive games for the money. He sneaked another look at the TV.

'The case of this young woman is still open,' Ranti said. She pointed at Ade's photograph next to one of the Olabo girl. 'Any information leading us to this man, please.'

'Is that not the flying paintbrush? And I hear congratulations are in order,' chirped Punchline the TV parrot, waving its wings to get the audience to cheer. Ranti looked bashful. Ade's heart clattered around his chest. He'd tried to call Ranti to explain what happened in Zaria but she changed her phone number. Was arresting him her revenge? Did he not make her laugh? Of course he did. That glow in her voice when they spoke surely it was of love. Or had she been pretending? For five years? It was not that long ago, outside the Mega Shopping Plaza in Victoria Island, while Ranti flipped through a technical brochure, that he mused on a name of their first child. Dreadilocks? Dandilocks? Webilocks, after his or her tight curly hair, yes, Webi for short. A short and neat name they would mischievously claim they got from an exclusive island where they conceived the child. Did he hear mention of Bambo amongst the TV cheers? He flicked his mind's eye away from the image of Ranti sharing jokes or a leg sandwich with that daddy's boy. At least a second slower, except on that occasion when Ade had a fever, how the man got on the team only the selectors knew.

Someone prodded him to hurry. Ade made a defiant sound, emptied his store, *odu*, from the first pocket. Sickening ejaculations of horror, reproach, disgust, disappointment came from the terraces. 'Switch off the TV,' he said, broiling in self-reproach. He lost the next game. Stomach fizzling with his acrid self-loathing, Ade chewed on a chalky antacid. Desperate to make up his losses, he asked for an I.O.U. but Tailor declined. Why abuse this noble gift God gave him by taking the pocket money of a bushboy from Bulawayo? As if in celestial judgement or mercy an almighty gust of dusty wind smacked into their faces, ending the negotiations and the sky turned the colour of crude oil. Generators rattled and died and from the starless sky lashed suffocating rain.

Drenched, Ade dashed for the car, cursing his cupidity. Ranti, not Controller, posed the greater immediate threat to his freedom.

Five

Ade could be anywhere in the fashionable world - Milan, Paris or London. In one window, a bevy of cadaverous Caucasoid mannequins dressed in golden lamē struck unlikely poses. What? How many million naira for one chair? And where to drive these low-slung sports cars? Ade's watch said twelve seconds past two o'clock when the taxi rocked and tip-tyred over the grunting shingle and smiling potholes to drop him off outside the tinted glass studio of Punchline and Juicy.

His head super-shaved and polished, chin held high, glasses wedged on, the gift, a figurine he carved for Ranti, in his satchel, Ade's stride shortened with apprehension as he neared her office. He turned left past the pair of water coolers and knocked on a shiny blue door. Was that too loud? Knocking on doors and opening them was once his sound point; now he crashed through them and landed with ugly paint on his face. He rapped the door harder and strode into the office. Please let Ranti be in and not bean-counting or in bed at home with that man, Bambo.

'Regarding what are you here for?' said the PA, notepad and biro at the ready behind her glass-topped desk. Ultra-slim in her pink short-sleeved blouse, she looked the woman for whom Ade's mate, Lekan, the pharmacy student, regularly died. Every inch of the wall was bedecked in impressive certificates of commendation. 'My name is Julius Afediyabamba. I have made several appointments but keep missing your oga.' He meant to scratch the back of his wet and itchy neck but his hand caught an electric cable on the edge of the table. 'Sorry.'

She frowned and slapped her laptop back in line. 'She is in a board meeting. You can come back another day,' she said, her tone terse, then she stabbed the keyboard a few more times and leaned back as though long-sighted. 'I don't see any appointment for Afediyabamba here.'

Apprehension peppered his throat. 'In my village they say a woman can be too busy for things in life. You must do the work for four PAs.' Ade pasted on his broadest imitation politician smile.

'That is what my mama says but Miss Ranti she works me too much,' said the PA, a needy look buffing her eyes. 'One day she get fever. We said she should go home. She said no, and she sent me to go and buy talcum powder so her face will not shine on camera.' The PA shook her head in admiration.

That's my girl. Give Ranti a project and she'd cross that last *t*, dot the *i* if it killed her, even in a bombing raid. But vendetta, no, not her style. Ade fished for more. 'Does sisi shogun have time for other matters? Last week on the show they were talking about it...'

The PA's hand jerked off the keyboard. 'Ah. Are you fake reporter?' Her gaze flicked on to the door. 'Ok, she is coming, now.' She sprang out of her chair to swing the door open and swaggered Ranti in with that slight turn of the hips in a gait that made her look as if she was going to cross a road. In a Nefertiti hi-top that owed its sharp contours to clever triangulations by rocket scientists she was wearing a light mauve round-necked blouse over a pleated avocado skirt.

Nodding the PA to sit, she clasped the phone to her left ear and swivelled to look up at the ceiling. 'I know sir, but as we say on the floor even the brightest forward-looking director in the world still learns from the dim past.' She had plucked her eyebrows and her honey-coloured face looked slimmer, more mature. Pride and regrets marched to mind. It had been going so well.

They met when they were nineteen. One windy evening he turned round after a 200m sprint to find, trackside, with a pear tree shivering behind her in the cool breeze, and the sun's sly rays slanting through the treetops to drape her square shoulders, Ranti wearing a serene contemplative look. A neat pile of Ade's makeshift hurdles sat at her feet. Conditioned by life with Madam Superbad to expect the worst, he feared that Ranti was going to set them on fire to mock his starry pretensions. But her graceful self-possession and her shy smile on her tilted face when she sensed his nervous gaze suffused him with shameless longing. Could she look at, let alone love, him? Him, the flying paintbrush, the boy with the face only a grandmother could love? But Ranti said she loved him and it took a while but from the way she looked at him and shot away from her friends when she saw him, to how she handed him an orange or saved him groundnuts and plantains he believed her.

'Talk later, sir,' she said and closed the call. 'Who is this man?' That soft creamy voice whipped up the memory of their conspiratorial chuckles when they shattered the bed slats during one coltish early fuck.

'He says he has an appointment, but I did not see it here on the system ma.'

'Arants it's me. Abs,' said Ade, terrified of making a fatal move.

Ranti started back, and to her face flashed embarrassment, guilt and shock. 'Oh. Oh. Abs.' Her eyes kept their bright probing quality and the tiny chickenpox

44

scar that she hated over her right eyebrow, still visible despite the makeup. 'Oh I know who you are now,' said Ranti, opening her stance. 'Abs from school. Filo, tell them I am busy. How is your sister? Tell me the secret. You've not changed at all oh.'

Ready to propose, marry, consummate there and then, Allah help him yes he would, Ade hinted at a need for privacy. Dissent flashed in her eyes, as if she resented taking orders in her bailiwick from him. She led him into a small spotless office. Typical Ranti. Only the most fastidious emperor refuses a meal served off her office floor. On her shiny walnut desk sat a black laptop, a smattering of unopened mail and a size A5 framed photograph of her father, the formidable man they called Coach. In the right corner of the desk, flanked by a bottle of water and a pencil holder, leaned a size A5 framed photograph that threw Ade into a disturbing melee of anxious curiosity and brassy jealousy.

Ranti shut the door behind her, marched past Ade to sit behind her desk. 'What do you want? No, leave them off, the glasses. So it was you at Chief's party with Yeni Martins? You looked different. You are bleaching your face? I should have known?' Her speech often ended with a questioning inflection. 'If the Olabos find out that you are here, hunh, hope you know what you are doing.' With her hands on the arms of her chair and the lights playing on her jet-black hair, she reminded Ade of an Indian goddess with four hands. The air conditioner hissed.

Trapped, his options fewer than those of a leaking tea bag, he said, 'I didn't do it. I can explain.'

Ranti's palm flashed into the air. 'So why did you run away? And why did you send me those messages?

You want me to be an accessory? Is that why you are here? To spoil things for me because you messed your own life?' Her higher right eyebrow reminded Ade of a beloved English teacher.

'I wasn't myself at the time. Believe me.' Who am I now?

Ranti cranked up the back of her chair and pulled a wretched face. Her creamy voice rose to a parodic falsetto. 'Why don't you try your multiple personality on someone else? What of the police? It wasn't me officer. I left my guilty selves in the bed or the bathroom, I cannot remember. The ones I brought here plead not guilty. As a matter-of-fact Ranti before you ask it was not me in bed with her my lord, but a rogue version, missionary, sorry, mercenary, version of me.' She tutted. 'As if you've not caused me enough trouble.'

Ade preferred her rant to cool and distant politeness. And the loss of her usual poise might provide a clue or the means to win her back. Ranti must have read his mind, because, with a shudder of indignation or contempt, she snapped out of whatever it was, self-pity, sadness, nostalgia and with a face set in ominous determination stabbed a button on her laptop. The computer yelped and growled to life.

'I've thought only of you and us since Zaria,' he said in a frantic hurry to stop her dismissing him from her presence.

'Us? Was there ever us or just one of us?' she said. Her lips wobbled. 'To reach this position do you know what I had to do to be allowed to even compete on an uneven playing field?' She rolled her fingers over the mouse. 'English degree in the day and diploma in media part-time. More should try it instead of drinking and joining useless fraternities. PJ is just the start. I want to set up my own production company. We had plans. You would have been halfway through the course by now. Ok, I agree that the High Court is not a stadium full of laughing and cheering crowds and sifting files in a crowded and boiling office is not the promise of winning a gold medal in Rio in 2016, but is that why you jumped from lecture theatre into the gutter. In a day?'

'Life in the gutter is not fun when you are rotting in hell,' said Ade. 'Why are you talking as if you did not know what happened?' He choked. 'You know what Microchip the Dean did to me.'

She clicked the mouse twice and looked up.

'Did Iya send you there to study or to defend the classmate? The girl couldn't look after herself? And why didn't you tell UAE sheik to go roll in the hot sand? No, because he promised you a stupid Diamond League contract…'

When did his disintegration begin? From birth, when Malomo his mother left, or when they picked Bambo over him for the Athletics team? So many to choose from and others of which he may be unaware, but in his humble biased opinion the unbearable agony of proleptic jealousy at the thought of Ranti and Bambo making diamond legs in an air-conditioned boudoir ranked highest.

Ranti's eyebrows responded with a disconcerting rise and fall to each modulated twist in Ade's carefully edited story. 'I cannot take this,' she said, her eyelashes glowing wet. 'If Coach finds out that I gave you one iota of my time he will burn me at the stake.' She slumped back into her chair and fanned her face twice with her hand, an old habit. 'Abs, what is it with you and

47

calamity?' Her voice cracked into a high-pitched warble. 'You make yourself small, which is why they pocket you, their hair comb. Yeni Martins. Is she not the one who came to collect the rent in the village when you were a boy? She must be by now nearly forty-'

'Thirty.' He snapped, resenting her deliberate exaggeration, then hating himself all the more.

'She was with that man's son in the stevedoring business…what does it matter now?'

Yeni lived with the son of a business associate of Chief's but issues, palpably gynaecological, did for their relationship. 'I did not come here for marital counselling,' he said, hoping he did not sound overly defensive.

'Who or what else have we been discussing for the last ten minutes?' She checked her wristwatch, arched that right brow, made a throaty sound and jabbed at a point under her desk. Seconds later two men in brown shirts marched into the room. 'Take that away,' said Ranti pointing at the photo of the Nollywood actor on the wall. 'Did I not tell Mr Pasan that I did not want half-naked women in my office?'

Ade let the breath out. Wasn't she decisive? So commanding. 'I thought they came for me,' he said.

'They did, but they cannot obey simple orders,' she said and with a good-natured puff of the cheeks got up to lock the door. A fruity whiff of her perfume raised his hopes again. 'Arants-'

'Don't call me that,' she said.

'I brought you a present. Not much, to show you my feelings. In here.' He pointed at his heart. 'You cannot overestimate how I missed, miss you, been through in my head, my pillows bear witness.' He handed her the statuette, to an inner growl of self-rebuke at the tiny jut on the eyebrows he should have sanded.

Her wariness dropped a notch, and she placed the statue beside the laptop. 'For a start, the thing, bust, is too big,' she said, with the tiniest of risqué flutters in her eyes. 'This is what I mean to you?'

Was she toying with him? He dropped his tingling hands to his side. 'Your PA says you've been busy. Fighting them off?' He glanced at the photo.

Ranti flicked mock sweat off her forehead. 'From morning to night they crowd me as though they are the beggars outside the mosque on a Friday,' she said, her voice soft with a short burr tagged on to the end. Ade's eyes latched on to her dewy lips and readied himself for an embrace.

But Ranti rapped the table. 'You must think I'm stupid, make a puppy face and give her a wooden thing and call her a pet name and she will wag like a doggy in the window. Back not five minutes and you are subjecting me to SWOT analysis.' Her phone bleeped. She muttered under her breath and slammed it on the desk.

What is Swot? Ade's heart skipped to his raging jealousy of the man in the photo. 'Arants, this PJ investigation. If you can just cool it for a few weeks. That is all I ask, for now, to give me time to clear things and prove myself to you.'

Her eyes narrowed. She scribbled a circle on a notepad and stabbed an emphatic full stop. 'Why can't your wife help you?'

'It's Controller, the head of Kakirikiri. He knows everything I've said to you.'

Her hands shot to her head, messing up her neat hair. 'Blackmail,' she said. 'This is worse than I thought. And Yeni is doing the same?' She dabbed her twitching nose with a crooked finger.

'I need is a few weeks to find the money for Controller, get the paper I signed back from him before he retires and I will be free.' He thumped his palm for emphasis, but Ranti shook her head. 'Abs, not fair. Not fair at all. I would never ask you to do this. You play your balls into deep bunkers and just as I am going to win in my game you crawl out of the mud and grab my club and say Arants help me, for old time's sake, leave your clubs to one side be my caddy because my need is greater than yours.' She tapped the stack of papers into line. 'You made your dirty bunker bed. Go hide under it.'

Six

Ade worked at Kakirikiri. The word suggests excitement, a playground ride, the cadence of a galloping thoroughbred, or the name of a great king of an ancient African kingdom, but could describe Ade's heart quake when he first saw the concrete perimeter fences, barbed wire and armed guards of the infamous prison. Chief and Yeni found him the job. Whether it was the intention to keep him out of sight he couldn't say but the Martins thought of everything.

A black van clanked up the road. What role did it play today? Morgue, mosque, church, prison cell, an ambulance, a clinic or a hearse? So lifeless was the cargo that some warders opened a book, Schrodinger's bet Peter called it, first on whether you'd find a prisoner in the van and if so, dead or alive. Psychopath. It was Peter and friends who should be behind electric bars.

Alone in an old box room before the afternoon shift debriefing, Ade sat chewing the end of his biro. The imperious heat stabbed at his face adding to his misery and dragging his mind to a crawl. His biro cracked and cut his tongue and its pieces put him in mind of shrapnel and Ranti's bombshells the day before. He couldn't get her contemptuous parting words out of his head. But Lagos boy, put yourself in her shoes. You turn up out of nowhere yesterday what did you expect? For the world to stop spinning, the sea to bow at your feet, full-frontal fucking fiery fellatio on the floor of her pristine office? Get real it could have been worse. Didn't she let you walk out of the place with your shame intact? Better than a smack in the mouth from Baba Ani's baritone sax.

As the black van rocked past his window trailing a hybrid smell of diesel, urine, vomitus and antiseptic to

Ade came the idea that he could still raise money from the plot of land Chief gave him. Lagos boy, why does it take imminent woe to wake your brain? Show the bank manager a photo of the building, coo over the photo of the man's twins and wife, and you could soon be laughing all the way from the bank to Controller and the precious files.

After work, with the dying day peeping through streaky clouds of pinkish grey, Ade raced to Tokunbo Street, where freed slaves from Brazil settled in the 19th century. Smashed drinks crates, kiosks, soggy food cartons and paper bags lay scattered in great disarray on the street, as if teenage dinosaurs had a rave the night before. The authorities could not say how many women and children drowned in the slums - maybe they did not know - but in Ade's Lekki no one died, except a distinguished admiral's reindeer and that was from homesickness and heat stroke. They say.

Stepping between two waist-high mounds of stinking rubbish, Ade hurried to the door of number 19, turned around, confused, scrambled back to the car and retraced his steps in the dark. Yes, he was on the right street, yet past the white door of Mr Ayorinde the accountant's office his gaze again flopped through a wide gap behind the leaning green transformer with the coloured wires coming out of its stand. Where once stood the concrete and steel promise of a three-story house, with the caryatids he designed to remind him of Ranti, now yawned a chasm bordered on the left by a bare wall reminiscent of a badly peeled sweet potato. His heart stopped, started, stopped again. Ade grabbed on to a telegraph pole.

A muscular adolescent man in a black T-shirt clambered down the pile of rubble with a springy sheaf of metal bars over his shoulder. 'Hey, leave them now, they are my things,' said Ade and jogged a few hesitant steps roadside after him.

'Contractor owes me money,' the man said, forcing Ade to duck under the wobbling load. A young woman tending corncobs over a charcoal fire knew Ade. She frowned and gestured over her shoulder at the Brazilian bungalow with the elegant but weathered cornices above its transom window. The house had the year 1903 scrolled beside its door in bold Italicised letters. 'Contractor don chop your money?' she said, with contemptuous insight.

Ade ignored her, and to suggest calm authority lifted his phone to his ear. But the moon came out, and he saw a fat man in a Sumo wrestler crouch amongst the wet ruins. Ade tore the phone and his glasses away from his face and saw with his smarting eyes a falling pair of trousers and two turds land inside the first "o" on a Coca-Cola carton.

'Ah, you beat me to it.' It was Bola, reeking of booze, in a bright orange shirt and jiggling car keys in his hand. 'Force majeure I'm afraid. I'm talking your house not the toll of gravity on that man's tender bowels. Free enterprise is for big boys, not for every frigging Tom and Dick and Harry. Don't worry, I won't tell Chief that you failed yet again to make a fist of a simple project.'

'But how come yours is still standing?' It was to keep a low profile that Ade asked Bola to buy the cement.

Bola shrugged. 'Chief will learn that you are a waste of space. You think he will give a toss about the plight of a molehill of bricks when his only daughter is, how should I put it, is the landlady of an unproductive factory?' And you the sleeping partner?'

Ade grabbed Bola by the shirt. A shove of a hot girder up the man's arsehole is what he needs to cure that sharp tongue. 'I hope nothing my brothers?' said a passing man.

'Thank you, the man is my junior brother, but he needs to learn that not everybody's dream can come true. They don't, do they, Julius? Dreams? By the way how is your search for capital going? You'll be needing it seeing what's happened here,' he said and patted Ade on the cheek with his wet palm. The neon lights on a pharmacy shop flashed his face into mocking grotesques. Ade sorely wanted to smash the man's face to pieces.

'Remember, Bola, every-day is for the big proud tyre, but one day is for the sharp nail in the road.'

Bola grinned. 'Dream on sleepy nail, your rubble awaits.'

Seven

Ade arrived at the Ayo benches late, delayed by a pile-up on the flyover. The lilting rhythm and juju riffs of the evergreen King Sunny Ade from the beer parlour lifted his mood. Thank the gods, no dreary Apala. Baba Lawyers lit a cigarette and heaved himself off the bench. 'Hey, Tailor Cufffingers don come. Go and fetch him,' he said and strode over to his favourite chair outside the beer parlour. Ade followed him, his scalp prickling from keen apprehension and embarrassment, glad that Baba Lawyers could not see his face in the shadows. Soon Tailor ducked into view with four kerosene lamps.

'I thought we agreed to leave Cufffingers out of your stitch-ups,' said Baba Lawyers, waving his cigarette at his friend.

In a razor-sharp grey safari suit, Tailor had a tape measure draped in perfect symmetry around his neck. 'Ah, ah, on my father's grave I am innocent.'

'I thought you said you had no father?' said Baba Lawyers.

'That is true, and I am his walking talking grave.' Tailor pointed to his chest. 'So what is the charge against me Tony my brother?'

'First-degree cradle robbing. Using confusion and befuddlement.' Baba Lawyers turned to Ade. 'Cufffingers did you at any point in this transaction see Tailor's stake money?'

The penny dropped. Ade collapsed, cringing into a metal chair. To his horror, it was wet. 'It happened. Spontaneous, not planned,' he said, squirming out of the puddle and dismayed that news of his humiliation at the hands of the mediocre Tailor must have got round the

Ayo benches. 'I was winning but the noise from the TV. PJ was-'

'Greed is to Tailor and his alchemists as hope is to the hangman, if that makes sense,' said Baba Lawyers. Tailor slapped a thick white envelope on the wobbly table. 'Ha, *o mase o* give it to Cufffingers before he begins to cry after a slight scratch. Don't cry for me Bulawayo,' sang Tailor to the tune of the musical, *Evita*.

'Let this be a lesson,' said Baba Lawyers.

Ade snatched at the envelope, delighted to have his money back, but angry for looking more of a fool to Baba Lawyers than he needed or wanted to pass off as a simple prison warder from Bulawayo. 'Had Tailor been practising?'

Baba Lawyers shook his head, dragged on his cigarette and pointed at the TV mounted on the outside wall of the beer parlour. 'Cufffingers. Each time you looked up at the TV in the dark the Ayo seeds moved in Tailor's favour. Literally. Yes, literally?'

Ade resented the implication that he did not know what the word meant but peeped inside the beer parlour to gesture for two cans. 'I don't think I will be able to pay you back in September,' he said, rushing the words before he choked on anxiety and shame. To his irritation, another snarling dwarf generator drowned out his words. Baba Lawyers stared at his glass of beer with a blank expression. Ade sucked in a deep breath and spat out the news again. 'September is looking a doubt, a cash flow problem,' he said, kneading his hands.

Baba Lawyer shuddered. 'You told me right there in that chair that you had adequate collateral.'

'It was the rain that collapsed the house. Ask Rashidi it was mad hell oh. Mud, water, cows, drums, chairs and table on the road. We nearly got washed away-'

Baba Lawyers raised a hand. 'Cufffingers, I know what a storm is thank you very much. The house got the rain, I beg your pardon, the rain got the house? I don't remember you showing me plans for a cardboard shack.'

'It was the contractor, Aganiko and Co,' said Ade, his humiliation the more painful for the respect he craved from his worldly friend.

'Aganiko the mudman? Gravity demands concrete the man uses sand. That man is not qualified to dig the grave for my pet worm. I'd cremate the poor thing. Under a generator. That's if we have diesel fuel.' Baba Lawyers winced and banged his beer can on the table. 'Bloody hell, Cufffingers that was my anny money.'

'Anny? Annuities?'

'Anny, aneurysm,' said Baba Lawyers. His fist thump of the table spilled more beer. 'Aneurysm, from Greek aneurusma, meaning dilatation. Muro, an old friend, found it in the aorta in my belly. The same thing killed my dad. Only fifty-four he was, and maybe his father too. 'Done well myself to get this far.' He made a rubbery sound with his lips and shivered. 'I can hardly go back and ask God for a refund can I, for faulty workgodship? And I can't go home. Haven't paid my stamp for donkeys and as soon as they clap eyes on my suntan they'll chuck me out or just do a patch up austerity job to balance the budget.' Baba Lawyers stopped. He calmed into a pensive mien. Ade stewed. 'Cufffingers. For the price of a raindrop in a monsoon I can say to you without fear of contradictions that if I don't raise the cash, bang, smashed before my estimated days by a pissed off aneurysm,' said Baba Lawyers.

Ade's head felt full of trapped wind. 'Sorry, I didn't know. But why did you give me the money?'

Baba Lawyers paused for a moment. 'Because you asked,' he said, in a matter-of-fact tone.

'What of the children? You see them often?' Ade said, hoping that they could help with money.

Baba Lawyers did not reply.

'They cannot help or you don't see them?' said Ade, softening the reproach in his tone with a loud slurp from his revolting can of beer.

'Prague, specialise in international jurisprudence. But travel here and everywhere.' Baba Lawyers looked at his feet.

Lagos boy, see how well they've done. 'You must be proud of them.'

'You take pride in something that has a mind of its own?' said Baba Lawyers.

'Is that not why you should?' said Ade, with great feeling. He fetched the envelope from his trouser pocket. 'Take this.'

'But where will you get the money you need for your project?' said Baba Lawyers.

'Please, take it,' said Ade, and grimaced at the terrible aftertaste left by the evening and the beer.

***

On a quiet night alone at home, if he was not carving in his shed, or mugging up on precolonial Lagos or wafting wistful eyes over the pages of his discarded Law textbooks - temporarily he hoped - Ade often sneaked online to watch Ranti on TV. But he did not want to risk the disabling agony of seeing her affection for Bambo. He sank on to the green velvet mat Iya bought him and began to repay his backlog of prayers. That done he set out his specific requests. Almighty Allah, The Beneficent the Merciful, he was sorry to have to ask and though both a blackmail and a bribe of sorts please could he find the money to pay off Controller? And please keep Baba Lawyers safe, and I don't care how you do it, by juju or by mutation or ghostly laparoscopy, make the aneurysm disappear. Please make Bambo leave Ranti alone and turn her heart only to this humble servant of yours. Whilst you are at it keep Iya out of harm until I can go there. Do this for me and I will never go to Bar Beach again, not even to watch or inspect and I will be off on the first plane to Mecca to the land of the custodians of the holy mosques.

Becalmed, faith reinforced, Ade recited two *suras* each for Iya and his sister Saro but none for his mother, Malomo. She lived for more beer than was good for her and didn't deserve his prayers.

Upstairs in the study he passed a lazy hour flicking through Yeni's sports car brochures. But for the shenanigans at the Athletics Committee and his intergalactic stupidity he might have bought one of the glittering speedy steeds himself. As Ade returned the magazines the crackle of a bulky pile of envelopes deep in the drawer roused his guilty anticipation. He peeled off the restraining band, and, ignoring his palpitating reservations, flicked open an envelope. How the crisp dollar notes fanned out and what a seductive, dizzying smell, the aroma of freedom. Temptation jousted with conscience. He was going to replace the envelopes and steal out of the room but an image of permanent servitude and incarceration, of the smug and arrogant Martins ignited his indignation. These warders of the world, the good and the great, the kidnappers of hopes, the untouchable, invincibles, the upright, lawmakers, the life sharks who take your life and lease it back to you without as much as a receipt. No receipt as they don't believe they stole.

Wake up Lagos boy. This is not a matter of to steal of not to steal, or what Iya or Ranti would think. This is the key to the rest of your life. You backed them and they cut you off at the knees and Yeni will not miss this contribution to your project. Was it not you who said you'd lick the Kakirikiri sewers clean if they led you to freedom? Allah brought you here today so for what do you delay? Permission from Bola or Yeni or Chief, from Jupiter or Mars, from chariots of Abyssinia or Mesopotamia?

Ade took the money. In a few weeks, freedom.

Eight

The district offices of the police force stood behind latticed walls within the hooting range of the traffic heaving over Eko Bridge. Humming Lover Man by Billie Holiday - he used to call it Brother Man until a friend corrected him - Ade leapt from the battered green taxi before it shuddered to a stop. He was wearing a light brown buba and sokoto and his watch said seven seconds past seven fifty-five.

Outside the gunmetal gates he took a few deep breaths and crunched on an antacid, affecting indifference to the melee around him whilst he mentally practised handing over the money to Controller and retrieving the file. Right hand both times. Show respect to your elders. His mind raced ahead. Is that not the flying paintbrush they'll say when he walked into a Chris Ofili retrospective at the Sheraton with Ranti on his arm and the emetic Bambo in the corner with a dewlap and the massive hernia hanging from his umbilicus bulging with envy. Ade oh, what a lucky man. The man don hammer oh. He finished with Yeni Martins but better still landed with Madam Shogun, Ranti of P and J. The useless boy, the cuckoo in the nest who should have been born a grasshopper - jumping was all he was good at, according to his miserable dad - had won the gold medal in life.

As the second hand ticked past twenty-seven seconds past eight o'clock, an orderly with the affectations of a tout came to fetch him. The dusky corridors, hushed huddles of petitioners outside each cabin door and the columns of ants, simulating moving cracks in the walls, always reminded Ade of a brothel, or doctors' consulting rooms.

Presently Controller's voice echoed up a stairwell, and he heaved into sight, towering over his large entourage in a white open-necked shirt. A tattoo of the map of Nigeria peeped over the top of his shirt from the base of his neck. He threw Ade the keys to his office. 'Go and wait for me.' Inside, a wide light brown desk in the middle of the room sat under the photograph of the bespectacled State Governor Fashola. A knee-high safe in the far right corner of the room drew his eye. There lay, behind that finger-marked grey door, the clue to the rest of his life, for which he buttered up his theft of Yeni's money by lying to himself and to Allah and made excuses for freedom and set himself up as a latter day Robin Hood, justifications that still left an ugly mark on his stubborn conscience. Yawning from anxiety Ade tapped his pocket for the reassuring crinkle of the dollar notes and sat on a wrinkly old leather sofa against the far wall under the barred window.

Controller's Sheki's grating voice rattled through Ade's head, reminding him of the invigilator during a typical struggle with the paper on Tort. The venal police officer ducked into the room, leaned the door shut, puffed his cheeks, and rolled his eyes in relief. Who did the police thief think he was? A celebrity fleeing adoring fans?

Ade leapt to his feet. 'I brought the money sir, as we agreed.'

Controller oinked. 'Don't shout. Why does everybody shout? How can we hear when we all shout?'

Ade brushed the smell of the police chief's sickly sweet aftershave from his nose. 'Sorry sir, it is excitement. Thank you for this chance…'

Controller oinked again from behind his desk. 'Don't rush me my friend. I have other matters to address before I can think this early in the morning. Number one is food matter.' He rang a bronze bell on the desk and barked through the door. 'Where this girl?'

A youthful woman scurried in to lay a steaming bowl of rice and beans, and half a dozen Scotch eggs before him. She bowed, curtsied and hovered.

'My belly, the best way to placate it is with assortments.' Controller heaped his spoon with beans and rice and dismissed the woman with a cursory wave. His slobbering, the jaws flapping machines in a satanic face, called to mind a carnivore showing off for the wildlife cameras. He popped the last egg in to his mouth and looked up at Ade. 'How much did we agree?'

Why is he asking? Ade sizzled with wrathful suspicion, but in reflexive respect for authority, said, 'as we agreed at Chief's party?' Out shot his wet palm with the wad of notes. 'Correct, sir, but you can check.' he Controller went on chomping. His pig tiny eyes narrowed to fleshy slits, and the ransom disappeared under the desk. When Controller rocked back in his chair to open the safe Ade shot forward, his brilliant future with Ranti flashing to mind.

Controller produced a slim grey file. 'It is the law of social chemistry that to make new and strong bonds, you must give and take, one low bow here, a favour there, a thank you there, a scratch of one back, a give and take, so you will be glad to hear that they are not going to move me from Lagos. Not yet and they speak no more of retirement. The committee even allowed me to tender a fresh birth certificate with years off for good behaviour. A fringe benefit offered to only a select few of us.' Controller flicked the file back into the safe and slammed the door closed. 'So you will see my friend that since we last met the ambient conditions have realigned to save me a costly professional reconfiguration. Shows that my ancestors are watching over me and not mere idle occupants of the beyond.'

Ade gripped his knees against a sinking feeling. 'I may be able to find some more if you consider this inadequate.' Which meant raiding Yeni's stash. How for do. The plumber has perforce turned stinking sewer.

Controller shook his head. 'I prefer things simple and straightforward to the point, without dissipation. That is why I joined the police force. It is for an excellent reason they do not call it police reason or police persuade or police cajole, but police force.' Controller tapped the ash off his cigarette with a flourish. 'Next month I ask only for five hundred dollars, a flexible and variable premium, as the underwriters say.' Controller bared his tiny yellow teeth.

Police thief were those teeth by any chance filed by lies? Ade's hopes sank to the dreadful conclusion that the man had no intention of giving up the files. His eyes darted around for salvation. A time capsule to send him back to his dismal date of birth or even further to the very first glint in his parents' eyes? 'But sir as you know I do not have that kind of money I had-'

'Ah.' Controller clapped his hands in mock dismay. 'You disappoint me. Take this as an investment in your continued liberty. Freedom does not come cheap. Many have died so that you may live. Even if the life is not to your immediate satisfaction you are alive and you grow to love the life you are with, not so?' he said, through a gigantic cloud of exhaled smoke.

What freedom involves stealing money from your wife? Ade's mouth opened and slammed shut in seething frustration. Self-disgust prodded burning tears to his eyes, and up blasted a sulphurous, unreasoning and terrifying urge to destroy Controller so strong that it snapped Ade's neck back. He needed advice.

Nine

'Cufffingers, sorry to keep you. I had to teach this man a lesson before it got too dark,' said Baba Lawyers. He wedged his green cap back on, gathered his grey dashiki, and swung his frame off the bench. Ari the Tailor tipped off the other end. 'Look, Cufffingers, my friend Tailor sways side to side in his seaman walk. No wonder, after six rounds with a member of an oppressed ethnic minority,' said Baba Lawyers, to loud laughter from the watching benches.

'I let you win because of a firm native action. My adversity policy as Provost of this College of Ayo,' said Tailor, staggering into the arms of a burly spectator.

'It is not adversity but diversity and not firm native but affirmative,' said a donkey-jawed man.

'I re-affirm that I meant to say a firm native action,' said Tailor, with a pointed stare at the man they called the uncivil servant.

'That's dangerous,' said Ade, pointing at Baba Lawyer's cigarette. 'Or so the doctors tell us.'

'Doctors tell you fuck all. It's shut up, pay up, and fuck off. I'll kill the bloody fag before it kills me.' Baba Lawyers threw the cigarette stub into a small puddle and watched it hiss to death. 'There you're dead, so there. What's wrong Cufffingers? You've got your unemployed stripper face on. For your consolation, since your thrombosed cash flow could do with a nudge or two I'll smoke the whole packet and write you into my Will.'

Ade took a long evasive slurp from his can of lemonade. He needed advice, but for unexplained reasons was not ready to confess all to his friend. The daylight dropped away and little boys and girls replaced the benches with metal chairs and tables. A box speaker played that rasping Apala music Ade and Baba Lawyers disliked and plates of steaming yams and fish stew arrived, with Baba Lawyers' extra serving of spicy bitter leaf. He stuffed it under that prominent overbite, mostly with his fingers, licking his huge fingers when saturated with stew. Gloomy prognostications stalked Ade whilst he waited - Ranti slipping out of reach, Saro and his mother in alcoholic limbo, Iya in despair at losing her house shaking her fist at the crooked rule of law, Controller chuckle-clearing his throat and gorging on loot, Baba Lawyer's aneurysm blowing up.

Baba Lawyers slammed his can of beer on the table with a satisfied air and tapped Ade on the elbow with a beer can. 'Come on out with it before it pops.'

'Do you know Controller?' he said.

Baba Lawyers' face dimmed and he stopped chewing. The bar-girl did not need a second invitation and whisked the bowl of fish away. 'Controller? You mean Bowtie?'

'You call him bowtie we call him Controller. He and I have a matter dangling between us,' said Ade.

Baba Lawyers slapped his thigh. 'Drat, should have known when you asked for that dosh. That's bowtie for you. One minute he is damning you with faint praise, the next he has his hands around your neck.' He blew the dust off his spectacles and put them back on again. 'A most greedy man. Hands out fines to lame beggars, or as he called it charged them for not having a receipt for their crutches. Tells relatives of detainees that the keys to the cell had gone missing and they needed money to cut fresh ones. One dad needed Controller's, or bowtie's special police permit to hold a child's birthday party, I could go on but life is short.'

'Cheeng,' said Ade making a sound of a cash register. 'That's the man. But the money I asked for was not for me, for a friend.'

'Well, tell your friend to watch every single pore on his back. If you have a weakness that snake will find it. The man, Controller or whatever you call him did me in whilst I was in the force. It started with a thief. You know how they test the same athletes for drugs over and over to make it look as if the authorities are doing something, but meanwhile, the real cheats are breaking records?' Baba Lawyers mimicked the breathless excitement of a TV commentator. 'Oh my word, my word, the Russian vials have broken the World record, leaving the other competitors hopping mad, bleeding and crushed in their wake.' He patted his cap back up his forehead. 'That happened in the force. One thief, Inspector Minikuli had two houses in London and one in Birmingham. He did not even bother to hide it but when I as much as hinted that something did not add up what happened? His pal, Bowtie writes this damning report about me. Me? Suspect promoted, I got investigated.' Baba Lawyers snapped a loose thread off his buba. 'Conclusion. I am not reflective, I don't get the new dispensation, and we are no longer in the colonial days of your father, insensitive to the national character crap.' He sipped his beer and pulled a face. 'First, they moved me to a stinking branch. They called it number one. The stagnant drain outside was as wide as River Niger in the old days. I was to answer to Bowtie, my junior and one other prick who is now a minister. That is another story. Tailor told me not to waste my time going to court. You won't get justice here in Lagos. We don't, why should you? Cufffingers where do you? Did you know that in fucking Dubai even the johns charge blacks twice the going rate for the privilege? The rest of the world must get a subsidised fuck. Africa, the mother continent, world subsidy for fucking and fucking everything else you can think of…wake up people,' he said, tapping his temples with his knuckles in his frustration.

Ade never knew what to make of Baba Lawyers' outbursts of African solidarity. He thought them patronising, especially when they appeared to absolve Nigerians of agency, but he was never insulting or crude and did not appear to have read or remembered the antifricanist literature. 'My friend likes this woman but he cannot move on because Controller has him by the shorts and curlies as you say it,' said Ade, squirming for dissembling.

'What did your friend do?' said Baba Lawyers. 'Or will Bowtie not say? And this friend sent you here to borrow money, and you gambled it at Ayo? He must be a close and forgiving friend indeed. From Bulawayo as well? Do you want me to have a word with him face to face?' He stretched out his arms. 'Suffer exiled Zimbabweans to come to me.'

'Now you are quoting Mugabe,' said Ade.

He shook his head. 'Mugabe is "welcome exiled Zimbabweans who don't agree with me…into my open firearms." I'll be happy to meet your friend. He's here isn't he? Or do you want to Skype him?'

Ade flushed. He nodded then shook his head. He did not know where to put his hands. 'Er, I'm not sure about that.'

Baba Lawyers wore the conceited look of a man listening to a fool's enthusiastic but garbled retelling of a hoary tale. He leaned over to whisper in Ade's ear. 'Because this Bulawayo legend does not even pass first muster as bullshit. It's ok Cufffingers. I promise. I won't press you but that depends on the number of wrinkles I find in your story. Want to go home to rehearse?' he said, in a tone drawing on mischief and amused forbearance. He ordered another beer. 'Whilst you mull over my offer I can tell you for the price of a pinch of nose hair that if you want to nail Controller, you will need DIG Kafu.'

Ade's elbows dug into his ribs. 'DIG? Should I know him?'

'One thing Controller does not want is a transfer from Lagos. This is his power base,' he said, prodding at his cap. 'DIG Kafu hates the man's guts but each time he gets near his quarry Chief Martins gallops in with his calvary.' He simulated a trumpet by blowing into his funnelled fist. 'DIG has been looking for a smoking gun, but Controller covers his tracks well, flits from place to place. Surrounds himself with a coterie of officers. Even subsidises their wages. How he does it no one knows.'

'It's Roadsweepers,' said Ade, with ill-justified alacrity, compelled by shame to chip in with a penn'orth.

'What if you ask the in-laws nicely? Will they not leave you be?'

'My wife is the man's business partner. I have to keep a Chinese wall between this and her business.' Ade breathed easier because that much was true. Yet Baba Lawyers' grey-green eyes strafed him. 'Maybe I should take a back seat and send my friend to see DIG Kafu.'

Baba Lawyers laughed in gentle mockery. 'These Chinese walls, what do you use? Steely or concrete or rubbery evasions?'

Ade sputtered, engulfed by embarrassment and led Baba Lawyers to sit on the dwarf wall on the quiet side of the green mosque. 'Promise you won't tell anyone.' Ade peeled the boot off his right foot as if to show a physio a sprained ankle.

'What am I supposed to be looking at in the dark?' said Baba Lawyers.

'That is my good foot.' Affecting nonchalance he showed him his left foot under the light from his mobile phone.

Baba Lawyers' head turned to Ade in cog-wheeled steps, his eyes widened and mouth dropped open. 'Don't tell me you are *the* Flying Paintbrush?'

Ade blushed. 'Shsh, a glimpse is enough for a while.' He stabled his foot but felt better for the admiring lilt in Baba Lawyers' voice. 'My mum did that, scalded it when I was small. It's a short story. Pastor said that he saw a vision in which I ran away. When she got home, she poured boiling water on it. I couldn't walk let alone run for months. When I learned to hurdle again, they called me the flying paintbrush because of the way it flashed over the barriers. A hated nickname stuck.' Ade gripped Baba Lawyers by the knee. 'If you tell anybody what I told you I will burst your aneurysm myself.' Ade told him how he met Yeni again and about the accident and Controller's blackmail. 'The man knows my case and-'

71

'Who else knows?' said Baba Lawyers.

'Ranti, my ex. You know the one who presents Punchline and Juicy.'

'A misjudgment and operational error if you don't mind me saying. One wrong word from her and your cover will go viral condemning,' said Baba Lawyers.

'So on top of your Master's degree in Psychology you are expert in the geology of women's minds as well? You haven't even met her and you jump to conclusions. I told her because I trust her and to buy time in the hope of a…'

'Rapprochement? It depends on the length of the fault lines when you split, or should I say on whose side most of them lie,' said Baba Lawyers. 'Look Cufffingers. What you think of what I think is academic. You do what you can and I'll see if I can wake up DIG Kafu. It may take time because the man can sleep for Africa. Even armed with a gob like mine it may take some time to wake him.'

Ten

It was Thursday the 24th of July four days after one Mr Sawyer brought Lagos the deadly Ebola from Liberia. At Kakirikiri, a dozen rag-bearded, half-naked male inmates carrying rusting metal buckets on their heads stumbled towards Ade, grains of excrement from head to neck. On their legs fly-spangled sores festered on crazy-paved skin that rolled in thick folds over their rusting leg cuffs. Ade brushed the dreadful stench from his nose and sped to Controller's office as fast as his inserts and the clammy heat allowed.

Eager to find any evidence for Baba Lawyers and DIG Kafu to use against Controller he'd arrived at six o'clock to empty his sham shredder. Against his instincts and Baba Lawyers' sage advice he was winging it again. How for do. He'd always improvised. We are who we are. Can we act any different? As he crept through the door, he sensed movement behind him, wheeled left to see, attached to her sprawling bosom and surrounded by files and newspapers and flickering laptop screens, a greying woman dressed in grey sitting behind a two abutting desks.

'What are you doing here?' she said. Her booming voice trembled Ade's heart. She rose from her chair to a height three inches taller than Ade. 'M Roja, senior governance officer, I am restructuring the office, seconded from Capital Territory.' She spoke with a leery authority of one who considered herself too good for the job, and the place.

'My name is Afediyabamba, warrant officer, but on, er, also, secondment,' said Ade. 'I came to clean Controller's office.' Capital Territory. Why couldn't she just say Abuja instead of wasting syllables?

'How come? You don't carry cleaning material?' she said.

Ade burned through several unsuitable replies. 'Err, I'm a team leader, er, but I start early to check on the latecomers. Can I empty the bins first?' He'd got to within feet of the shredder when Peter, one of Controller's close mates, sauntered in, smelling terrible of stale tobacco and his body. He pointed at the bin bag in Ade's hand. 'Is that a divorce settlement or golden handshake?' he said, pointing at the bin bag in Ade's hand. Moustachioed, in his late thirties, Peter lived in teeming Ajegunle with his wife and three children. He had a postgraduate degree of sorts and resented Ade as the unschooled immigrant who struck lucky with a local chief's daughter.

'The bag? Oh yes, you saved me the wahala, the girls on my team asked me to cover you up so they do not have to look at your face. Health and safety.' He half-turned to abort his mission but Peter barred his way.

'Excuse me ma,' said Peter, 'ask this worthless troublemaker what he is doing here so early.'

'Look, I have other things to do,' said M Roja, and with a short, sharp contemptuous glare at Ade strode back to her desk.

Peter snatched the bag from Ade and barged past to drag the shredder out from under the table. 'I've been watching you. Let us see what you want with this thing.' He turned his attention to the lid of the shredder.

Ade backed off, riddled by anxiety. 'Wait, that voltage stabiliser thing can blow,' he said, combing his brain in desperation for a way out. If Controller found out Ade was spying on him, he'd spoon out his eyes out.

'I know what I am doing,' Peter said and wrenched his arm away from Ade, but as he leaned over to the switch in flew Moji, her trolley with the faulty castor wheel scraping the concrete floor. 'What are you doing sirs? That thing can kill oh. You didn't hear that Florence's hand and mashed pepper nothing different between them because she disrespected this thing?' Moji snatched the bin bag and the lid of the shredder from Peter and with a polished deftness tipped the contents of the shredder into the bag. 'Leave this kind of work to us, but of you want to learn I can teach you, oga Julius.'

***

Back at his desk after lunch and disappointed by the failure of his plan Ade picked up his biro again, doodled and peered round the alcove. No sign of the shuffle and clank of Moji's shoes and her trolley on the floor. Had she gone home? Did she think so little of him that she did not bother to court his gratitude or approval, say goodbye before she disappeared? He only wanted was to thank her for saving his neck and ask if she had found Cordelia. Full stop. So he liked her around but not on dangerous ground, that's all, no more. His phone rang. He groaned. It was Controller. The police thief expected another payment in three weeks, give or take. By the way any news on Bola's campaign?

'Bola has enough financial firepower to atomise any rival, but he is launching his campaign again soon,' said Ade. Controller did not sound impressed. Ade feigned poor reception and closed the unsettling call. Where was she? Why was a simple polite gesture proving so much more difficult than finding the assets of a late dictator? Pride yielded to impulse, and he called Moji. Her breezy voice mail message with the jolly "bye" at the end offended him. She was only a junior, not even a warder, yet she tangled him in the strings of her aprons. Ridiculous. Lagos boy. Leave her. If she doesn't want to help you that's her problem. Find Cordelia another way. Had he not enough palaver on his fate?

Ade crept to the first floor where Moji often hung out. There he found her friend, Beatrice, stacking the plastic buckets. Had Ade not heard that his friend was in a disciplinary meeting? She asked as if he'd pissed into the baptism font in front of the Pope.

'My friend? Ah, you mean Moji? Why talking in semicircles,' he said, her insinuation of an improper relationship with Moji rousing his self-conscious anger.

'Beatrice shrugged and wiped her face with the sleeve of her brown uniform. 'Okay. You can make the face like a Benin sculpture but you know what I talk is true. Was it not because of you that Peter is making trouble for her?'

That man again. Recall of Peter staring at Moji's cleavage that morning made Ade boil. Another one of his list of men to swing from Eko Bridge by his balls? Ade carried the buckets to his desk in the alcove to wait for Moji. Yeni called. He ignored her because it was about the temerity of Damola, their neighbour with the children and noisy fountain to have a fourth child. That prospect raised Yeni to near violent indignation. As Ade pored through the rota once again, the rear window opened on an official car crawling to the main gates. A man leered and hissed at a young woman across the road. It was Moji. Tetanic with possessive anger, Ade leapt out of his chair. Two officers got out of the car and the leering man in it squealed away in a swelling cloud of dust. Ade sat down angry for almost making a fool of himself. 'Oga, I am here,' said Moji. She appeared out of nowhere carrying a short stack of buckets of her own. Ade's heart slipped on the banana skin. She had changed out of the brown uniform and to his guilty disquiet, hidden her lissom limbs under a baggy pair of cream trousers. 'These are yours.' He pointed at the buckets Beatrice gave him.

For a beat or two Moji looked blank, then recognition flashed across her face at the same moment that the thought occurred to him that Beatrice set them up. He rocked back in his chair, in horror that he may be the butt of office gossip. If careless talk got back to Yeni she would crack his cranium between her heavy duty electricity generators. When Ade gingerly pushed his stack of buckets towards Moji their fingers touched, and a sweet and sour trill zipped up his belly. He'd just finished a quick silent prayer to Mecca for his unease when Peter marched up to stand within breastarc of Moji.

'Is she debriefing you?' Peter said, licking his nicotine-stained lips and moustache. 'Julius, the knight in tarnished armour was late again. Donkey was lame?' He chuckled to himself.

Ade shot out of the chair. 'Should I not have been told, oh sorry as a graduate you prefer the word, informed.'

'Julius, from which river do you get these crocodile tears? River Nile or the Amazon or are they all your own work for a change?'

'They come from the deep south blues the toilet brushes beat out of stinking shits such as yourself.'

Moji's mouth dropped open. She swung the stacks round and tried to sidle past Peter but he stood in her way. 'Lekki man, you don't know that the girl has overstepped the mark with the inmates?'

Overstepped? Ade quaked to fearful emotions he couldn't explain.

'Just because I gave them water, the girls in KIYO, that is it,' said Moji, her eyes ballooned by fear.

Ade had recently bought a few odds and ends for Moji to smuggle into an inmate. 'I asked her to take them a bucket of water. Blame me,' he said, in expiation for doubting her honour.

Peter's eyes narrowed to polished slits. 'Is that why we talk to her and she refuses to answer?'

Moji dropped the buckets. 'Oh, no not at all,' she said, implying with her pained expression that she wanted Ade to shut his big mouth.

Peter leaned over to shake his fist in Ade's face. 'If not for that Martins man, Chief, or what they call him, you and I will not be in the same vicinity. And you Moji, a last warning.' An officer called his name from a passing car and Peter leapt over the wall for the proffered pack of cigarettes.

To Ade's admiration, Moji soon regained her poise. 'Na wa oga Julius, the way you bounce Peter. When you called him a shit it made my head spin as if I was on a spinning roundabout.'

Every time she called him by that name, Julius, she slapped on another stinking layer of guilt. 'Big or small roundabout?' he said.

Moji looked at her feet. 'Is she your girl, this Cordelia?'

'Nah, I told you. I knew her family vaguely when I was small,' he said with an emphatic shake of the head. 'I just want to help her. Did you find her?'

Moji pirouetted back to Ade. 'That is what I thought,' she said with patent delight. 'I told Beatrice not to waste her time, oh.'

'Beatrice? I thought Beatrice got married last month. How? I mean how many times.' His tongue twisted the words the wrong way. 'How many times? Not how many times does she get married but how many times has she used that excuse that she is going to get married?'

'As many times as I have to tell you the real words of that song.' Her eyes smiled at their shared joke.

'You mean with the fog together Maria Carey.' For the sake of appearances Ade sat down behind his desk and picked up his biro.

Moji shook her head and voice rose in cheerful exasperation. 'Not in the fog together, but we belong together.'

Ade ignored the warnings tinkling in the back of his mind. 'I know what I heard with my twin ears. It was on the radio this morning.' He had to leave soon to beat the worst of the traffic but her amiable manner and other indefinable qualities detained him.

'Oga, you too funny.'

He pulled a doleful face. 'Then why does Peter not agree with you in grading my funniness?'

'Because he is an empty bucket made of toenails. No imagination. But oga Julius, what were you trying to do in that office?'

'I was looking for my missing joke book. Peter must have hidden it.'

She sounded disappointed and pulled a thick sheaf of papers from her bag. 'Is this not what you wanted?'

'So you knew that the thing was a bobo machine?' he said, ashamed of his earlier evasion.

Moji replied with another ironic smile, unfurled a sheet and read, her eyes jerking back and forth over the lines while her scimitar eyebrows taunted each other over her shallow frown line. 'Too much grammar oh,' she said, thrusting a sheet at him. 'What do they mean? Analysis of intention, symmetry of exposure of contact cases in close proximity? Maybe they are using big English to cover that they do not know what they are doing.' Her wide diastema reminded Ade of his hero Ed Moses. In Lagos the wide tooth gap was a sign of good luck. He'd like some.

'It will take many more drafts to cover that woman's backside,' said Ade, then recoiled, fearing that he offended her. 'I mean to say the papers will make a breeze when she uses them as a fan.'

'Fan? The fans are my friend are blowing in the wind? Is that not how you sing it?' Moji chuckled, laughed and her tiny eyeteeth glinted. Four polished spears. Guards of her honour?

He liked the childlike way the nineteen-year-old turned an "m" into an "n" making sometimes, sound like songtimes. 'I know the words now. It is "the answer my friend blowing in the wind."'

She stuffed the papers back into her bag. 'Oga Julius this bobo shredder of yours will not get you to pass go. Why do you not ask for my help? You think of me only as a basket mouth?'

Ade flinched in self-reproach because he'd given her the nickname, basket mouth. Moji, the prison quidnunc, *amebo,* had an extraordinary tendency to exaggerate, see a garden cat and call it a prowling tiger. 'You know I don't mean it. I just give people that I am fond of nicknames.' To divert his disquiet he wafted at an imaginary moth.

'Hey, is that blood on your finger?' Moji said.

Ade sucked on the papercut. 'It is fine.'

'If you say so,' she said.

'It is nothing, really.'

'Oga, ha, ha, I see lemon in your eyes every time I want to help. If you don't want my help, just say so but for me, as we are working together I take us as brother and sister even though you are from abroad.'

Her anger and the filial reference both alarmed and dismayed Ade in equal measure and he castigated himself for distancing her by acting the superior officer. 'How for do,' he said, uneasy about these incremental betrayals of Ranti.

Ms Roja huffed past, eyeing them both with great suspicion.

'Don't mind the woman, let her go and mind her own business, her asymmetry of big yansh,' said Moji and she tossed her head back and laughed.

'Oga Julius, you know what men are like when woman fever catches them?' she said.

'As in Mills and Boon?' said Ade, not sure where this was going.

Moji made an ironic huffing sound. 'I'm not talking of storybooks. I am saying that the doctor in the Sickbay doctor get fever for Beatrice. Beatrice says that he told her that they check the inexperienced girls in KIYO for the corner corner business that Controller is doing.'

His phone rang to some boring ringtone that replaced the old James Brown riff that went with the flying paintbrush and could betray him. It was Yeni again. Moji stepped away to lean against the wall. 'But I am coming. I will be there before eight,' he said, to interrupt Yeni's tirade. 'Something came up at work. Harassment case. One of my colleagues and the man is well known for it.' He signalled to Moji to wait and affected a casual air by scribbling on the desk, but her phone rang as well and she snatched up her buckets and he could only watch in helpless irritation, heart tattooing itself with its dim opinion of him, for not getting any closer to either Controller or Cordelia, as the object of his sin-ful attraction tittuped along the deserted corridor turned left and out of sight. Later, he checked his phone for a text from her but it was Team Leader Ojo summoning him to a meeting that Ade hoped might lead him to Cordelia. He owed her.

Eleven

An orderly showed Ade into the long rhomboid room. The ubiquitous portrait of President Jonathan Goodluck hung above the baggy colonial-era furniture stacked along the sidewall. He looked like a man trying to cap a gushing oil well with his backside. Ade sensed that amongst the smell of coffee and dusty files hung the ghosts of foregone conclusions, but he prodded his glasses back up his nose and put on the blank foreigner look that he hoped might lure the officers into an indiscretion with which he could skewer Controller.

A dusty ceiling fan gamely stirred the stuffy air. Opposite Ade at the long table sat Deputy Team Leader Peter, and Team Leader Ojo, his bulging eyes red from drink as usual. Between them the chairman, his cheeks not dissimilar to those of a greedy hamster, reclined in a striped orange and brown *agbada*. His lips glistened with the dribble that he dabbed at regular intervals with a knuckle. Warrant Officer VV, named after the vroom vroom sound made by his ancient scooter, sat to the right of Peter. From the swarthy folds of Peter's vast face radiated unplugged hatred. Between them they did not have either pen or scrap of paper. They stared at Ade, fencing with their eyes, daring him to speak. Ade gathered himself. 'Well, sirs, they say. Never too premature to deliver a pregnant pause. I believe you called me to discuss the latest deaths in custody in KIYO.'

'Another of your *yeye* memos. Do you think you know more than us? Do you?' said Team Leader Ojo.

'Chair, sir, it was not that. I am only doing my job in case they ask from headquarters as it was in my section that the deaths happened, making two, not

83

counting Onuwo. This year fifty have died. And the girls the Roadsweepers arrested last month are they here on this site in KIYO or in the main prison as the place is packing them in, sardines, and the water they give them to drink is not fit to use to flush toilet let alone to put in the mouth and why diarrhoea-'

'Hey my friend, one thing at a time. This is not a cowboy film where the Indians shoot their arrows at once,' said the chair.

Peter guffawed. 'Then they run up one by one to catch bullet with their belly.'

'Or in their eyes,' said Team Leader Ojo. Squat, with short receding but suspiciously black hair and a devout Muslim's flat spot on his forehead, his chin evoked the squared off bottom of a smartphone. Ojo claimed to be in his forties but often betrayed his true vintage by his personal and detailed stories related to the "Wild West" in the 1960s.

'Chair this is what I was telling you. The man is always using a machine gun to catch mosquito,' said Peter. 'Chair, ask him please, can you make tea without boiling water? What does he want here in a maximum security facility? Hot showers, butlers, tea-breaks, designer t-shirts to tee off in at the club, things that many of us with postgraduate diplomas, who have never stolen even a biro in our lives do not have? Is that what you call justice, ernh, sinners become our lords and we turn into servants?' Peter got up to pull his trousers away from his crotch and sat again in a huff, wriggling his bristling moustache.

'I am only asking for clean water for them to drink. Many are not charged or convicted, but would you like them to lock up your sister for 24/7 to beg for chewing stick, for water to drink, to wash, not to talk of toiletries, they were fighting this morning over one pad, and I hear they are even talking of putting women in the male section.' Ade added the last bit on the spur of the moment but the guilty flinch by the usually doleful and apathetic Vv disturbed him. Shit of no nation. So they *did* mix the sexes in the same block, not yet in the same cells, thank Allah, after what nearly happened last time when male inmates escaped from their cells. Poor Cordelia, blame me. The chairperson yawned. Ade bristled. He expected resistance to his tentative proposals for minuscule reforms but not this arrogant and callous indifference to deaths, and disease and abuse.

Chair jabbed a finger in the air. 'Julius or whatever they call you. Where you come from do they address elders in this fashion? Don't come here to take liberties because we are a tolerant people here in Lagos. Digging and shaking everything we say until you get what you want to hear fall out will not work with me. And this thing you call truth, do you see it sitting in this chair or this room anywhere?' he said, with mocking glances around the room and up at the fan. He dabbed his lips and his bulbous cheeks. 'Truth did not come today, and it sent me instead so let me decide whether I can bake from these ingredients a dish that the majority of reasonable people in this vicinity can slip to their hungry stomachs.'

So this is why they say the truth never dies. Confronted by monstrous lies it hides, biding its time or waiting to be found. If this was an inquiry, he was a flying broomstick. His ruse had failed. Against his better judgement he was going to attack Peter's predilection for sexual harassment, and refer to a bitter taste in the mouth when Moji rumbled through the door with a trolley of refreshments - a few chunky white bread sandwiches and oily sausage rolls. Ade's heart slipped on that banana skin as it always did when he saw her recently. He risked a surreptitious smile. She blanked him. He squirmed on the chair, staring at his clenched fists. Because he gave her the time of day, asked her for the odd favour, to pass on a few messages to inmates, find out where they kept Cordelia, who did she think she was? From now on it was keep your distance. They could call him what they liked, see if he cared.

'Morning. Sirs, how do you like your tea or coffee?' Moji said, sounding as chirpy as a stand-in gameshow host.

'Wet, cupped, weighty and swaying full of milk, how else?' said Peter.

Ade's ribs snapped taut with a near overwhelming urge to shove Peter's teeth deep enough for a colonic inspection.

'You know what? How stupid of me not to know that ogas prefer their tea hot and burning in their lap,' she said. She poured everyone but Peter a drink, which from his smirk, then wink at Ojo he must have taken as a flirtatious snub. As Moji straightened back up to her great height, she flashed Ade a smile, which struck his floundering heart like the shock from a defibrillator. Ade perked up, blushing and with a complicit nod at the serviette under his cup and the merest hint of a smile, Moji backed out into the sunlit corridor.

Whilst the others tucked into the sausages Ade read Moji's note. He took it back. She'd only gone and found Cordelia.

***

Sick Bay, a converted chalet kitchen, complete with colonial chimney breast and wood-fired stove, stood twenty yards inside the highest point of the perimeter wall. On a stretcher in the middle of the dim, dank room, a square-shouldered girl sat with her back to the door, the number 243, printed in bold red numbers on her prison gown. She looked too small to be the Cordelia Ade saw on Bar Beach but he could not be sure. You shrink, gutted, after they take your name away, seize your belongings, search every orifice and starve you.

'What are you doing here?' said the prison doctor. As thin as a twig, a patch of grey hair peeped above his ears.

'Walk in dead is late again, so I came to cover straight from my meeting,' said Ade, brushing the pungent smell of disinfectant from his nose. Olaiya was always late, the explanation for his nickname, walk in dead, so late for his funeral they started without him. Tingling with apprehension, Ade shut the door behind him and tried to steal a glimpse of the girl on the stretcher. A gigantic pile of thick black hair lay under her feet. Ade swallowed the last crumbs of a sugary antacid and walked round the stretcher for a proper look at the girl. When he saw the mole on her chin, he knew at once that it was Cordelia. The reciprocal spark of recognition in her eyes disturbed. 'My sister, what is your name?' he said, trying to sound the calm Lagosian.

'You mean to say you don't know me?' she said.

'You know her from somewhere?' said the doctor. The doctor snatched a long rubber band off the table and tested it for strength. 'Stand there, *o jare* and let's finish and go.'

87

'How can you know you don't know someone when you don't know you know everyone you know,' said Ade, sweating like a rutting pig.

'Doctor, don't mind me. That is how mama Cordelia tells me to greet everybody for business,' said Cordelia and made a sad sucking noise.

'So why did you not greet me like that?' said the doctor, sounding more than a trifle miffed.

Because she's off duty great doctor. Ade signalled for Cordelia to get on the trolley. 'Doctor, I can fill the forms and take her back to the cell if you want to go and meet the officers outside sir. And I can sweep her hair off the floor.'

The doctor looked puzzled. 'Look my friend, stop your leafy shaking. You think I want to sell her hair? Hold her there and don't waste my time,' he said. Ade squeezed her upper arm and suppressed a retch as blood spewed into the 50ml syringe. 'Why are you taking so much blood?'

'Ha, ha, what concern is it of yours? Is it your vein the blood is coming from? Is it your blood the needle is drinking? Are you the one who is going to analyse it for potassium and renals? Hold the cotton wool there, my friend. I have to teach you that too?' After, the doctor sat under the window to fill out the forms, whistling the Billie Holiday tune *Autumn in New York*, the one Ade used to call Your tum in New York until Moji corrected him. The doctor tapped the biro against the wall. 'This thing is not writing, wait here,' he said holding the pen up against the light as he loped from the room.

'Sorry for the other day,' said Ade, skipping round to face Cordelia. 'Where is your room? I want to help.

They say you know why they are doing these blood tests.'

Cordelia gave him a puzzled look. 'Welcome,' she said in a trembling voice. 'What have I done that is new under the sun, in this Lagos, enh? Woman has no right to eat?' She said an escapee, an inexperienced girl of fifteen told her that they kept her in a ship's container near the wharf. 'The man who came to inspect is the *oga* of Roadsweepers. He has big belle and his voice is like a locomotive and he tests the girls for export. If your blood test is good they take you to rehabilitation, hunh.' She made a cynical sound. 'So-called rehabilitation. From there many did not return.' She said they took the girls overseas where they became surrogate mothers for rich barren women and their husbands after which they threw them on to the streets or sold the girls to other traffickers.

Ade put his arm round her. 'Cordelia, don't cry. I have a friend who will help you. I didn't know they were coming that night. I am really sorry,' he said.

'Not your fault. What will be will be. Just my bad luck that day. I tell you one woman managed to escape from abroad and return. The thing her eyes see mouth no fit to talk.' Cordelia said she begged God to get out of here. She was tired of Lagos and wanted to return to her village. 'Anything is better than this fear. Fear that they will catch you and do you by force, fear now that they will take me abroad because I am tall and they say I must have big waist bones for giving birth.' Her face lit up a fraction. 'But maybe by the grace of God my blood will fail or the X-ray machine will break and they will not be able to complete the tests.'

If her blood failed that meant she was ill in any case with anaemia or one of the many fevers, Yellow, Dengue, Malaria or one of the silent killers or new fevers no one has heard of, from overseas. As he bent over to pick up the soiled cotton bud Team Leader Ojo and Peter and four huge security guards charged into the room wielding walkie-talkies and batons. The cotton bud dropped out of his hand. Oh what a holy stir-fried mess. Ade's hands shot up to cover his head. 'Why this my seniors? Is it my fault that walk in dead is late again?'

'Who gave you authorisation to enter here?' said Peter as one guard prodded a baton at Ade.

Cordelia screamed as three men dragged her off the trolley. 'Kill me then, kill me. I want to die than go to main cells. Please tell my people I dey here, they are in Akajaoku, oh.' 'Shut up,' said Team Leader Ojo.

Her screams of terror and distress clawed at Ade's spine.

'Who are you looking at in that way?' said Peter and struck Ade on the head with a baton. A pair of muscular hands stopped Ade retaliating. The right hook he had in store for Peter sank back in cold vault, earning compound interest, until that day of revelation when he would unleash it with all the armed force he could summon.

Team Leader Ojo prodded Ade in the chest. 'Julius, you have vex me big time this time. From now and immediate effect we demote you to permanent assignments on the Sanitation team. This is for code violations, and persistent insubordination and interference and trespassing without authority.'

'Can man trespass *with* authority my senior?' said Ade, the words escaping before he could stop them.

'Shut your mouth. If not for Chief Martins who sent you I would lock you up and throway the key,' said Team Leader. 'Get him out of my sight.' The muscle men frogmarched Ade straight off the premises and dumped him a block away from the prison gates.

***

Miserable, and angry for disappointing Cordelia, Ade sat on a rusting drum in the furnace of a July afternoon, a furry red bloodstain fanning along his shirt. Pedestrians crossed the busy road to avoid him and motorists slowed to stare, then, hassled by toots of impatience sped off shaking their heads in pious pity. Ade had a blinding headache, but he counted himself lucky to have a head in one piece, recalling that careless swipes with official batons left poor Dennis the quiet unable to walk or speak. As he looked round for someone whose phone he might borrow to call Rashidi, Moji loped out of the prison gates. She was wearing a flowery pink blouse, and brown court shoes. Her smile, dimpling the corners of her mouth was a warm sunny winch round the cockles of his heart. But when she saw his bloodied shirt a worried frown clasped her face and, gesturing to her companion to go on without her, she scurried across the road to stand on a tongue of crumbling tarmac a few feet away. 'I heard,' she said.

Of course. Ade wiped his bloodstained hand on his sock and stood up. He stepped back out of her space as a couple of other members of the administrative staff approached. 'Please look out for Cordelia. I don't want her to suffer because of me.'

'You and this Cordelia. But one wonderful thing is that they demoted you to our team. We can help this your friend, Cordelia if that is what you want,' she said, a

91

childlike eagerness in her voice, then with an abrupt change in demeanour added in a subdued tone that on the team he could help Beatrice and the others organise the rota. 'When do you start?'

'Immediate effect.'

She saluted with a breezy air. 'Right sir, oga sir. What can I do for you, sir? Put what you want on my head or wrap it around my neck, sir. But next time you want to head-butt their batons make sure you wear a steel helmet, sir.'

Ade had not laughed that loud since Bambo's shorts fell round his knees on the home straight during a 400m flat race. 'Ok, ok,' he said, his eyes smarting with happy tears, 'I will order a helmet, but you must let me make you thick body armour to wear for when Peter is on duty.'

'Don't worry, I can handle that man,' she said, her eyes narrowing with her impish grin.

Ade fiddled with his shirt, his fun spoiled by his intruding conscience.

'My place is not that far. Come, you can wash your head and face and wait for your driver in the shade.' Moji pointed through a mesh of old telephone lines.

Ade shrank back. Go to her house? He wiped his stinging scalp with the swab she gave him. 'It's ok, I will manage, and the blood has dried. I mean I'm coming, you are right, too hot out here and the walk will cool my head,' he said and in his embarrassed haste staggered backward into a hawker's pile of pineapples. After trudging a mile one stride behind her in bashful silence, with the blood beginning to drip from his head again, they reached a single-storied house. Painted green on one half and a shade of orange on the other, it had a shop to the left on the ground floor. Moji led Ade round to a tap at the back of the house. Tepid tap water ran vivid pink off his head. She pulled a crisp dry towel off the clothesline and dried his scalp just as Iya used to when Ade was a boy. Moji reminded him of Iya. Ade wondered what Iya would make of her but a sense of betrayal yanked his on to the safer contemplation of Ranti.

Moji flopped the towel around her neck. 'Now your shoes.'

He jerked his left foot back from her so hard she nearly slipped on a slimy wet patch. 'Sorry, I'm good, don't worry,' he said.

She tutted. 'Ah, if you don't take off those socks, in this heat, the blood will glue your foot inside your shoe,' she said and slapped the towel back over the clothesline.

'Thank you.' Did that sound appropriate? 'Thank you for saving my head from bleeding to its death. And thank you for finding Cordelia,' he said.

'Every five minutes it is Cordelia.'

'Is she my woman? Ah, ah, no, I told you many times. I know their family,' he said, to a tug of disquiet. 'Hey, my head is beginning to ache again. You have a painkiller?' he said, rubbing his temple.

'You have a headache because you dug another senior service hole with your head. Next time give me a warning,' she said.

Her kind smile snapped a pennant taut in his chest. 'Is that because you have a JCB to dig me out or bury me deeper underground?'

She pondered for a moment. 'To dig you out,' Moji said with a sparkling grin. Then, if you vex me I can bury you back anywhere at any time.' She blushed. And so with delicious guilt, did he.

Later that evening he called Baba Lawyers to tell him what he learned from Cordelia. But to his chagrin, Baba Lawyers was, as a senator once said, economic with his encomium. 'Cufffingers, you know as well as I do that to bury a big beast like Controller you need a big hole and more than a shovelful of sand. Concrete man, concrete and by that I mean a gigantic steaming pile of shit. Nothing less will stir DIG Kafu from his sleep.'

Twelve

Bola relaunched his campaign on the last Saturday in July. So many relaunches, the man should work for NASA. Controller ordered Ade to attend. He had a pleasant surprise but Controller's track record suggested otherwise.

The floodlit tennis match outside had just ended with a net cord and an apologetic whoop from the victors when Bola Martins swept into the packed Orange room - the members' dining room with bright orange walls. He was wearing a silky sequined red calf-length top and a cap the same colour. He waved down the standing ovation and clapped his hands. 'Waiters. Servo,' he said, light flashing off the sequins as he turned and bowed from the platform. 'I say, my people, if we win the election, with the calibre of the people in this room no longer will those international mother fuckers, IMF, try their latest drug on us then blame us for not swallowing faster when things fuck up. No, my brothers and sisters we will sweep past them with a haste unrivalled even by the Security Council's response to nuclear tests by brown people.' They laughed and started to chant. 'We are PDP and will win, APC go and lie for inside dustbin.' The other guests joined in, drumming out the rhythm on the tables with cans and plastic bottles.

Ade found a table in the shadows, well away from the hard-core party hacks. He was counting the number of waiters and making a mental note of what they were wearing should Yeni ask for a report, when Controller squeezed through to his table. He was wearing a shiny green and white cap and bright yellow *agbada*. 'Where is madam?' he said.

'She travelled,' he said, a lie. Yeni spent the last two days in bed and he hoped she was not pregnant, or, as they used to say, in the family way. A disaster in any book.

'Greet her for me. Tell her to call my office as her container has arrived and will need clearance. Now I want you to meet my very good friend Professor Seinde Kosimbe.'

Was this the pleasant surprise? Ade half saluted out of respect for the professor, technical adviser to the WHO and prominent member of the Emergency Operations Control leading the fight against Ebola. 'Very good to meet you sir. Thank you for your hard work.'

Professor's toothy grin flashed on and off as though it took too much out of him. 'Thanks for your kind words. You will excuse me if we do not shake hands, practising what I preach,' he said, in a nod to Ebola. 'Our race against this virus is similar to racing a hurricane, but we are hopeful that we can win because if it took hold here in a city of fifteen million.' He shook his head. 'It will be worse than Naples and Sodom and Gomorrah multiplied. But heard wonderful things about you too Julius.' He had a good wide fleshy nose on him but pinholes for nostrils.

'Good things? Ha Seinde. As a professor of microbiology you of should know that given enough time we decay, sweet or not,' said Controller. He winked at Ade, and with his friend, sat opposite Ade.

A professor and a police thief shoulder to shoulder? Only in 21st century Lagos. 'An honour to meet you sir.'

Controller beamed. 'Seinde and myself, we grew up together, same street, shared the same trousers and pissed into the same bush at times, but not at the same time. If it were possible, we'd share our underworld, dicks, prostate the whole lot,' he said, with a mischievous poke at his friend's midriff. A woman sitting at the next table gave Controller a dirty look.

Professor flashed his teeth. 'Julius, Sheki tells me that your camp is amassing massive manpower for next year's elections.'

'Or erections as Prof Atchili used to say,' said Controller, and he snapped open a can of beer.

'I am not in their camp or any camp,' said Ade.

Controller raised an eyebrow. 'Don't make me laugh. From the day we are born until we die we are in camps. We have rich camp, poor camp, tribal camp, religion, born to be wise, born to be stupid, lazy, or diseased camp. When you married Martins you joined their camp, end of story. Accept it. You cannot clamber up the class ladder then turn round and dismiss your good fortune in the social taxonomy.'

Professor Kosimbe leaned away from the smoke rising from Controller's cigarette. 'Sheki can tell you stories. These people, Martins, Chief-'

Controller nudged him quiet. The professor looked peeved and Ade pretended not to notice the tension between the men by beckoning to a waiter. 'Prof, ask anybody. What I know of party politics is smaller than a microwaved amoeba.'

'But I am not political either. I still consider it my duty to help the displaced, the disenfranchised and the-'

'The disowned the disjointed, dis-everything, the dysenteric and indecent,' said Controller and tapped his protruding belly.

'You saw Apapa road?' said professor.

Ade rolled his eyes. 'That was no road.'

'A gallimaufry of sand, mud, and gravel,' said Controller.

'That is Sheki for you, descriptive to a t. The reason the road to the major port in the country reminds me of a war zone is that Chief, Bola and the others are ruling this country and if they win they will condemn us to another difficult century. Do you not see the irony in the waves of our people dying on ships to get away from here? I ask you this. If they brought slave ships now will your people get on or not?'

'A hyperthetical question,' said Controller.

'Give humans rice and rights,' said Ade, alarmed because Moji barged in to mind. Not for the first time that evening.

'Give rice and promise rights, say the Chinese. It works for them,' said prof.

'So did slave camps. But in Nigeria they say they take rice and rights and light and pocket them then laugh in your face,' said Ade.

'I thought you said you know nothing of politics?' said Controller.

'I said *they say*.'

'Enough of this circumbendibus,' said Controller. 'Julius, I have a perfect mission for you which I am sure you will enjoy in your inimitable way. Seinde wants to run for governor. I've hinted at this task before but we need specifics now. Your in-law's spending, his contacts, plans, data to help us get Seinde into the House.'

Ade fanned his face with a menu. The distinct lack of bargaining chips glued him to his seat. 'If you mean Bola. The man is a sadist and I speak from experience.'

Controller stabbed the ashtray with his cigarette. 'That is as useful to me as fish scale is to a drowning camel. I reiterate. We need a lead before this Ebola thing takes hold.'

'We hope not,' said Professor Kosimbe.

'But if I can help, will you kindly consider the other matter, Controller, sir?' said Ade.

Controller gave an anaemic smile. 'I never say never and I never say for definite unless I don't mean it.'

And I wish you a white-hot trident up your dick. Trolleys arrived creaking under salvers of shark, crocodile, fried braised egret, pigeon, guinea fowl, rice dishes, cans and bottles of beers and wines and vintage champagne, the last reserved for the cream of the VIPS. Must have cost an average town a lifetime in human-hours, but Yeni said a fortune many times greater awaited Bola in the Senate. Ade ate the tepid dish of tinned moinmoin in despair, disappointed that he had again drawn a blank, while Bola made his usual politically correct speech blaming foreigners and the World Bank, IMF, UN, EU, Fulani terrorists from Timbuktoo for ruining the country. During the long and loud applause that followed, Controller and Professor Kosimbe tapped their noses at Ade in conspiratorial bonhomie and staggered, arm in arm, out of the hall. As the hall emptied, Bola, looking as eager to reach Ade as a biblical pestilence swayed across the aisles bumping into tables and shoving the waiters out of the way until he reached his reluctant victim.

'Is this your wet trouser of Sinbad the tailor face? On my happy day? Haven't you had enough to eat or did your team lose? Wimbledon is it, that bargain-basement club? They will soon go under,' he said, leaning over to peer at Ade through bloodshot eyes. 'Those squatters tell them that...'

A waiter had been waiting. When Bola ignored the tapping of a bronze salver on a chair, the waiter nudged the glass.

'Take your fucking hands off me you pointless simpleton. Can't you see I am wearing silk?' said Bola, straightening up to shake whatever malign virus inflicted on him off his sleeve.

'But your bill remains, sir,' said the waiter, with a frightened frown.

Bola snatched the bill from the waiter. 'Get Sulu for me.'

'Sulu is no longer working here sir. And we need to tally as one o'clock don passed and my supervisor Mr. Odu vexed with me last time when you no pay, sir.'

'How much is it?' said Ade trying, without success, to wrest the bill from Bola.

Bola jerked away and bumped into a table. A bottle smashed to the floor. 'Do you know who you are talking to, this rat?' said Bola. 'Tell your supervisor that if he is not careful I will get them to lock him up in Kakirikiri and when they release him he will come to beg. Doggy style.' Bola laid on an obsequious mien, tapping his lips with clasped hands. 'Oh, sir, sadly me, sir, don't you remember me, sir, I used to serving you at the club please give me something to chop for the sake of my pickin and my only mama in this world,' he said in a withering and effective impersonation of obsequiousness. 'Go man. Wait for me. I'm coming.'

Under a dim light, and muttering to himself and to a passing colleague the waiter gave a stunning portrayal of a stubborn mule. From how he held the tray out shoulder high, on a steady palm, and Bola in his unshakeable gaze he got a retributive kick from the confrontation. 'People do not know when to stop to drink when the barrel is empty,' he said to another passing colleague.

'Did you say something remnant human?' said Bola.

Ade pulled Bola away from the waiter. 'Bola why don't you just pay the man?'

'What has this got to do with you? Oh, how could I forget, still sniffing around for a loan are you? Nothing if not persistent. Can't take a fucking hint? Tell your yawning pockets that I've got other things to do with my money and I'm getting pissed off that everyone thinks they have a say nowadays. Tell those fucking geriatrics in the village that if they are not out by Friday I'm going to drill into what's left of their rotting teeth lessons they will not be able to dine out on for weeks.'

Thirteen

Monkeys leapt across the road, and shimmied up leafy iroko trees. Across a distant hill tumbled a bushfire. Gongs rang in Ade's head. Who are you, who are you? What am I? Her only grandson, that's what. Her only hope. That's what I am. Iya, Iya stay alive, I'm coming. If the worst happened, he counted his life not worth more than a toothache. The car lurched downhill through wispy smoke and in yards the track petered out into a quagmire of a rat's tail. Oh, shit of no nation, he'd taken the wrong turning. Tears of anguished fears tore to his eyes. He reversed the car and on a vague hunch swung right round the smoking ruins of a grass hut. Old landmarks, the lanyard hanging from a giant gourd, the babalawo's tiny grotto daubed by palm oil, the coconut trees under which he practised his hurdling technique had gone, replaced by diggers and lorries axle-deep in mud. But through a copse he spotted the stack of rusting motor engines outside the cabin of Mama Hercules. The acacia leaves looked as if they'd been lynched by the heat. Beyond it, rinsed in smoky light, leaned the Zaremba he built for Iya eight years ago to mark his sixteenth birthday. Ade leapt from the SUV, ducked under a low hanging bunch of green plantains and ran a short way to Iya's gate, terrified of what he might find during Bola reckless campaign.

The gate rattled and swung back and forth behind him as though to cane him for staying away. Iya's house, a mix of bare brick and whitewashed mud, its tin roof covered in moss, backed on to the forest in a compound fifty strides deep. The zigzagging rows of Iya's short and brisk broom strokes looked days old, shallow and blurred and pecked at by the chickens. Inside the gate a pair of mating lizards scurried, still entangled, into the undergrowth. On another day he would have envied their carefree cooperation but the acrid and now familiar odour of diesel fuel yielded to the putrid aroma of rotting flesh. His eyes shot to the pen on the left border where lay his tawny goat with its legs pointing to the sky, like those of an overturned sofa. A ragged gash in its side teemed with maggots. One day Bola would pay. No mistake. Let nobody say different.

He rapped on Iya's door with the knocker in the shape of an Ayo board, pressed the door open and peeped inside in apprehensive expectation. A pot boiled, smelling salty and of offal. He knew that smell well but where was she? He took a deep breath and stepped over the threshold. Except for two jagged islands joined by a sooty chiasma above the cooker, the plaster had all but peeled off the walls. In the far corner, the photograph of Iya's beloved grandfather, Jinadu, stood in a faint ray of sunshine.

'Who is that?' It was Iya. The crunch of his feet on the concrete floor must have alerted her. She swept the curtain back and stepped through the doorway. 'What else do you want? Have you not killed enough?' Iya had short grey hair parted down the middle. Behind her lopsided spectacles darted narrow, close-set eyes. In the left eye sat what seemed like a speck of chalk that the younger Ade used to call a catarack. She froze in a slight crouch, squinting through the cracks in her spectacles, looking wiry and unimpeachable but no longer unbreakable.

'It's me Ade, Ade,' he said, limp with glorious relief.

Iya's glasses flopped to her chest and hung by a frayed electric cable. 'No, it cannot be. Olorungbami.

103

God help me. Malomo's son? Here in my house, like wind blows you here? Where have you been? What do your face and your nose?' She fanned the smoke from the cooker away and stepped towards him.

'It is me. I wear these glasses and shaved my hair since what they said happened but it is not true.'

'Why?' She said the only message and letters she got about him came through that nurse and what she gathered from the radio. 'How can you leave me like this? Do you want to kill me? After Malomo and Saro you were my only hope of not letting those people win and turn us into their servants again. I knew you didn't do what they said but what can I do? I didn't want to say anything because that may make things worse for you.' She rocked him in a bony embrace and her smell of candlewax and her minty homemade perfume. They sat down on the bed opposite the firewood stove and whilst he inspected her himself, she ran her fingers over his scalp, face and hands as though to convince herself he was truly there.

Ade roasted. He would have much preferred expiation through physical pain. Kindness he did not deserve killed him. 'Iya I came to take you away. Do you not smell the bushfires?' He flicked cold perspiration off his forehead.

'See what they did to a goat that did them nothing,' said Iya, shaking her head. 'Is Bola not the junior brother of that Yeni who used to come to our house in the white obokun to collect rent?' said Iya and she got up to prod the boiling contents of the pot with a ladle. She was wearing a yellow top over a brown loincloth and a pair of leather slippers. 'Where have you been all this time?'

'Not now, let us go. I've seen what those men can do,' said Ade, rattled by the reference to Yeni.

'If I go they will take this house.'

'If you stay you think you can catch their bullets with your teeth with juju as in Nollywood movies?'

Iya chucked a fistful of kindling into the fire. It fire spat and reared up. 'OK we will eat first. *Efor riro* remain five minutes. You like yam?' Iya made haste for nobody when she was cooking or hungry. 'Iya, no, we have vegetable where we are going,' he said, his armpits itching at the unpleasant prospect of a tiff for which had neither inclination nor time or energy.

'Where are you taking me?' She sat on the bed beside him again.

Ade covered his blooming unease with an attempt at light-heartedness. 'I will see when we get there.'

Iya's eyes pricked up, and she pointed through the window with her ladle. 'Ade ah look oh, is it the men again?'

A jeep rumbled towards the hut, its twinned headlights blinking through the bushes. Unlike Ade, they had come the right way, turned left at the palm-wine tapper's. Ade's heart pounded like a pneumatic drill. If they arrested him and the Olabos somehow linked him with Iya, they would slam him behind bars before he could spell his name. 'Iya this is why I wanted us to go. Wait here, begin to pack, we are not staying here.' He scampered out to bow before the jeep, hands held together in a show of unsurpassable humility.

The passenger leapt out of the front seat. 'Squatters,' he said, with concentrated malice. He was wearing a sweat-streaked khaki uniform.

'Chief sent me to bury this goat here in case of disease,' said Ade.

'That is not my concern. Squatters must to be follow us go for headquarters.'

'Ha ha my brother, how you talk like this for this time. Night nearly fall. Make we settle now, ah, ah.' said Ade, wringing his hands, imitating the act put on by even the most hardened prison inmates in Kakirikiri. 'My brothers, wait there.' He ran to the car for the sealed brown envelopes he kept for such emergencies and thrust one into the man's hands. At that, the mate tumbled from the jeep, cigarette stub in hand. Ade handed him an envelope too. Allah please don't punish me, it is no bribe, but a consultancy fee, like the money *oyinbo* people gave to the custodians of your holy mosques for buying their jets.

The men grinned, weighing each other's windfalls in their keen eyes, raced to the jeep, no doubt off somewhere else to reap where they did not sow. Ade dashed back indoors. 'Quick bring only what you need. Where we are going is not that big.' He hoped to smuggle Iya round the back of the house and into his shed.

'They have gone? How much did you give them?' Iya fiddled with her glasses. 'If I go with you how will Malomo or Saro know where I am?' She shuffled over to her grandfather's photograph and clutched it to her chest. She was going to take them as well as her favourite threadbare prayer mat and beads and her box full of medicines and necklaces.

Ade counted to ten, heaved a deep breath in and took her by the wrist. 'Iya, Bola's men do not care,' he said, slowing his speech for persuasive effect. 'I have

106

seen them in action. To them neck is neck to cut or break, and a gun is for offloading into anybody who crosses their way. Take a few things and let us go. Only one mat.'

Iya looked lost.

'Ok take that.' She wanted her old jewellery tin that contained prayer beads and all the other miscellaneous bric a brac with which she kept herself amused. He shook his head, harder this time. 'No. Not the crate.' If she opened it she'd want to spend all night reminiscing. He helped her pack and bundled her into the car, rushed off to turn off the stove. Iya seemed about to open the door, but with an angry stare and a grunt, he buckled her back in and this time, perhaps sensing the strain in his restraint, she placed her hands on her lap in reluctant surrender. Ade started the engine, reversed, heard the thrum of another engine and saw the lights from the jeep twinkling through the forest towards Iya's hut again.

Bastards. 'They must have opened the envelopes.' He'd stuffed scrap paper in with the naira notes. The car lurched back through the forest but one officer gave chase on foot, leaping over the charred undergrowth and round a trapped digger. Ade put his foot down, spinning the rear wheels in the mud. The engine stalled, and the other man cut Ade off with the jeep beside a ditch. 'Are you ok? Iya, ok?' he said, his head throbbing.

'Are you sure you can drive this kind of motor?' said Iya.

The officer lumbered up before Ade could restart the car. 'You think you wise pass us?' he said, between huge sucks of breath and the intimidating taps on the car with a pistol. 'Oya, let's go, Paul will follow us.

Headquarters or your house. Oga, it is up to your choice,' he said and clambered in next to Ade.

Ade stole a glance at his fake wristwatch. Tuesday the 29th of July, a few seconds to half-past five. Yeni might even be home already. He started the engine, and they raced home with the siren of the jeep blaring behind him until they got close to his estate in Lekki where he coasted the car to the house, found the men five dollars, promised to find some more, which they all knew was a lie, but, based on the laws of diminishing returns, an offer they would be foolish to douse. Ade escorted them back through the estate gates, left them in the middle of nowhere, nipped round the back of the house to smuggle Iya into his shed minutes before Yeni arrived. She sounded in a worrying excellent mood and Iya did not.

Fourteen

Iya shuffled in through the makeshift dividing curtain. 'Oh, just come back? How was work? Who is that?' she said, pointing at a figurine lying on the rough-hewn wooden worktable. A pallid bulb glowed from a cord swung across the eaves.

Ade shrugged. It was a statue of Ranti but he did not want to encourage Iya down that or any other line of questioning. He glanced at the door. Where was this boy Zaki? Not lost around the back streets. It wasn't even that dark yet. Iya sat down, her slender scaly fingers intertwined on the table. 'I am glad you still carve but is this where you normally sleep?'

Which meant why have you put me in this shed. Ade used an old prefabricated hut at the foot of the garden as his hideaway. It stood ten strides behind a copse of pink-flowering bougainvilleas and in it he often carved or read or watched Ranti on his computer, passing the time until he had to face his wife in the principal house. 'I will move you later when I know that they are not looking for you or us,' he said, to gurgling self-hatred and guilt.

Iya seemed content for the moment and went back to talking about how she taught him to carve Ayo boards with the grain and how she used trees to date important events, for example, when a house was built, when a chief died, or a child was born. This was safe ground. 'How for do. You taught me well. Remember when we used to sell Ayo boards at Federal Palace?'

'And you wanted to give that girl discount? Because she is a fine girl?' said Iya and bared her receding gums in a hearty laugh. 'That day I begged Allah, please don't let him be like his father. The man likes women too much.'

Was that rhetorical, a warning or an alarm? Ade stewed in bitter disgust at the memory of that man, who made up half of him, but who refused to pay his school fees because Iya brought him up as a Muslim. He was probably looking for an excuse to disown the boy after what happened between Malomo and Buraimoh. Yet he was one to talk when it didn't take him long after he booted Malomo to bring in Madam Superbad and that pair of fiendishly wicked daughters.

Iya gave him a playful tap on the knee. 'Will you carve one of me? I will pay you.' Minus tuition fees she said, after a brief pause and clapped her hands in delight at her joke. In a bright green top over a brown loincloth, for the first time in the three days since he brought her from the village, she seemed to have had a good night's rest. Iya wiped her face with her prayer beads and got up to sing Ade's oriki, his praise song. It promised that he would grow up a pleasant boy, an omoluwabi, and marry an agreeable girl and they would live happily ever after. After that, the pace quickened and Iya broke into a brisk dance as she segued into the extra bit on the end of the oriki, a coda that sounded like rap, or like a call to arms but in a strange dialect. 'I will record it for you to keep and play to your children one day because it is important to know the history of this family.'

'You always say that.' During the black days that he spent at home after his dad chucked his mother out for her adultery, his oriki used to give him hope, but it now made him sad because its predictions had not come true. Quite the opposite, and he'd ended up here in a gigantic mansion but without an iota of control, even over the fate of most of his gametes. Gormless gonads, manufacturing millions of gametes whether he liked them or not and he couldn't even tell which ones to keep or discard. Talk of a man's control over his body. No institute for men like him. 'As soon as Zaki comes, I have to go. Food will soon be here,' said Ade with another anxious glance at the door.

'Good. I am hungry. But you said your wife travelled?'

'Now she is tired and resting in the house,' he said, to tightening in his stomach.

Iya blinked. The cataract glowed in her left eye. 'Hunh, she knows I am here?'

This was another roundabout way of asking why his wife had not come to pay her respects. 'No. I told you that I don't want anyone to know that you are here because of what happened with those men the other day. I will explain but not today,' he said, resenting Iya for forcing him to lie to her over this trivial matter when larger elephants sat in the room.

'No wonder.'

'Iya, no wonder what?' he said. Ade hated that phrase - no wonder. 'Iya, I know you are going to ask what happened at the ministry. But you cannot just go there swear affidavits and the next day you get documents. It takes time, sometimes weeks, months, and ten thousand naira is nothing nowadays,' he said, and, creaking under the weight of his mounting deceptions, he fiddled with a chisel. He'd been nowhere near the Land Registry. He may be stupid and pig-headed and he loved Iya, but no way was he going to blow his cover just after the villagers lost their case. Not at least until he'd finished this business with Controller. Then he'd find out if Iya had a good enough case in her own right.

Iya was about to say something but went quiet. Ade knew that look. He gestured for her to go on.

'Are you not studying? Where are you working?' said Iya.

'You mean where I am working?'

Iya's turned to face him square on. 'You are going to answer me or not?' she said with the air of an impatient judge.

'I am in the Service.'

'No wonder.' She flipped over a piece of cardboard and under it lay an old identity card from Kakirikiri that Ade often used to brush the dust off the worktable.

His toes stiffened. 'Where did you find it?'

'Why do you ask? Is it not yours?' She pointed at a toolbox on the edge of the table.

'Oh, that is from Kakirikiri, I am on secondment there in a section called KIYO.'

'Is that why they gave you this name, Afediyabamba?'

For the thousandth time he wished he'd told Yeni and Bola to run off and boil their teeth and leave him alone when they asked him for the favour in Zaria. He glanced at the door, desperate for Zaki to arrive. 'I have to use that name because I don't want them to connect your case with mine.' At that moment and to his immense relief the main door scrunched over the sawdust and in hopped Zak with a black sports bag. Ade smelled spices and boiled plantain and fried yam.

'Wait, don't go, eat with us,' he said.

Zaki looked horrified to have even given the slightest impression that he considered himself worthy of sharing a space, let alone a meal, with Ade. He pulled his shorts up. 'Eh, no sir, it's no prombulem, sir. Let me shut the door for mosquito not to enter.' His tiny lips turned down in apology.

'Let them enter, they will fry in this heat, just eat,' said Ade.

The boy's smile, the first Ade had seen on his face, a delight. 'Zaki, how are your people at home?'

Zaki's hands shook. He dropped a plate on to the table. 'Did I vexed you sir? Please don't send me back.'

Was that because they relied on the money Zaki sent home or because they had sold him retail or wholesale and wouldn't want him back? 'No, I was not talking about that. But when you reach the house if madam asks tell her that I sent you somewhere. You

112

hear? Don't forget. If she starts her wahala tell her that I am coming,' said Ade, chiding himself for upsetting the boy but also disappointed that the boy might dislike and fear him as much as he did Yeni.

Zaki bowed and left. Ade picked up the statuette. 'Iya I have to go. You eat. Even you and that tapeworm inside you cannot finish all this.'

'Is that a challenge? Wait there and I will show you,' said Iya.

'I don't know where you put it. Tomorrow Zaki will come and clear everything or I can do it if you want.'

'Because you are a big man in a big house, you don't want to eat with me again? You don't want to tell the truth about what happened to make you change your name at work? Is your real name a shame?'

He'd made it to the door, inches to freedom. Irked, he spun around. 'Iya, it's not that,' he said, but the simple whispered questions as she popped a prawn into her mouth set him off. 'Iya, I've made many mistakes.' He bowed his head, shut his eyes tight and leaned against the door.

Iya put her arms around him. 'Don't shake your head like that, my son. Sit here, not there here, beside me, bring your stool. You make a mistake? And so? Even nature is not perfect. Do you think I don't know that you are inside real *agbako?* Yesterday I am looking through a window and I see how Zaki and the boys are running *kurukere* like cockroach, spinning about like that Baba Gami the barber's chair. I said to myself, they must fear the madam of this house. Do I know her people? How come he married so quickly and did not tell me? But whatever it is we will come out somehow together, Insha Allah.' She patted him on the head. 'You

113

are a good boy. Don't let bad things change you into a bad person. I remember when you were small you were the only one who would pack the jerseys and carry to the shed after you finish playing football and when you wanted something you did it. No matter what. You are still the same, when you want something you try. Remember the day you followed me home from your papa's house? That is the Ade I know, a boy who will take his head to crack any coconut so that others can enjoy.'

'Ah, Iya I don't think so.' He glowed inside that at least she and perhaps the girl in his class bullied by the Dean and Moji still thought well of him. But he could never forget the day he ran away from home, his seventh birthday, the day Princess Diana died, Sunday morning 31st August 1997. He chased after Iya's bus to flop, sobbing, into her lap and swore that never, never would he do what his mother did to him; leave his child, never, unless he died.

'Iya, I cannot sit here talking when food is ready inside and it will go cold and so will yours.'

'Wait, let me show you this first. Yesterday you ran away before I had time. Better to understand the past or it will punch you in the back of the head.' Iya broke off a piece of yam dipped it into the stew and popped it into her mouth. She beckoned at Ade and pointed under the bed. Ade dragged out the frame made of thirty or forty slim slats, some black or charred and held together by twine, cord and wire.

'History is to us what tail is to animals,' said Iya.

'The tale we grew to replace our tails,' he said, in a playful, portentous voice.

'If you let someone else look after it for you, you go shock, like electric.' As when people go for plastic surgery. 'They open their eye after the operation and their lips are like bananas,' said Iya.

An awkward smile raised itself to his lips. But he, a man with a bleached face and trimmed nose, could hardly laugh at the cosmetic mishaps of others.

On Iya's face settled a mournful solemnity. 'Listen,' she said with quiet emphasis. 'This is history, how we used to do things before they come and dabaru everything with their big English.' She brushed a fly off her nose. 'Are you listening? My grandfather, Jinadu, my mother's father.' She paused, closed her eyes as if in reverie and smiled, opened her eyes, stroking the slats as she spoke. 'Baba Agba Jinadu is the one who made our family come from under the table of others to eat our own fine food. That house and that land is what I have kept. They can say what they like in their court but it is my own and all the rest and I know it and they know it too.' She sipped from a glass. 'Maybe one day it is Malomo who should be the one teaching you all this,' said Iya, in a saddening voice.

Ade whined inwardly. About Malomo he could not bear to hear. After dad threw her out and replaced her with Madam Superbad, night after night tapped and slapped, beaten into new shapes if he made a mistake in his homework, or forgot the name of a state governor, or how many gallons of petrol it took to fill the car, sent to bed while his stomach begged for anything, anything at all to caress, even orange pips, he had yearned for his missing mother to come and get him. But when he wished, waited, and prayed to Allah for months and she did not come and Iya told him that Malomo was living with Buraimoh, his heart turned to stone against her and for years to most girls and women - except Iya. 'Iya thank you now I have to go.'

'You, you have a child yet or yet going to have?' she said, in a tentative voice.

Ade turned the statuette over in his hand with a quizzical air and shrugged. 'Early days.'

'Talk, you have pickin or not?'

'No pickin. I said no time yet for that,' he said, peeved that she looked relieved.

'Why you look as if someone poured hot pepper in your ear?' Iya flinched. 'What was that? Did you hear it? Like coconuts dropping on the ground.' She shuddered and leapt to the front window.

'No don't open the window. I think it is Zaki,' said Ade, in great agitation. 'I have to go before she kills him.' Then, as he charged from the hut, he feared what Iya would think of him when she learned about Yeni and him.

Fifteen

'What happened?' said Ade, and, trying to recall the basic first aid he learned at school, dropped to one knee on the flagstone floor beside Zaki. Blood oozed from the boy's head and for a moment Ade recoiled in horror from an image that reminded him of himself as a defenceless little boy. 'Yeni what is wrong with you? You banged his head on the wall did you not? Look at blood everywhere, even there.' He pointed at the marks on the wall. 'And on your fingernails and your clothes.'

'How many times have I told him not to run inside from the rain?' said Yeni. 'He fell because he is not used to this kind of floor.'

'You mean how many times have you beaten him senseless?' At least the woman retained enough humanity to lie. 'It is not his fault you know, that this month has not worked out. I know-'

'Thank you Mr Twitter mouth. Why don't you go and broadcast our problem on satellite so that every common houseboy in Lekki will know? You will like it if I put all your private things on Facebook?'

'Sorry.' Ade leaned over Zaki. 'Are you ok?'

The boy nodded. 'No prombulem, sir.'

'Look at him making sorry face. Ask him what he was doing inside your trouser pockets,' said Yeni.

'Is that all? I asked him to take the tissue out before he washed them.'

'But the money I left for Mrs Owopade the treasurer and this piece of shit goes and took it.' She prodded Zaki with a toe. 'Tell your oga where you put my money or you will smell real trouble,' said Yeni.

That Yeni had discovered the missing money gripped Ade's throat like a thorny vice. 'Sorry I meant to tell you. If it is the money in the envelopes in the drawers with the brochures, I took it. Emergency with the property.' His voice faded to a rough and guilty whisper.

'Don't insult my intellectuals,' she said and tapped the back of Ade's head. 'If it is women you are spending my money on you will not last more than my spit in this Lagos.' She licked her forefinger and raised it to the ceiling to make her point.

'Don't you ever slap my head like that again, ever,' he said, through gritted teeth and grabbed another napkin off the table to press to Zaki's head. 'We cannot just leave him bleeding like this.'

Yeni kicked her foot free. 'We? We? When did this matter become a matter for *us*, ernh? Take him to the hospital if you want but if they take pictures and pass to cunts 'r' us don't come and beg me when they charge you to court.' She clucked and clapped her hands. As she left she turned round in the doorway. 'Ok, why not call Dr Opa?' she said in a softer voice.

'It's Zaki's brain that needs treatment not your bloody uterus.' He wished he hadn't said that.

Yeni whinnied and stomped off. Seconds later one of the newer house girls crept in. 'Yeah pah, Zaki don die oh, don die oh.' She wept, slapping her head and ears and hopping on the spot.

'Get me a bandage or towel from the cupboard in the downstairs toilet,' said Ade but she went on weeping and only stopped when Yeni reappeared now in a spotless light blue frock.

'Eh, Julius, this temper of yours is something bad oh.' The colour dropped from her face and she crumpled to the floor.

The house girl screamed. Ade leapt across to break Yeni's fall. He laid her head down next to a table leg. She was conscious and breathing, her pulse, 54. He raised her legs into the air as per previous attacks and she soon opened her eyes and heaved a deep breath. Most of her attacks lasted only seconds. Stress and dehydration, noxious stimuli all precipitate, the doctor had said. Today she did not look that bad and had a good colour, the tone in her legs and disdain for everyone and everything soon spread from her eyes to the rest of her face. Ade propped her up in a chair, handed her phone back and dashed the blood-soaked Zaki to hospital.

An emergency operation removed the clot on Zaki's brain. Back on ITU the nurses seethed at Ade, addressed him with such unconcealed contempt you'd think him a defendant at Nuremberg. He hurried off, tail trapped between his legs by the anxious thought that it would take only one phone call to P and J and they could expose his secret and charge him for child abuse.

Sixteen

Ade flicked on the bedside radio for the early six o'clock news and wished he hadn't, because Controller came on, gushing about a Gold medal, this time awarded by the Civil and Historical Society. They said he penned an influential pamphlet on land tenure in precolonial Lagos. Ade winced. This country is truly kidnapped. At this rate the man will be running for governor, have statues erected in his honour. How for do, they've built them for mass murderers all over the world. A few won the Nobel Peace Prize for blowing people into jigsaw pieces.

Yeni prodded him in the back and flicked on the low lights. 'Where are you going at this time when you are on the afternoon shift?'

He needed to feed Iya without Yeni finding out. The blast of freezing air round his ankles and Yeni's sharp prod in his back did not help his mood. 'To Expresscare. To see your handiwork. If not for that surgeon who knows what would have happened.' He drew his pyjama tops around him against the cold and got up so that he could smuggle some food to Iya before Yeni got downstairs. After he turned down the air-conditioning he looked out of the front window, with an envious glance at the egrets flying east in a spotless sky. A long white saloon pulled up. 'Oh, stony shit.'

'What is it?' Yeni leapt to the window. 'Fucking effrontery. What does cunts 'r' us want here? I will show her *jaguda* way today if that is what she wants. I told you not to take the boy to hospital? See what you've caused, now?'

In a raging panic, Ade hopped, left foot first as always, into his silk socks, moccasins with inserts and a black pair of trousers and bounded first downstairs to warn the house help that madam may be coming downstairs, then called Iya. 'Iya, quick, she's here,' he said, tripping through the doorway like an exhausted triathlete.

'What? Your voice is shaking,' said Iya.

'It's the TV people. If they find you, I'm finished,' said Ade. 'Ah, it must be the nurses or maybe it was Damola, our neighbour that Yeni does not like, must have heard about Zaki and told PJ. They are running a show against domestic abuse and the hospital has my photo and address and I don't want them to know that you are here. Wait there, don't come out. I will bring food later. Drink the biscuit, sorry eat the biscuits,' he said.

'Why don't you-'

'Iya, wait, not now. I'm trying to think. Just go behind the curtains and wait for me to call you-'

'Who are you talking to?'

His scalp seemed to leap from his skull. It was Yeni just outside the cabin. 'Nobody, the yeye man who calls himself receptionist cannot even tell me which ward they took Zaki to.' He leaned against the wall to catch his breath whilst he clawed his mind for a plausible follow-up lie.

'Cunts 'r' us is in the parlour. She says she is not going anywhere until she sees you. Did you see police?' said Yeni with a slight tremor in her voice that did little for Ade's nerves.

Ranti got up to greet him in the vast living room. She was wearing charcoal-grey trousers, a white silk shirt with a mauve top right quarter and looked every part of the up-and-coming executive. On another day he would have told her how proud he was of her but he lurched past her to fumble with a light switch, turned the bright overhead down lighters on instead of the dim wall-lights he wanted, found the right knob at last and turned the lights down. 'Migraine. I cannot stand the bright lights shining off the vases,' he said and put on a strong Zimbabwean accent for Yeni's benefit. He sat down in one of the outer chairs just in front of the wall.

'Me, I suffer too when it is hot,' said Ranti.

Since when? Was she play-acting, or playing with him before she noosed him up for the gibbet? Her face gave nothing away. Not even that right eyebrow. 'Why are you here?' he said, in an anxious whisper.

Ranti sat down two chairs away and pulled some files out of a briefcase. 'For the record can you confirm your name and address, sir?'

Her neutral tone put his back up. 'Should I not wait for both of us to be here?'

'Sir, I ask only a simple request.'

'So do I,' said Ade and to his relief, Yeni marched in with a pot of coffee on the cracked tray she kept for guests she disliked, which meant everyone except a few recent business "aunts." She was wearing an orange top over a brown mid-calf shirt, no extensions in hair that she seemed to have roughened again to make it look as if they had been fucking each other's brains out. What Ranti made of that and the expensive furniture he dared not contemplate and he sank back into the shadows and with anxious amusement watched the women swap barbed glances.

'How many sugars, or are you a bitter person?' said Yeni.

Ranti gestured refusal over the bowl of sugar. 'Sweet enough. You have or had a boy called Zaki in your employ?'

Ade's mind raced back to the condemning looks on the nurses' faces. He gulped and nodded. 'I took him to the hospital as a precaution after he fell.'

Yeni waltzed over to sit down on Ade's two-seater between him and Ranti. 'They are too clumsy. If he was here, I will not let him serve you today. All the boiling water will be on your company dress and my floor. Julius, not so?'

'How is the boy?' said Ranti.

He gave her credit for asking and was about to answer when Yeni butted in. 'Very ok. But for you coming to disturb us this early in the morning he would be calling them at the hospital now as we are sitting here. Not so Julius?'

Don't overdo the Julius, she knows who I am, Yeni. 'Absolutely right, I was going there when you arrived.' Ranti had not laid a finger on either of them yet and he breathed more freely.

'Do I know you somewhere?' Ranti leaned forward, a questioning frown on her face.

For seconds his heart slapped about, like a flag in a gale. 'Ah, everybody says that I resemble someone they know. That is why I stopped going to the market. Too many requests for selfies.' He squirmed further back into his chair.

'How can you know him anywhere? His name is Julius Afediyabamba, and he is my husband.'

'His name and the fact of your marriage, I do not doubt at all, ma.'

'What is it you want?' said Ade, the force of his indignant defensiveness taking him by surprise.

Ranti shrugged and flicked open a reporter's notebook. 'It won't take long,' she said.

'That is exactly what that quack said to my tooth until three hours later I took my mouth and ran away with it from his room,' said Yeni.

'Am I right to say that the scan showed subjudue, subdue?' Ranti's attempts crumbled into a pleading smile.

Ade leapt to her aid to make up for snapping at her earlier. 'You mean subdural.' He'd learned that word at the hospital only the other night.

Yeni, on hearing the warmth in his voice, turned to glare at Ade.

'This girl called Abi or Agi found you with the boy. Yes? No?' said Ranti, again with that irritating condescension.

Ade suppressed the urge to snap back. Was this unalloyed revenge or about Yeni, or just power? He would never have guessed it in all their years together. But then the mote in his eye was just as large. Was he not the Marcus who puffed himself up like a pompous army officer with the Cordelias at Bar Beach? 'The girl may be right,' said Ade.

'Right as in correct in every detail?'

'Correct in that I was there, not as an explanation for what I was supposed to have done there.'

'Can I see where they sleep? I assume not in such a beautiful room.'

Beautiful room. There she goes again. Is that why she is here? Curiosity and envy, contempt, inverted snobbery, reverse psychology? 'This place? No, Zaki

125

does not sleep here. This is where we entertain intruders,' said Ade, with the emphasis on the last word.

Ranti's mouth twitched and whilst Yeni churned her knees, she made a slow and long entry in her notebook. When Ranti flipped yet another page, up shot Yeni from her seat. 'Calm down,' Ade said and pulled her back.

'Calm down? In my house? No way they can just wake up one morning and say they are going to search my house. No way.' She threw him off her. 'Inspection? Now whatever the call you PJ woman, get out and off my property and take your stupid cameraman with you. And I will make sure they search you before you go because if even one drop of salt is missing, you will smell hot chlorine and pepper.'

'When your houseboy turns up with more blood on their clothes than in their veins, it is in the public interest for us to investigate.'

'Sheeoh, you will not find your pubic interest in my backyard.' Yeni glanced out of the front window.

Ranti raised a faint dismissive chortle. 'Will *you* take me round to the back of the house sir? I just need an idea of the layout for my preliminary report.'

'Preliminary my arse. No way is he taking you behind any shed,' said Yeni and just then Bola waltzed in wearing a pinstriped black suit. His barrister's wig and a briefcase swung from his left hand. 'My dear TV girl, leave the premises or I will bury you so deep under the fallout from your crass stupidity it will take more than an army of autocues to disinter you,' he said in a loud baritone. Ade cringed in begrudged gratitude to the man he detested even more than Controller. 'Thanks,' he said.

'Tell that over-promoted ex test tube of yours to keep her beak out of my family's business,' said Bola. 'Or, else. Well, I don't have to spell it out, do I?'.'

Ade clamped his tongue, more concerned about how to get through the next awkward evening with Iya,

Seventeen

Iya slid through the gap in the raffia curtain, sat down at the table and pointed at the fractured frame. 'Look, Papa Jinadu's photo, broken,' she said, wiping her face with her prayer beads. 'It broke when I tried to hide it when you phoned me this morning.'

Ade unwrapped the fresh-baked bread and set it down on the table to let it breathe then found an empty biscuit tin under the table. 'I'll put it in here. Maybe Baba Noru can glue it back together. Sorry.' She so loved that photograph.

Iya scoffed. Baba Noru took a year to repair one small stool, better off doing the job herself. She took the cover off the steaming dish of stewed haddock, sighed and replaced the lid. 'Hunh, is it because you don't want your wife to hear me eating from a plate that you bring me plastic bowl as if I am a small child?' She pushed the dish away. 'Tell me what happened between you and yellow? Yes, Ranti. That was her name wasn't it? A fine girl. If it was her living in this house she will not leave me inside a shed. Sorry, let me respeak. If it was her you are with *you* will not fear taking me inside the house. True or not?'

Iya liked Ranti even before she met her, since she learned that on his first nervous visit to Ranti's house he found, to his pleasant surprise, her father, the fiery intimidating Coach, mimicking a penguin in a game of worst impressions gets to eat the chicken wattle. Later that night Ade went to bed consumed by envy for the family life he missed as a child. He told Iya that a content family like Ranti's, like the family of the little bear in the story of Goldilocks, is what he wanted for his child.

Iya wiped the plastic plate dry then glared up at Ade. 'Answer me. I am right or not? She does not want me inside. Just like your father's wife used to do when I visited you.'

He ducked the latter comment. 'Ranti? I already told you what happened. We had a small quarrel over nothing but before I knew it that was it, we finished.'

Iya shook her head. 'You think I just dropped like chicken shit?' A cough spasm doubled her up, almost throwing her off her stool. Ade held her steady and for want of anything better to do, tapped her on the back, willing the spasm to stop. She straightened up at last, eyes silvered by the tears from her coughing spasm. 'Thank you my son,' she said after three deep heaves of breath. She gave his arm a reassuring squeeze. 'Now tell me the truth.' She stopped for another deep breath. 'Why did you and yellow scatter and you go and marry this one here?' She gestured at the house with her head, blew her nose and looked away. 'This is what I was praying to Allah not to happen. For my son to marry somebody that does not agree with him. Marriage of allergy. The same thing that Malomo did.' She placed the bread on her plate. 'But Allah knows best,' she said, deep sadness in her eyes.

He almost hugged her, but anxiety restrained him. 'Iya you say Allah knows best, but you didn't say that when you were singing my oriki that promised me a likeable girl.'

'It does not work like that. Your oriki said that an *omoluwabi* would marry an agreeable girl.' But if he was not an *omoluwabi* how could he expect to marry a fine girl? Iya shook her head. 'Your palaver is even worse than that of Malomo,' she said and with a wistful warble her voice faded into silence.

'Worse? Do you think I will ever do what she did? Leave my child?'

Iya scoffed. 'Always you prick Malomo in the same wound. I did not blame you when you told your papa about Malomo because you were only six and did not know what you were doing. And you did not know the consequences.'

Ade winced at the memory of the day he found his mother in bed with Buraimoh. He was six years old.

'Can you hear me?' Iya tapped him on the knee to get his attention. 'Are you listening?' said Iya. 'Are you remembering all the problems it caused? You thought it would pay you to tell him but you see the result?' His dad saw him as a cuckoo in the nest and in weeks replaced Malomo with Madam Superbad and her two girls. 'And now my only grandson is in Lekki like a big man but he is like a donkey with a rope around his neck and he is going round and round until the rope is too short and he cannot move, but he tells himself that things are ok because they give him grass to eat and water to drink. No wonder.'

'What do you mean by no wonder?' said Ade. That condemnatory, patronising, deterministic phrase scoured his insides like a cactus sponge. No wonder, they say, in unison, clapping their hands and tutting as if that explained everything as if to say cards dealt and marked at birth for this one, that was it, the end, cannot escape, immutable, how else was the boy supposed to end up? 'Iya if it is a matter of no wonder, why did you agree to look after me? Was it to look at me as I failed so that you can file it away and compare it with all the other cases of no wonders with your friends? And you always side with my mother. She burned her own son's foot. You know what I went through at school because of that foot?' Ade clenched his eyes shut, tried to contain himself but the bitter memories of the put-downs, the overslaughs, the taunts, the hunger, misery, tear-stained sheet of his early days racked up and up. He burst into confession. 'Iya, it was *bi ere, bi ere,* like play, like play, I didn't know Yeni was going to be like this.' He wiped his eyes with a bunched fist. 'Sorry, grandson is supposed to make you happy. Not all this *apakati*,' he said, between sniffles.

Iya wiped his face with her sleeve. 'Ade. Why, ah, ah. I told you before, even nature makes mistakes, plenty of them for that matter. Do you not see the mistakes nature made begging on the street, some have no legs or hands, or no nose, or eyes like mashed egg? It is because I love you that I am harsh with you.' She embraced him.

The warmth and stiffness of her sun-dried blouse reminded him of when she used to tuck him into bed after a glass of coconut milk. 'It is Ranti that I need. I want her back.' He stewed with apprehension, unsure whether Iya would praise or condemn.

'Hunh, my son, think well. Do you want her because you love her, or because anything is better than this?' she said.

'Ah Iya, this is why I didn't want to tell you. I love her full stop, how can you even say that?' he said, angered by Iya's smug look.

'Every action is a reason trying to get out and sometimes when it comes out people don't see it even when it is dancing in front of their faces. If you do not tell me the whole story of how you went from yellow to

131

this one I am going home.' She hung her head whilst she caught her breath, then got up to pack.

'Wait,' and out flooded the rest of his miserable confessions about what happened in Zaria, the false statement, Controller, everything. When he finished Iya did not speak. She bit her lip and the look she had in the photo of her as a youthful woman at her husband's graveside returned to her face.

Ade felt much better for unburdening himself. 'Eat. The food is getting cold. I can go and buy some more if you want, but I will have to go round the back.'

Iya lowered her gaze from the ceiling and shook her bowed head. 'This is my fault,' she said. 'If I did not make mistakes with my case, my grandson will not be in the pocket of the Martins. How can I struggle for forty years and this the result? It is because they have money that you followed them like that in Hausaland. That is the reason why you did what they said. I saw this habit in you from when you were small. I warned you did I not?'

He blanched at the shameful memory. Yeni, well into her teens, used to accompany the estate manager to the village in a chauffeured Merc. She often wore her hair in red barrettes, feet in snow-white socks and shiny ox-blood sandals. Once, in a hissy fit, she threw a bottle of iced water out of the car window, just like that, as if water, the first thing the space missions look for on any planet, did not matter. Only rich people could throw it away like that. They turned the tap and there it was. With Iya, clean water was something you worked, prayed and fought for, showed that you cared for by walking a long way to split it from its family in the river with promises to love and not waste it and show it respect. One

Saturday morning he'd waited all morning in desperate anticipation for her to appear and when she got out of the car his heart lunged into his throat. Her arrogant pout, pert nose in the air, pinched surely against foul smells, eyes narrowed against village dirt, cornrows adorned with pearls and a sliver of a smooth neck above a pink blouse made him ache with the futility of his longing. What must it be like to be one of them? They did not have to worry about anything or what people thought because what you thought always counted for more. Aged twelve or thirteen, eager to catch Yeni's eye, he flashed her a wide smile to show off the teeth he scrubbed with a spot of toothpaste mixed with ash that morning. Yeni looked straight through him. In response he pummelled himself in frenzied self-castigation. What was he thinking? Why would she look at him, a drunkard's son? The girl lived in a palace, face made in heaven, your nose an insult. You can run and your teeth are strong, but what is special about that? Even rats can run and have strong teeth. As Yeni's car swished past the weak-kneed Ade, Yeni threw a green bottle out of the rear window. He scampered over to pick it up, as an archaeologist would to some precious find. Though cold and wet and covered in sand, she had touched it and held it to her lips and so would he, surely a sign that one day their lips would meet. Tingling with reverential excitement, he gave the bottle a frenetic brush down and raised it to his mouth just when Iya looked out of the front window. In a calm but scouring voice she explained that he was better than that. His shame convinced him to train as a lawyer so that his children would not grow up like him.

'Those days are past. I caused this mess and I can find a way out. Controller, our oga is making the prison into a business park with the girls,' he said, struggling to shore up his crumbling composure.

'Controller? Is that not the same Sheki Ggagba who writes in the newspaper about land in Lagos? He is paying the officers out of his own money I hear.'

'Not you as well. He is a thief. It is not his money, it is the money for drugs and to buy vans to take the inmates to court. If a thief builds a house or mosque or borehole for the town, is he still not a thief? I am sick of it when everybody sings his praises. That Mexican drug baron who tarred the village road is he still not a murderer?' he said, warming to his thesis. 'Someone takes your land by gun and builds roads and railway to empty your land by force is that person still not a thief? Even if as he runs away if his horse shits manure that you can use on your farm is he still not a thief? And he will come back and say the cocoa is his because it was his horse.' Wilder, crazier, angrier, illogical examples galloped to mind but Iya stopped him with a firm wave of her hand and a wry smile.

'You are like baba Agba sometimes, when he vex that is how he talked,' she said, the distant twinkle growing in her eye.

The allusion to the great Jinadu his great-great-grandfather made Ade blush with keen pride.

Iya went on. 'Controller and what you say reminds me of a story Baba Agba Jinadu told me. That nothing some people will not do for money.' She sipped from a glass of water, blinked and turned once again to Ade to start her story. According to the story, in the beginning the sun had all the power and energy and the moon was

134

sad and cold, no water no electricity, nothing. But it was wily, that moon. Watch me oh, said the moon, and gave the sun a list of all the sins, murder, fratricide, theft, genocide, stealing, lying, the sun could add to it if it liked but the moon bet that there was nothing that human beings would not do for money. The sun disagreed; are they not the children of the great almighty who made us all? Look how splendid I am, shining with an unquenchable light. It took the list from the moon and placed the bet. In minutes the sun lost its bet due to genocide and ethnic cleansing, whole people wiped out. The sun wept. It had never lost a bet before. Moon said it would give the sun the chance to win its stake back. They rolled over the bet. Again to no solar avail. Every day they doubled the stake and every day the sun lost and every day the moon got free heat and light and all its energy needs from the sun.

'Ha, that story is almost as good as the one I told you about Controller. But mine is true.'

'But who told you about Controller's business?' said Iya.

'You hear these things.' Ade tossed out Moji's name and chased it with a bogus cough. 'She is a girl at work with me.' He let the happy image of a smiling Moji in a yellow tabard tarry a while.

'Ah, Ade, from Ranti to Martins to Moji. Not enough sand in your gari?' Iya traced an angry doodle in the sawdust with a foot. 'You have to be careful when it comes to women. You know the cut?'

Ade pulled a face. 'Where they do terrible things to little girls down there?'

She nodded as she let out an explosive cough. 'That cut was one of the starts of trouble for me and my mama.

135

My mama had it and when I was born it caused many troubles so much that urine is coming from her birth passage, the smell is so bad my papa ran away.' She paused for breath. 'That is how it started. Baba Agba, may his soul rest in perfect peace, did not want his only daughter to be on her own. He agreed that his right-hand man will marry her and he will get land in return. Are you listening?'

Ade nodded and dragged his stool up close.

Iya went on. One day, Baba Agba fell off his white horse not far from Ita Faaji in the centre of old Lagos. On his deathbed, he called Akakambo to thank him for taking his daughter on and in return he granted his right-hand man half his land and the other half he left to his daughter for security. She was sure Baba Agba wrote it all down but when he died the documents disappeared and Akakambo and his new wife forged fresh papers and took over the entire estate. 'That little place I am living in now is what is left,' said Iya. A distant cousin secured it for Iya's mother. For years a widowed Iya and her daughter, Malomo, almost died of hunger but learned to make a stew out of the roots of stubborn grass. They boiled, roasted, fried, and crushed those roots. How they survived, she does not know. Fear of returning to those days still kept her awake at night.

'Iya you are swimming up the wrong river again. Going back to what I said about Controller and Baba Lawyers-'

'Wait. I've not finished.' Iya blinked twice, kneaded her lips with her teeth. She opened her mouth to speak, stopped and started again. 'Do you know that the wife of chief is not...no, wait another time.'

'Iya, don't do that to me, go on.' He pulled his stool up closer.

'You should know. Bola and Yeni are from the Akakambo side that stole Baba Agba's land from us. Chief's wife, the one they call Princess A is the grandchild of Akakambo's wife.'

Stunned, Ade flopped backward, anger and shock bumping his heart about like a runaway off-roader. So Chiefs are thieves and thieves become chiefs but the true owners, evicted from their land, condemned to a diet rich in raw cellulose, stubborn grass? He wanted to smash Bola's head and hold it up bleeding to those poor and angry villagers. Free cheers, hip, hip, hooray, he's a jolly dead fellow and so sing all of us oh. 'Iya, I didn't know.' He tugged at his collar because his chest and neck felt tight as though he had an undersized vest on back to front.

She patted his knee. 'Don't blame yourself. How would you know? I didn't want to say so, not to poison your mind. I kept postponing but better to hear it from me.' Iya fanned her face with her hand.

'I was going to say that I know someone who will help us. My friend, Baba Lawyers.'

Iya threw her hands up in jocular exasperation. 'Which one is Baba Lawyers again oh?'

'He is my friend at the Ayo place near Alagomeji. His actual name is Tony Ware from-'

'Tony Ware? From where?' Iya went quiet, rolled a piece of bread in her palm and tossed it into her mouth. 'Real oyinbo or one of those counterfeit ones we see in Victoria Island?'

Was she referring to him as a counterfeit too because he had Baba Lawyers as a friend and lived here

137

in Lekki instead of in the village with her? 'No, this is a real oyinbo, with big front teeth. He is from Essex but married a Yoruba girl. He is taking me to see Mr Durosote.'

'I used to know one Mr Durosote, lawyer, Ogun state. It is not his son?'

Ade shook his head.

'What is he? Businessman?' Minister? Pastor? Senator?' said Iya.

'No.'

Outside, a man hummed Amazing Grace, the hymn that Ade used to call a maize in crates.

Eighteen

Ade wiped his sweaty scalp and checked the handkerchief. To his immense relief the nick he made during a hasty shave after Ranti's call had stopped bleeding. In khaki trousers and a blue long-sleeved shirt, Ade looked out of place amongst the suited diners who looked, from their mammoth beer guts and bling, to have all the time, money and appetites in the world. Had Ranti chosen to meet him at this rich people's place at such short notice to mock him or tantalise, leave him raw and hanging from a hook whilst she waltzed off to Bambo's joint? Or to betray him? The steep slope of the lawn down to the rocky beach would make escape difficult, but Lagos boy she could have arrested you at the house the other day before Bola arrived. Calm down - you are too poor for paranoia.

The hotel concierge swiped Ade's forehead to check for fever, a sign of Ebola, and a waiter ushered him down the lush deep green lawn. He chose a table for two a few feet from the water's edge in the welcome shade of the tall papaw trees trading graceful shots in the odd gust of breeze. It was one of those dispiriting sweltering days. A steamer chugged past, towing its tiny shadow over coppery water. His watch said a few seconds to half-past two. Half an hour to go. Sizzling sounds came from the hotel kitchen.

Ranti arrived twenty minutes later, smelling of coconut and jasmine and wearing a cyan blouse over a white pair of trousers, her Nefertiti haircut, as usual, an epitome of symmetry. A black pearl necklace offset her honey skin. She was wearing sunglasses.

'Sorry, the new driver likes seven-point turns in narrow streets, reminds me of someone else who auto

139

sabotages,' she said. A waiter arrived with the lemonades. Ade lit the candle in the bowl. The flame flickered but stayed on. A good sign? Lagos boy put the beer down, speak now or lose her, but as he chose the words another fussy waiter sailed up with a sizzling platter of club sandwiches. 'Hmm, delicious, been waiting for this,' said Ranti as they polished off the last crumbs. She took off her sunglasses. Her eyes smiled as if glad for the true view of him. Faint with hunger for her, up with those spring onions he wanted to be, between the lips, the faraway glow in her eyes recalling better days. 'I thought you came to arrest me. Arants, I would never hurt a child. I've not slept since. It is as if my bed is hot ash.'

'But who made the bed?'

Ade threw his hands up in the air. 'Ah, ah Ranti, that is not fair.' The table rocked when he slapped his elbows down. To drown the awkwardness and the sourness in his mouth, he sipped from his can of lemonade, shuddered with disgust and spat out a dead fly. A leaden mood engulfed him. Ranti took a platinum credit card out of her bag ready for the bill. 'You know why I am here? Your dear wife called my office to say I wanted to steal her husband back from her.'

'Do you have any proof that I told her who I really was? This is typical Ranti. Buy a toothbrush you have to examine every single bristle before use. I am telling you now that I did not tell her anything. Think about it. After all, Arants, you are the investigative TV journalist.'

'Abs, sorry. It is just that I risked my job to come to your house that day.'

Ade calmed down. 'What do you mean?'

'I managed to get your file from Funmi. Funmi Omati, magnifying Funmi would have had you arrested for mass genocide instead of domestic palaver.' Ranti placed the credit card on a saucer. 'They suspended me from the team for breach of process. It is internal. So far.'

'What?' That job meant all the world to her, and she did that for him? He cupped his hands around hers. 'Thanks, sorry Arants, I didn't know. I was thinking that you asked me here to shine your brilliant portfolio.'

'I'm sorry for the way I treated you when you came to my office. We had been through tendering, reorganisation, renegotiation and all the rest, etcetera etceteras. It was a shock to see you, but no excuses, I behaved really badly and I wanted to make it up to you. Forgive me?'

Ade nodded. Of course he forgave her. He swatted a fly away and clasped her hand between his and told her that he would see a man called Durosote who could help him. In the shimmering sunshine, a Pharrell Williams hit boomed from the deck of a passing pleasure boat. Ade hummed along in his head, flipped his glasses off to wipe his face.

'I'll see what I can do about the investigation but you have to be quick,' said Ranti.

'I'm always quick, that's my problem,' he said.

'Don't start.' With a demure smile she slid the credit card back into the bag. Coming from Ranti, that smile passed for a green light to debauchery. 'Arants, I don't want to believe that this is the end for us, take it that we are on a sabbatical, at worse enforced leave, or a suspension and now we have the power to lift it. And with your help we can make it still.' Sidling up, Ade brushed a silvery flake of eyeshadow from her cheek,

141

and his eyes closed in heady anticipation of a kiss and the ebb and flow of blending lips, of the firmness of her breasts against his chest, of his lungs exulting in her warm breaths, breaths of heaven, breaths of Ranti fill me now and never stop. But firm fingertips repelled him. 'Abs, you haven't changed. Impossible,' she said. Gutted, he retreated and wobbled his chair into a new positions before he sat. But what did impossible mean? Impossible, as in futile, or that she wanted him but not yet, or because he would never escape Yeni, or that she did not trust him, or was impossible code for yes but first let's play hard to get? A passing steamer gave a short toot. A waiter sailed down the steps to bring them a jug-full of iced water. Ranti tipped him. 'It's only money,' she said as the waiter skipped back up to the hotel.

'Only those who have money can call it only.'

'You don't hear those who do not have love call it only,' said Ranti.

'What do you call it then? Easy come and go?' said Ade, sensing that he may have overreached.

'I call it essential. What do you call it?'

'Ranti.'

Her look of meek contentment stirred him again. Desperate for her verdict, he had to try again. Ade leaned forward but Ranti's lips, a fraction back from where he expected them, felt firm, dry and unyielding, like a camel's hoof. His stomach meowed, and he dropped, back once again, mortified, confused and almost terrified that he did not feel as distraught by her rejections as once he would.

'When do you meet this Odusote man who will help you?' she said.

'The day after tomorrow.' He coughed to clear his sore heart.

Nineteen

Across the wonky table sat Mr Tunji Odusote, crackling into two phones, one held to each ear. Flies too fat to fly dotted the tables, like wide-bodied jets during a pilot's strike. The syrupy lagoon water thumped the hull and another stomach-turning smell slinked on board. Like tobacco smoke it clung to skin, clothes and the soft furnishings on the creaking chairs.

Ade gave Baba Lawyers a rhetorical nudge. Had Durosote, the socialist banker and treasurer of the Workers' Freedom Party chosen this cloacal location on masochistic or ideological grounds? With one long and final flourish, Mr Durosote closed his ten-minute call, tossed his head back and raised the beer glass to his lips for the heeltap. 'Waste not want not,' he said, in response to Ade's bemused stare. He was wearing a red tie over a baggy white shirt with its sleeves rolled up to the elbow. 'I see you look uncomfortable. Sorry, it is not the Sheraton but I think more clearly here amongst the incredible working class. The salt of the earth, the resilient, the ubiquitous and the merciful though unpowerful. This thing those private equity vulture capitalists call restructuring is to load the company with debt, take billions in dividends, run the thing into the ground and jetstream to the Gulf,' he said. 'You hear the noise we are making over Ebola? It is because it affects Lagos, where capital is most at risk. Dangote gave one million dollars to fight the thing. Thank God for that. Let us not be churlish. But do you know that we have the highest number of deaths to HIV/Aids in the world? Not to talk of TB. Yet about that, we are so quiet. The clown Zuma in South Africa tells us to go and shower. Where?

144

In our mothers' tears? His swimming pools? My friend Julius, are you by any way inclined?' he said.

Inclined? 'Me? Erm, straight, straighter than a polygamous rabbit,' said Ade, in panic.

Durosote looked most unimpressed. 'Tony is your man ok?'

Baba Lawyers scratched his head through his green cap. 'I think he misheard or misunderstood and I have to admit so did I Tunji my friend.'

Mr Durosote gave an angry grunt. 'I could not have made myself any clearer. Will you be inclined to work with our team, in the wider interest is what I was asking?' Prematurely grey and bearded, he flicked at the flickering fluorescent bulb hanging off one end above his head. 'Ticking bulb, like Nigeria.' His dense corneal arcus made his eyes look like radio dials.

'That is why we are here, to help, to stop the country ticking the wrong way round, backward,' Ade said and got up to fiddle with the starter on the bulb. In seconds it stopped flickering, and it glowed so bright that a waiter shielded his eyes. Durosote looked impressed. 'Tony my friend, how can I help your friend?' he said, leaning back, hands behind his head.

Ade tugged a scraggy beard that he left uncombed to underline his radical sympathies. 'If I can speak for myself, my reactionary brother-in-law's senatorial campaign needs certain impediments because his victory will spell doom for your electoral aspirations on Lagos Island.' He hoped he sounded plausible after a fevered tutorial in political jargon with Baba Lawyers. 'We have some psephological figures, projections, and models to be more accurate, compare the local government election results in-'

145

'Hunh, Tony. Your friend is not as dense as I thought. If I accept the basis for your hypothetical proposition, on pedagogical grounds, then what?'

'Professor Kosimbe wants to run as a senatorial candidate for PDP. He is not as charismatic as Bola Martins so anything to boost him and undermine Bola gives your party of the people a better chance.'

Durosote threw his hands up in the air. 'Tony did you hear? Wonders never cease, oh in this Lagos. That fisherman Kosimbe wants to be governor? My earwax is more interesting than that man. Why don't these academic types leave the practical side to experts, ernh?' He downed his beer and twirled the hair over his right ear. 'Ok assuming that we are on the same side, if only temporarily. Then what?'

Ade bowed in exaggerated humility. 'I am ashamed to admit that my motives are based more on marital politics than on the lofty national issues you pursue with such unsurpassed fierce and intellectual vigour. That my wife is not overjoyed by the imminent nomination of her brother is common knowledge…'

'Cronyism. Pah, all the big isms, tribalism, racism, cronyism, nepotism, antifricanism and the other corruptions of life on earth are like sex, often practised out of sight, but effects plain to see. But thank your stars that the odd conflict between the ruling classes permits a glimpse of the ugly plans they have for the rest of us.' Durosote tapped one clenched fist with the other. 'It is our servile adherence to precedent that nails us to poverty. Nothing wrong with worshipping dead people but why have we Africans to take it so seriously? The people we are copying have grown out of it. Boy, bring more goat's meat *o jare* make man enjoy small before decay. Goat meat, Julius?'

Ade shuddered to think what Iya would make of the heretic banker. 'Er, maybe next time.'

'Pah, wake up. Eat and enjoy is the best diet for life.'

'Your tie, fine,' said the serving boy, as he wheeled away.

'Why is the boy asking? What's he going to do with it? Pull an omolanke with his teeth, hang the neighbour's goat, flog an unwilling accomplice?' said Mr Durosote.

'At least they'll know Armani did it,' said Ade.

Mr Durosote's eyes assumed a leonine anger. 'You think that is funny? Tony, tell your friend that his bourgeois sense of humour does not sit well here with me.' He punched his chest. 'To drag my people from the gutter means I must get in there with them?'

'Sorry, Tayo, Cufffingers misarticulated,' said Baba Lawyers.

'The man is here ten minutes, and he mishears, misspeaks, mis-hits, misses everything, like an emigre. Are you an émigré?'

'In a way, but-'

'Forgive him. He's nervous because he is in awe of you. Apart from a few in the City of London you know that you have no peer in this particular specialism,' said Baba Lawyers.

Mr Durosote relaxed, and a mischievous smile wafted a glow from his eyes. 'Go on, say it. I reassign and realign capital. It lands in your bank account clean and tidy, like a girlfriend or boyfriend lands in bed. Without insider knowledge you will never know where the money has been, or your partner for that matter. But

147

mine is in a good cause, my hands the antiseptic and my conscience the guide. Rogue traders are more plentiful than H_2O molecules in the seas and I hold their feet to the fire. Fleecing is too soft for them. That is for the gentle movies.' He caressed his chin. 'Ok, Julius Cufffingers. To subvert these oppressors would send a loud and clear message. Through whom can we exploit this corrosive sibling rivalry?'

'Iya.'

Twenty

The top brass had converted NN G Niger into a bar for senior civil servants. It was just after five o'clock when Ade found the former battleship riveted to the wharf by a rusty chain. With Iya beside him he sat down across a tiny table from Professor Kosimbe and Controller in a cabin about 12 feet square. The blood-red sun, perched over the corner of a glassy tower block, seemed only a few feet away. Ade tried to look calm but the cabin walls seemed to expand and contract in time with his heartbeat. Iya coughed, her ankles swollen again. Ade handed her some tissue paper. As soon as this was over and Controller gave up the files, he would take her to see Dr Opa.

'Mama, I apologise for Sheki's lateness but should you not see a doctor about that cough? She appears short of breath to me,' said Professor Kosimbe. Straightening his rainbow bowtie, he beamed at the youthful woman sitting on his lap. 'Ok, Yolande, this is not for your ears, my dear.' Yolande, in an electric blue blouse, kissed him, winked, flounced out on bright red stilettoes a size too big, her clattering footsteps rattling the clock on the cabin wall. Professor smiled at her fading footsteps with sickening smugness.

Don't get cocky, it's not your looks, sir. 'Excuse me professor, do you know Oremi village?' Ade said.

Controller nodded was about to reply when Professor Kosimbe nudged him quiet. 'Wait, Sheki let him land.' He drew the land out into leeaarned like a southern redneck. 'Oremi? The land dispute area?'

'What they did to me is like a worm inside my heart. I will not let them rest. Thieves. No home training. They bring machetes, guns and bulldozers every day. Is that

149

good? After all, I did for their father. Just because the court says they won the case and we should move? I will never agree and is that how to treat people who have been there for fifty years?' She inspected the nose pads of her glasses.

'All Iya is asking is to work with you to bring them low. What do you have to lose?' said Ade.

'Time. The other campaigns have both velocity and momentum by now, we cannot afford wishy-washy plans,' said Professor Kosimbe, flashing his white teeth. He looked most conceited and how on earth did he breathe through those pinholes?

'And time is one thing neither you nor your grandmother have much to conjure with.' Controller glanced at his gold watch, his podgy face the picture of bitter irritation. 'Excuse me ma, I don't want to disrespect mama.' He said Iya was lucky to still have all her marbles and most of her teeth at her age and she had a close grandson to boot. They could never beat the Martins and as he understood it, the other side had a secure root of title to the land as well as money and connections. 'Go and settle. No court in Lagos or Abuja for that matter will see it your way.' He turned his pig-tiny eyes on Ade.

Ade shot forward. 'Well, if that be the case can we can forget the cheque.'

'Which cheque?' said Professor Kosimbe.

Controller looked like a man trying to stifle an untimely belch. Ade had hinted at a cheque for a substantial sum of money, engineered by Durosote. Ade feigned reluctance for a second or two before he gave the cheque to the professor who stared at the figures in pious awe. 'Ok, tell us what you have in mind before doubt-'

Controller shot forward, yanked it off his friend, swivelled his incredulous gaze from Ade to Iya to professor then back to the cheque. 'Let us examine your plans before doubt smears our intentions,' he said.

'Iya wants to work with you to make sure Bola loses this election, she needs your support,' said Ade. He told them that Iya had contacts with the local youth, in places they would never imagine. For example, she said, some area boys and girls were related to her friends. All professor and Controller had to do was agree to the outline plan in principle and leave the details to her. 'We made the cheque out to your campaign but we can change it to a charity if that is more convenient, or we can return it to our bank,' Ade said. They had to make up their minds, and soon. Controller belched and tapped the table with a cigarette he looked desperate to smoke.

Twenty-one

Two days after the meeting, with Ade in near syncopal suspense, Controller called at last. They met in the late afternoon in a damp and derelict backstreet police station in Ikoyi. 'Julius, it was good of you to come. What we have to discuss is not for the airwaves,' he said, waving Ade into a high-backed chair. In mufti, his belly strained his white shirt. 'Now tell me the truth. Is Bola spending that much and where is the money from?' he said, flicking a switch on a tiny transistor radio. A highlife tune and a local news bulletin fought for supremacy with the static.

Mr Durosote's figures had exaggerated Bola's campaign finances to just within the bounds of credibility. 'I could not believe my eyes either at first but when I think about it he launches a campaign almost every week. The bags of rice he bought for supporters to distribute, like rice would go out of fashion. Rice everywhere, people could not believe it. Some of them said if he can do this maybe Bola can import snow for them to melt and drink. And come and see many Russians, Chinese, Indians, and South Africans there too.' Dizzy from his rapid-fire lies he reached out for the arms of his chair to steady himself but it had none.

'Who are his main backers then? Russians or Chinese?' said Controller.

Ade shrugged. 'All I can say is that he seems to have funds unlimited. And the money is not from Yeni. If Bola broke a leg, she would ask how many.'

Controller sighed, slid out of his chair to lock the door. Spreading his arms out like the famous statue in Rio, he leaned towards Ade and dropped his voice to an even lower whisper. 'Ok listen. The matter we discussed

152

the other day with Seinde can turn out a triangular win. And they are the best. Most stable, according to geometry. Was it Euclid?' He turned up the radio, cleared his throat, tore a leaf out of a notebook and placed it on the desk.

Ade put on his stupid foreigner expression. 'That was the general idea, sir, win-wins for all sides. Was that Pythagoras?'

'That is Greek to me. But English flexibility is the key my friend,' Controller said, brushing a moth off his shirt.

'Sorry to bring this up but I hope you will consider my situation also.'

Controller emitted an impatient sound. The moth had left a stain on his shirt. 'Let's finish this first and leave Seinde and other matters out of this for the moment. He is excellent in fact in his field but when it comes to practicalities he thinks too much of hypotheticals, contaminations, downsides and possibilities. The grim over the bright.'

'But what else would you expect from a professor?' said Ade, considering that he had not slept well for 72 hours, the agitation bubbling underneath, the tension in his calves and buttocks, the calmness he managed to portray surprised and relaxed him.

'Take this pencil,' said Controller. He scribbled, "what is Iya's request?" on the piece of paper.

Ade leaned over the desk, wrote, "have you heard of the Agidi ceremony?" and handed the note to Controller.

Controller tossed his head back and let his voice boom round the room, drowning out the jangling guitars on the radio. 'Agidi? What sort of white cap chief do you

153

think I am? My family has a high table during the *Eyo* parade and we advise the elders when it comes to choosing the next Oba. Candomble priests from Venezuela stayed in our family compound in Isale Eko last year, 2013, or was it 2012? We are going on a return visit next year and, guess what, to Argentina, if they do not devalue their peso again and cannot afford our tickets,' he said. He leaned back in his chair.

'Maybe one day when all this is over you and Iya can sit down and learn from each other about traditional Lagos life,' he said. 'But let me deal with my side, Iya, and you look after your friend.'

'Brilliant idea, Julius wiser. From divisions of labour does capital grow,' said Controller. His eyes poked out from under fleshy lids, polished by greed.

Ade steadied himself. 'Iya says she needs girls with fear in their veins. We settle you on the same night on delivery but Iya as you know wants this to be the start of a business relationship, provided we settle this file thing also sir.'

'You ping me the same question again and again. Let me reciprocate with a pong, a hypothetical question of my own. Say you get the file. How do I know that Iya will carry on business?'

'She will carry on the business because she wants me to be independent of my wife. After all, I cannot eat files.'

'Then, we have a deal. If all goes well I will give you the file,' said Controller, in that tone of mock resignation adopted by market women to convince that they've given you an unbeatable bargain. Ade could almost hear the cash register jingling in his voice.

Ade kneaded his nose. 'Sir, if your son came home with a deal like that would you not ask whether he had a coconut shell for a head? I need a signed understanding, something I can show Iya, if only for my self-respect,' said Ade, hoping he had put up plausible resistance.

Controller tapped his shirt pocket for a cigarette and shook his head. 'That is my red line. If your Iya does not accept my conditions then take your plan and go,' he said with a flinty smirk.

Twenty-two

'I thought I told you to rest your feet on the stool?' Ade said, pointing to the tools that Iya laid in neat rows under the table. 'Look at your feet, the swelling is almost reaching your legs. And you are slowing down I am sure. Only thing good left is your appetite.'

Iya looked down and wriggled feet that shone with oedema. 'Look good to fry and eat with rice. But my mind will not rest and the food will not do good until Controller is inside a cell. What did he say? I didn't hear you well on the phone today.' She picked up a plastic spoon, decided on the fork again and opened a spicy bowl of stew.

'We agreed the 16th or 17th.'

'Any signature?' She did not wait for a reply and gave a resigned shrug. 'The man is too wicked. Did you see those eyes? Like marble, like the eyes of those soldiers arrested for killing innocent civilians. Alhamdulillah, the Agidi is a week after the full moon, we must not miss it or you will have to start again. Come.' She opened another dish, let the lid drip condensation on to the table while she popped a piece of fish into Ade's mouth.

The fish was too salty and peppery but the gesture made Ade feel like a good little boy again. Disconnecting Iya's phone from the four-plug extension hanging off the table he dialled for more credit. 'That should last until after the Agidi ceremony. But don't use it all up calling boyfriends.'

Iya tucked the phone away. 'I tried to bury all that, but the urge refused to die because it is still owing me arrears,' said Iya with a cheeky smile.

Ade shuddered in pantomime disgust, 'Save Ade oh, from comical Iya. She burst my gallbladder with the laugh I laugh oh and I go bitter for this Lagos oh.'

'Must you always have the last word?'

'My name is *full-stop*,' said Ade, with an expansive air.

A glow of deep affection rose to her face and when she said Ade called to mind Jinadu, pride ballooned Ade's head full to bursting. He never tired of hearing that he did have something going for him after all and was not just destiny's toy.

Iya replaced the lid on the bowl of noodles. 'How is that friend at work, Moji?'

Ade's heart slipped on that banana skin again. 'Why? The second time you asked.'

'Ah, ah don't bite my tongue out of my head keh, Ade, do I need a certificate to want to stop some *koni koni* girl dribbling you about at this delicate time of your life?'

Ade looked out of the window to hide his angry face. The sun slid behind a doughy cloud. Moji dribbling him about? She had not even met the girl. 'Iya, but why do you still go on with Agidi? Cutting junior girls down there, urgh, where are their mothers? Their fathers?'

She jabbed her fork into a mound of noodles. 'Everywhere in the world, I am sure people want to belong to something. That is why I had it too. After, they treat you like a woman, tell you how to bargain in the market, how to manage water, plant yam and tomatoes, how to cook, about men and the rains, many things.' She raised the noodles to mouth.

'What of infection, bleeding, scarring?' A question he asked to reassure himself and to assuage his guilt for planning to use the Agidi girls to trap Controller.

'You are going to ban having children too?'

'Not the same thing.'

'That is what you say when your argument does not fire. Without respect for culture and tradition we will be like animals doing anything because it is what we like.' A cough spasm doubled her up. Ade gave her a drink. 'Thank you my son. What was I saying? Yes, about the cut. Let overseas people do what they like. I do not want to force my way on their way.' She gave her nose a mischievous tweak and added, 'even though my way is better.'

'Ah, so according to your way we should leave Controller to do what he likes with the girls in the prison because we do not want to force our way on his way?'

Iya's eyes registered a blend of amusement and pity. What sort of lawyer could not tell the difference between culture and crime against human beings? She said Ade was only angry because he had to use the Agidi ceremony to get out of a self-inflicted mess.

The jibe hurt. 'Does Niari come to sing for enjoyment or to drown out the sounds of the girls screaming and crying for the good of precious culture and tradition?' said Ade unable to resist a tilt at the moral high ground.

Iya threw feet in the air and laughed. 'Where have you been boy? The cut in our area stopped just before Abacha died. Around 1997.' The crying and wailing and singing by the girls during the ceremony was for ceremonial effect. 'Your problem? Thinking you are the only one who can swing words around till they cannot remember what they wanted to say. I did not explain what happens at Agidi nowadays because I wanted to find out if you were serious about the plan.'

'So did my-'

'Did Malomo have the cut? No,' Iya said, with a vigorous shake of the head. 'I refused. Before they finally agreed for all our area to stop I begged and begged and wrote petitions to the elders and the *Oba* and they agreed for the cut to stop. Many others followed our lead. Just a few stubborn backward places left. I wish it all to stop now but not by force or war.'

Ade hugged Iya. Widowed and homeless she did not take to drink or go off with men and saved Malomo her daughter from the cut and sold carvings and Ayo boards to get Malomo through teacher training college. What was Malomo's excuse? Bad husband? Driving each other to distraction, to addiction, into the arms of other - or was she destined to alcoholism by her genes? Or was it the limited choice of men, and she picked the best of a nasty bunch? Or was it her childhood? Or what happened to Iya during pregnancy? Nowadays they talk of problems and disease dribbling down the generations in new ways - famines in one generation causing diabetes or mental illness in the grandchildren. Was that her problem?

'Did you hear me? I asked you if the oyinbo friend is the one who took you to this magician Durosote?' said Iya.

'Baba Lawyers? Why?' he said, peeved by her sceptical air. 'We were talking about the cut and you ask about Baba Lawyers?' he said.

'Is that his actual name?' Iya stifled a wheezy cough.

'How many times? Tony Ware is his name, widowed, married a Lagos girl. Two children, both lawyers who travel a lot and I have not seen them at the Ayo place. He goes to see them from time to time. Why do you ask?' said Ade, offering a glass of water, and hoping for a change of subject.

Iya's ears pricked up. 'Lawyers? Can they help? Hunh, was it not oyinbo law Akakambo used to take our land and now you think the same oyinbo people can help you?'

'Iya you sound like Ranti. On a shiny sports car the first thing Ranti checks is economy and brakes. I did not like your agidi plan but shut up and agreed. But mine you give not one grain of credit. Did my plan with Durosote not work? But you roll your eyes on talk of Baba Lawyers. Was it Baba Lawyers who took Baba Agba's land?'

'I am worried about you, that's all.'

Ade snapped. 'Iya worry not. You think I am stupid that's why you asked me not to talk to Ranti. You thought I would get her into trouble at work. I knew what you meant, and it hurt but I didn't react. The other day you called me a donkey.'

'I didn't say that.'

'You said I was a donkey and rope going round and round. Again I did not react, not because I am dumb or anything. Then you claimed that I did not know Yeni well enough before marriage. You are right but that is old news. Can you know the inside of the mind or heart of another person? Did dad know that your daughter would turn to drink? Did mum know that dad would take fists to her?' Ade fired away. Some couples were just lucky, lucky not clever or more discerning, they did not

160

know any more about their partners than he knew about Yeni and they also must have been fucking blind, learning on the job, hitting and hoping for the best or for the not that bad when they first met. He charged on in this cynical vein and ignored the tiny voice begging him to stop, that this is not what he believed, that he wanted Ranti, and that Iya was old and the only one on his side, respect Iya Lagos boy before the only one in your corner turns away from you. But Ade went on pounding, voice rising to drown out dissent, ripping words from his deepest hurts and firing blindly at Iya.

Iya remained silent through the rant, nodding as though to a deep inner clock and chomping on a slice of bread, but when Ade mentioned Saro, his missing half-sister, she winced and squeezed her eyes shut and in that split moment guilt sliced him from crown to feet. And Ade shrunk in his own eyes to less than a rat dropping. 'Sorry, Iya,' he said. He bowed his head and mumbled deep-felt apologies. Didn't mean it, didn't know what came over him, he was not himself, it was tiredness and trouble at work. He waited in great fear to see if she was going to sweep him up and chuck him away.

Iya opened sad eyes, fiddled with her spectacles and looked to the ceiling. 'Foresight, oh, hey, where are you oh, foresight. Good. Go quick before Ade the great, the grandson upon high, blinds with electric plans, oh, I beg you, he doesn't want to listen to anybody oh, so foresight go and rest.' She wiped her forehead with a handkerchief. 'Ah, Alhamdulillah, Ade, foresight sees that you don't need her. She came all this way from the near future, which is a very far place, and now she has to go away. When hindsight sees that her friend is not happy she will cheer her up by taking her up to the top

161

of a tree where they can laugh when the fools pass by crying carrying their heavy regrets and mistakes.' A hint of mischief mingled with the residual pain in her voice.

Ade shook his clasped hands in another apology.

'It is ok. *Omo mi* I know how your *agbako* makes you feel - burning, cutting, crying inside but never ever talk like that about your sister or your mother because my head bangs with the memory of what I fear more than anything. For myself and all of you.' Iya placed a warm hand on Ade's shoulder.

'Iya afraid? Of what?' said Ade, locking eyes with his grandmother.

'I fear not to die, why should I? But I fear to die for nothing, or to die like nothing.' To die as if she never existed, without leaving a mark, that was the definition of purgatory. '*Omo mi, jo,* please. Promise that you will not live or die for nothing. Don't let me die for nothing or as if I was nothing.'

Twenty-three

Their plan could not be simpler. Baba Lawyers and the elite team from the anticorruption EFCC unit would pounce and arrest Controller when Iya handed over the marked notes in exchange for the young girls abducted from the Agidi ceremony. Controller's nemesis, DIG Kafu would do the rest.

The Agidi night arrived. Brilliant moonlight polished the car bonnet as Ade bumped the car along the dirt track to rest outside the old water treatment plant - an abandoned gift from a multinational quango. He cut the engine and read the flaking numerals on his watch. One hour, fourteen minutes and a few seconds to go to this postponed moment of immense gratification. The sharp smell of fresh menthol again filled the car as Iya rubbed the ointment on her chest. 'Is the oyinbo friend ready?' Iya said. She wheezed and looked tired under the whisky-yellow glow of the courtesy light.

Ade's tongue made a disconcerting Velcro sound against the roof of his mouth. 'It wasn't him, Tony, on the phone. This cough. Tomorrow or Monday we are going to the doctor. No more arguments,' said Ade.

A long and wheezy cough rattled the bead and cowrie necklaces hanging from Iya's neck. 'It's catarrh, hunh, because of the dust and things in the shed. But who are you calling this time?' said Iya, prodding more ointment up her nose.

'Nobody,' Ad said, but the slow sweep of Iya's discerning eyes rushed more heat to his face. He slowed his shallow breaths and swapped phones so he could listen to the Agidi ceremony through an open line to Niari whilst Iya got through to another friend. For a few frightening moments, Niari seemed to have run out of

163

charge or credit, then over the phone came the reassuring sound of dragged metal chairs, bursts of tinny applause and ecstatic screams of *Niari, Niari* mixed with shouted greetings, whoops of delight and general ribaldry to match that from the locker rooms of the most disinhibited schoolboys. After more hollow scraping against the floor, clashing of saucepans and the tinkling and splashing of water came a faint hum and crackling, like that from an open fire. Niari's magical nape-tingling singing over the plaintive chords of a kora wafted over the line. She sang about a junior war captain in Oba Kosoko's army who drowned near Epe on the way to fight Akitoye and his British allies.

'I thought you said she couldn't sing,' Ade said, moved to tears.

'No. I said her mama was a hundred percent better.'

'Iya, you should have been a lawyer.'

'I am. Only without their expensive certificate,' said Iya and closed her eyes. Niari started to sing an up-tempo tune. A girl's anguished scream rang out. Ade shivered in horror and his feet dug into the floorboards in agonising fellow feeling for the inexperienced girls. Then followed a sharp noise, like the sucking of teeth, a slap, or clap of hands. The wailing stopped, replaced by the sound of shuffling feet and of pouring grain. The hollow crunch of a calabash came over his phone. 'Iya, I thought you said it was all pretending.'

'It is, the girls learn quickly how to make the correct noise and sounds.' She paused to stab a stare at her phone. 'O ti ya,' Iya said, meaning the moment had come for Ade to send Controller and Baba Lawyers the prearranged text, "Pako saved the penalty."

Four and a half more excruciating minutes crept past in glittering moonlight. Ade peered through the misty window. His teeth chattered and his hands shook so much that he gave up the attempt to fasten a button on his shirt. He trapped the phone with a thigh before it clattered to the floor. Iya stirred. He froze and turned away because if she saw his sweaty face in a flash she would sense calamity. Ade made a sucking sound in a pretence of frustration and yanked the door open. 'Iya, wait, reception is poor here,' he said and leapt out of the car just as the moon disappeared behind a cloud. The dark leaned right up to Ade's face, like a blackboard. When a furry animal scampered over his feet Ade nearly exploded from his heels. He waited, while his eyes rubbed away some dark, then tapped Baba Lawyers' number out yet again. Voicemail replied. Fuming, Ade sent another text to say that they'd been sitting there since forever. Where was he? Again no Baba Lawyers. Ade cursed. Logical, clinical, erudite and effective Baba Lawyers, the psychologist and police officer with a mobile X-ray of the mind inside in his head, had never let him down before. Could it be the aneurysm? Why hadn't he gone home to the UK to treat the bloody thing and get his kids, are they not lawyers, to pay? No, oyinbo, too proud to beg. *Ko tan* now? See where pride got us now - in dark and fucking morass within touching distance of quicksand.

He heard the thump of plastic on metal and turned as a dark van pulled up, headlights dimmed. A rake of a man in a loose-fitting gown jumped out of the passenger's side. He had a phone in one hand and swung a short baton in the other. Ade charged up to him.

'Where is your oga? Inside? The girls?' he said, to dispel ambiguity.

'Wait here,' said the man, and he tucked his baton into a side pocket to make a phone call. 'Oga, wetin I go do now?' The man turned to Ade. Seconds later, Ade's phone rang. 'Julius loser I presume?' said Controller.

'Are you here in the van?' Ade said, casting about in desperation for Baba Lawyers and men.

Controller chuckled-cleared his throat. 'I have been doing this job before many countries sucked from the breasts of their founding mothers. Boy Julius trapped in a dough of his own baking, or mouldy mould? Wasting police time, compromising a crucial investigation, obstruction of justice, but one requires time to consider a fair and judicious resolution, dispense with the need for one of your miserable memos.'

'What about the girls Roadsweepers took from the Agidi compound? If you did not want the deal why take them?' Ade said and exploded towards the man. But the van revved up, knocking him sideways into the undergrowth and sped off into a blue mist. Ade tried to get up but slipped back into thick slime.

Out of the corner of his eye he saw Iya open the car door. 'No, wait,' he said, but she floated towards him mouthing inaudibly, bead necklaces swaying down to her waist. 'Iya wait, go back. I'll be ok, it is only my leg.' Iya stopped yards away as though struck by a blow, reeled, her hands went out to Ade then grabbed her chest. Righting herself, she swayed sideways, rocked back and in split fractions of a second Ade decided that he could not clamber out of the mire quickly enough to save her. Her spectacles caught the moonlight and with a sandy screech she wheezed, her glasses crept down from her face, crashed to the ground and Iya landed on to her face with the necklaces flicked out from under her. No, no, please no. Fear rocketed Ade from the slime. 'Iya, Iya, I'm here.'

'My chest,' she said, croaking and wheezing. 'I need to sit up.' He propped her up in the back of the car, secured her with a seatbelt. Her head lolled back but oh yes thank Allah she breathed. Iya's weak smile plucked lumps from his heart. 'You are a wonderful boy. They will not win. Remember what I taught you. Tell your own too...' She paused for breath.

'Wait, rest don't say anything.'

'Thank you my son, where are you taking me? I'm getting better now. Fresh air from the windows helps my breathing.'

He rushed her to the hospital. The first two hospitals, fearing terrorists or armed robbers, refused to open their doors. Ade charged to the island, bundled Iya into Nicholas's Hospital near the Marina.

'Didn't you know she had severe aortic stenosis?' said a doctor with a grey beard, an hour later.

'What is that? Had or has?' said Ade, each breath a shovelful of glass splinters.

'Sorry, but it was bad my brother, nothing anybody could do. She is no longer with us,' said the doctor.

Ade's brain rubbed around inside his skull like a foot in an oversized shoe. It took an hour of pacing the dewy concrete outside for him to grasp the concept first that Iya of all people could die at all and that she just did.

Twenty-four

Nothing prepared Ade for the dense despair, the mercurial emptiness and disabling apathy or the spasms of angry self-contempt, some strangely masochistic. Punched drunk by his loss, he wanted to be left alone but did not want to be alone. He wanted comfort but was too proud to seek it and avoided Moji. Yeni seemed indifferent, which was bad enough, but when she accused him of overreacting, Ade, incensed, wounded, and disabused of even his modest estimates of her humanity, retired to Iya's prayer mat as though to gather her essence before it leaked to someone more deserving. There, hindsight found Ade, taunting him for dropping out of Law School and for the pathetic envy and neediness - because he wanted to get up Ranti's nose - that led to the disastrous bond with the Martins because they were up there and he in the doldrums. Hindsight teased Ade for accusing Ranti of hanky panky with Bambo when he had no basis. It replayed the biting sunny day the athletics agent, Mualla duped Ade, mocked him for the naiveté that lost him his place on the national team to the inferior Bambo, and for thinking he could outwit Controller. What were you thinking? Making plans with Baba Lawyers against that man in Lagos? Flying paintbrush, you need a good clean.

Prayer helped pass the time, but also embittered him. Did Allah not know that the flying paintbrush wanted a wonderful family, not silver or gold or glory? Why did Allah let doctor Adadevoh, who died on the same day as Iya, succumb to Ebola when she saved the city from disaster? Could Allah not swerve Ebola round her or her round it? Why did Allah act as an indifferent schoolmaster or parent, watching from the touchline,

168

whistle in mouth, arms across chest, whilst the kids played a game called life to the death? Then, a scorching jolt seared up his brain stem and slung him back to the mat frightening him into begging for forgiveness.

If it was despair that cleaved him to the mat, it was anger that cleaved him from it.

He went to meet Tailor in a town where the river narrowed on its way to Badagry, the old slave port. Serried clusters of shacks on the river banks leaned over their five o'clock shadows as though for a better view of the seagulls fishing in the mud banks. Ade waited at the foot of an ancient humpback bridge near a fading mosaic of Dosunmu, the Oba, on board Prometheus. A palm wine song he used to sing with Iya floated over from a beer parlour, stood tears to attention in his eyes. As he turned away from the embarrassing stare of a schoolgirl an impatient street hawker knocked Ade backward into wiry arms. They belonged to Arirueri the Tailor. 'Cufffingers, sorry I am late. Papa was not well. *Eyin Iya a da oh.*'

'*Amin.* I pray that I can *be* that wonderful legacy. How can Baba Lawyers do this? Where is he?' said Ade. The man had better have a good and proper explanation.

Tailor clasped hands. 'I don't want to involve myself in a quarrel between father and son, oh, I beg you. Come. Dead bodies used to lie here, the ones who died of fear or fever or committed suicide before they went to hell,' said Tailor as they shoved and sidled through the crowd on a wooden footbridge.

'The ones who died. The lucky ones?' said Ade, a painful question he long pondered but which slipped from his tongue that afternoon.

'Why not go and ask them?' said Tailor in a testy tone.

'They didn't answer,' said Ade.

Tailor pointed at a long boat. It sat in mud at the bottom of a slimy flight of concrete and wooden steps.

'There? Baba Lawyers lives there? Are we lost?'

'Take it easy with the man. He is not well and think of Iya.'

Wrinkling his nose against the sickening smell of fermenting household waste, Ade inched down the steps, passing one hand over the other on the rusting arm rail, right hip aching from the impact with the van on the night Iya died.

'Vincent, is that you? Is that the fish and fuel?' said Baba Lawyers, in a strong Lagos accent.

Mystified, Ade tapped the hull again. 'Cufffingers here.'

'Oh.' Baba Lawyers appeared from the bow of the boat, wearing a red cap and an orange Day-Glo, cheeks hatched by wrinkles, like those railway junctions drawn on a tiny map. He pulled a shirt sleeve back up his bony shoulder.

'Janus, so this is where you hide your two faces?' said Ade. His jaw tightened.

'Dreadfully sorry. Thought of nothing else since I heard the news. But Cufffingers. You look thinner than the spread on a miser's sandwich.' He put an arm around Ade. 'Come in before a flapping mosquito wing blows you away.'

Ade slapped Baba Lawyers' hand away and followed him down a steep stairway into a musty cabin. About ten by six feet wide, the room had grubby green walls, two flick-up tables, on one of which stood a foot-high pile of old newspapers and a cracked electronic blood pressure machine. 'I'll kill Tailor for bringing you here but what is done is done. Drink?' Baba Lawyers kneeled to lift a floor panel.

'I went to Alagomeji, you weren't there. Was the great Baba Lawyers avoiding Cufffingers I asked myself.' Ade crouched to fasten the starboard window with a belt and eased his sore hips on to a creaky chair. Baba Lawyers scratched an elbow and lowered himself into the chair across Ade. 'So today is the day you can try one of your amazing stories on me.'

Baba Lawyers blanched. 'Tried to warn you.' He paused, took a deep breath. 'Caught between a rock and a harder place, believe me, I was. Ah.' The cans dropped out of his giant hands and he went grey and sweaty.

Not you too. Ade leapt to Baba Lawyers' side and laid him back in the seat. 'Is it the thing?' He pointed at Baba Lawyers' abdomen and felt his friend's brow. To his horror it was cold, and wet, just like Iya's. He gasped, terrified. 'What of calling your sons. Can we not Skype or Facetime?' said Ade, the sweat dripping off his nose.

Baba Lawyers opened his eyes, shook that majestic head, sat up and took a deep breath. 'I could have guessed this would happen. Now that you've seen this place, they carried this boat here on a skip, you still think my kids are international lawyers?' His face crumpled and looked as if would rather belong to anyone else. Baba Lawyers doubled up for a few seconds then unfurled again, heaving deep breaths through his mouth and pinkness rose to his face. 'Hope this ticking nuisance won't blow up in front of my bloody backbone. I'll tell you for the price of second-mouthed mouthwash I don't take kindly to this thing having the casting vote on my life.'

'Can't just sit and hope in a ramshackle boat,' said Ade.

'I've lost most of that. Hope, that is.' Baba Lawyer took his cap off, stared at it as though begging it for an answer, then, he put it back again with a resigned air. 'I have kids.' Baba Lawyers winced. 'Let me start a bit earlier. Cufffingers, you know I married a local girl?'

'We all know that. I did the same myself. That we have in common, as I told you,' said Ade, the edge back in his voice.

'Remi was her name. One of the few women in the force at the time. Pretty and knew it. Off my rocker with her. Got married, naturally. Back home in Essex you'd think I'd died and gone to Hades We had one boy, one girl.'

'I thought two boys,' said Ade. The floor made a sticky sucking sound under his feet as he pivoted back into his seat.

Baba Lawyers blushed. 'Never said two boys. That is what people assumed, but what did it matter? Still doesn't. Then Remi became a wahala woman and my easy bicultural life became a mystery, a maze, with high walls of prickly…misery. What did Tony do to deserve this…didn't fit anyone up, or take backhanders, ok, the odd packet of cigarettes for turning a blind eye, but for this? Anyway…this evening in the car on the way back from a party. They told us to wait but Remi insisted she had to get home in the storm. Kids in the back Remi in my ear; *yakkity, nigbati, sebi this sebi that, useless man, call yourself a senior officer etcetera.* As her mouth goes faster so is my foot pressing harder on the throttle.

172

Started to tip it down, giant raindrops as long as a piece of string and as thick as a finger, took the wrong fork in the road, and…suddenly suddenly suddenly as the song goes…we are riding this bronco of mud and water, smacking into telegraph poles and trees, sandy water is clawing at my eyes, ears, and nose. Crash, car rides up on the side of an abandoned bus. How one got the little ones out only God knows.' Baba Lawyer took his cap off. 'Hear a cry…look round. Remi trapped in the seatbelt. Does time stand still? No…it rushed on ahead, doubled back with a report from foresight.' Baba Lawyers frowned and stared as his cap. A large V-shaped wrinkle appeared on his scalp. 'I tried but did I try hard enough?'

Ade sat up to shock drilling through to his bone marrow. Was Baba Lawyers saying that he couldn't save Remi because it was futile, or couldn't in the sense that to do so would condemn him to desolation? But how many times had he also lain in bed hoping that time would spool back or, without willing the means, hoping that Yeni would just go away, leave the flying paintbrush alone? 'Baba Lawyers, nowadays they have counsellors,' said Ade.

Baba Lawyers shook his head. Bags wobbled under his eyes. 'It's the kids who should have seen the shrinks. Kale, or Tom, was twelve, the girl Efun, or Carina, eleven…I lost them also on that day. I would go into a room, and they would leave or go quiet. When I left the room, they would start talking again. I suppose the last thing they remember is this flaming row between their parents, then they almost drowned and they saw their mother die.' Baba Lawyers stared at his cap as if it were a crystal ball.

'Where are they now?' said Ade. Had they seen a terrible thing, not cowardice or fear, but the glint of calculation in their father's eyes? Was it murder in their eyes?

'Where are they? Went off the rails.' He closed his eyes and rubbed his palm with his forehead.

Only those lucky enough to be born into a family with an excellent record of accomplishment have rails to leave. 'Can I help?' Ade said, disappointed that his friend had not confided in him, but then he could hardly talk.

Baba Lawyers opened his sad grey-green eyes. 'I last heard from Efun a few months ago. She was in some camp, then disappeared again. Cockroaches have a much higher per capita GDP. The boy I still seek, hoping we can be a dad and boy again. We live for hope.' Baba Lawyers cleared his throat and bowed his head. 'Believe me I was all set to come that night to nab that man but a mole leaked my plans. Controller was on to me. If I as much as lifted a pinkie for you ever again he would tell everyone about the kids and me.'

Ade's hands leapt to his face. 'Controller knows? How?'

'Everything. Lock stock and barrel.' Baba Lawyers leaned forward. 'Cufffingers. Those people I play Ayo with are my family.' If Controller destroyed the trust in him, he might as well die. 'The only thing that keeps me going while I look for my son and wait for my girl to come to her senses. I was too bloody scared of him. It won't happen again. Promise.' He clasped his nose between his palms and closed his eyes, and rocked back and forwards, like a devout man in prayer.

Ade left home that morning intending to take his anger out on Baba Lawyers, offload on him some blame for Iya but now saw that that would have been a spiteful indulgence. Poor Baba Lawyers, widowed and estranged from his children. 'But you could have explained what happened. I'm sure your proper friends, Tailor, and co will understand,' said Ade, asking Baba Lawyers a question he asked himself many a time.

'It was too late. And I suppose I thought it was safer hiding behind my bars until I sorted myself out. When it comes down to it is that not what life is all about? Hiding behind bars?'

'Yours or someone else's?'

'Anyone's,' said Baba Lawyers.

'Or is life about trying to break out in one piece?'

Baba Lawyers leaned forward and said in a quiet voice, 'in one piece, yes, but in what bloody shape?'

Twenty-five

Dressed in white, Niari and a pair of Iya's cronies fanned their faces with hands, bills and programme notes against the blistering heat. Sad and dignified, they stood on the higher lip of the grave, their shadows slanting across Iya's swaddled body lying graveside in a rough wooden coffin. A keening whimper from mourners on an overlooking hill set Ade off, but he shored himself up with a gulp of air.

After a long dirge, the Imam closed a tattered prayer book and four lean pallbearers lowered Iya into the dark void. Ade stole a last glance at the peaceful face and like a demolition ball, the thought struck him that Iya's tiny knuckles, the hands that stirred pots of stew, sliced yams, carved Ayo boards, wafted flies away so he could enjoy moinmoin, helped build props and hurdles, the lips that turned the phrases he loved as much for their sound as for their content, would never move again.

Ranti nudged him, looking the part of a dutiful wife in a black pillbox hat and black ankle-length skirt. She pulled the strings to complete the checks for Ebola and get the pathologist to release Iya's body. Could this be the start of their beautiful reunion? Choking back a sob he nodded his thanks to her again. Ranti squeezed his hand and prompted him with a tiny genuflection towards the mound of earth. Sensing the anxious sympathy of Niari and friends, blinded by starry tears, Ade felt around for a handful of soil and tossed it across to Iya's feet. It seemed wrong to strike her on the face. As the clods drummed into the bleached slats Ade waved at Iya, tucked his hand into Ranti's, and, bowing and thanking and nudging through the milling throngs, hustled away, until held up by a dense cluster of mourners.

'Can't thank you enough. Rushing in without thinking. This is the result.' Ade pointed back at the grave. 'That.'Another ache waxed in his throat.

'Don't blame yourself. Heart disease,' said Ranti, the kind burr in her voice melting a chunk of the griefberg in his heart. Ranti nudged him again. When she gestured at the main gates Ade's heart slipped on that banana skin again. Moji in a brown scarf, white blouse and her brown shoes, stood between the gateman's porch and a hearse. A tender aching sweetness surged through him and he wanted to hug her tight for going to the trouble. In response to her inquiry because he looked sad - bananas under his eyes she called it - he'd told her he lost his grandmother. She must have wheedled the rest out of him. 'It's Moji. She's the one bullied at work,' Ade said, with painstaking formality. An unwelcome quiver laced his voice.

'Who told her?' said Ranti, in rasping contralto.

Did she want to choose who attended his grandmother's funeral? 'I asked her to see if she could find out where they put the girls Controller arrested that night. Then she saw my sad face.'

'Anyone else coming from the prison?' Ranti looked bemused. Moji did not look too sure either, the initial flash of pleasure on her face doused by Ranti's proprietorial demeanour. Ade beckoned Moji over with a stiff wave. She fiddled with her crumpled handbag, paused for a beat before she loped up the slight rise through the crowds. 'May mama's soul rest in peace. Sorry I am late again as usual.'

'Late but not absent,' said Ade, thawing to the private joke between them. Ranti's drill sergeant affectations restricted him to a weak smile and after just missing Moji's breasts with his awkward attempt to cheek kiss her, fumbled, into a limp handshake.

Ranti cleared her throat, three times, each report louder than the last.

'Ah, sorry, Moji this is Ranti and Ranti, Moji. Moji has been very helpful to me.'

Moji's bright face crashed so hard Ade's ribs cracked like a whip. 'I mean not only helpful but of general help,' said Ade, mortified by his insensitivity. Helpful? Why did you say that Lagos boy? His scalp boiled.

The women touched fingertips. 'Abs, anything I can do just ask,' Ranti said and turned an anti-clockwise quarter circle to close off Moji. Ade stepped backward to open his stance to both women, stole a look round for Niari but, surrounded by gawping admirers, the singer was too far away to help defuse his tension. 'Ranti presents and produces PJ,' he said. Moji looked blank. 'You know? The TV show?'

'What is PJ?' said Moji. She sidled up to Ade.

Ade thrust a bemused glance at Moji. He was sure that he had heard her give PJ a good rating.

'We try to educate the public, inform them of these events and scandals, injustice, abuse of power, etcetera etcetera,' said Ranti.

Moji straightened up so that Ranti, standing so close, had to look up to her. 'My job is simpler than that, it is to do what oga tells us.'

A pallbearer brushed past. Ranti jack-knifed forward as though shot, scowled at the man, turning her arm this way in great affront. 'Someone should nail a sense of balance into that man.' Ade glared at the man's receding form in a loyal show of support. 'But he said sorry,' Moji said, her eyes decrying Ranti's overblown reaction. Ade took Moji's point, but would rather she did not make it there. His toes drew up - like a slug's antennae withdrawing from danger - and as he turned to shield Ranti from another tottering pallbearer, Moji gave him a sharp tug on the wrist.

'You know what? I don't know what is wrong with this leaking basket I have for a head, oh,' she said, tapping her temple with her knuckles. 'I have a list of the girls they brought that weekend. Some are for sure *keh* the Agidi girls you asked me about.' She fetched a folded piece of paper from her bag and leaned closer so they could read the list together.

'This is magic. Fantastic. Incredible. And you have the names and addresses of many of the families too. Unbelievable. Excellent work Moji.'

'Number 243 helped. She is desperate to get out of there before they move them. There are rumours,' she said, the promising glow in her eyes waxing stronger by the second. 'But this means *we* should be able to get them out before Controller starts his mago mago rehab system as 243 calls it.' She meant Cordelia.

Ranti flinched, and a look of faint disquiet settled on her face.

Ade turned to Ranti. 'Arants, this was my fault, the result of the Agidi night. But for Moji I don't know how I would have been able to sleep at night.'

'Ah, oga Julius, always you blame yourself, even for the colour of your own shadow,' said Moji. She beamed and turned to Ranti. 'I did nothing really, but he likes to boost us. That is why we like him on our team, though his eyes are on better things.'

179

Did he detect a drop of caustic irony? 'Me?' he said, aiming to disarm or reassure through genial banality. 'Me? How can a demoted man have any ambitions in that place or anywhere?'

Ranti turned to Moji. 'Exactly what do you do there?'

'Clean. I began work there a year ago, mainly the offices and sometimes the cells. KIYO is not too bad. But the main prison is like hell on earth,' she said, stressing each word.

'That is what I thought,' said Ranti in a sardonic tone.

What you thought, meaning what Ranti? You thought Moji was a cleaner the moment your eyes clasped her or that you agree that the cells are like hell? Or was he tilting and turning her words to find offence? 'We do our best but it is not easy,' he said A prickly silence mushroomed between them, as tangible as the cloud of dust churned up by the mourners. A fly crawled up towards Moji's breast. Ade's fingers twitched but propriety kept them twitching by his side. Then Moji saw the offending insect, waited for a beat, puffed air over it then resorted to a finger flick. When her cheap polythene blouse crackled with static Ranti started back in a show of great alarm, as though to a backfiring car or from splashed mud. Moji's shoulders hunched and her eyes sank in pained bemusement. A blue pickup chugged up the slope ahead of another sizeable group of mourners. Ade stepped back with Ranti beside him, churning and ransacking his dishevelled mind for the right words, but when the van and mourners passed, Moji had gone.

Twenty-six

Ade didn't know or care whether it was a Wednesday or Thursday because several sweltering days had passed with neither hide nor hair of Moji and he still dipped into shame and despair about his role in Iya's death. He'd spent most of the late shift behind his desk in the alcove overlooking the prison gates berating himself and envying the freedom of the brilliant white egrets pecking at a sandy knoll and the raft of soldier ants floating a sliced corncob gingerly round his foot. Nodding in reply to a greeting from a porter who looked all but done in by the heat, Ade put aside the draft rota for September and returned to his peace offering. After days of toil should he start again with mahogany? Dimples had always given him trouble and Moji's sat close to her mouth when she smiled. Had he captured the wisdom behind the lightness of her eyes? When the alarm went off to mark the end of shift on a clock above his floor, Ade leapt from his seat, stuffed the figurine, inventory and draft rota into his rucksack, and set off in search of Moji.

After half an hour wasted perambulating between Ado and Edoko Streets looking for the two-tone house with the bent pole in front, he found Moji's house painted white instead of yellow or green. He strode to the shop on the ground floor with the alacrity of a military despatch rider and made a show of fishing the draft rota out of his pocket. The shopkeeper disappeared through an inner door and minutes later, Moji, in a pale blouse and maroon calf-length skirt, sauntered, round-shouldered and pale, up from around the side of the house. 'How did our oga from Lekki find this place?'

'Special juju satnav.'

'Then get a refund. You are lost.'

Taken aback, Ade lifted the knapsack off his left shoulder. Go on, speech ready to go tell her you missed the jokes, smiles blazing to her face, spreading from eyes to the high arched cheekbones and to the lanceolate tips of her eye teeth. But it was easier to conceive than deliver, and ordinary words stuck to his wooden tongue. 'I came to see if you are ok,' he said, cringing.

'Why would I not be ok? Is Beatrice now my doctor or bodyguard?' Moji made a sound, a cross between the hiss of a snake and a click of a lock just like Beatrice did at work. Desperate not to lose face, though he felt like a dustbin filled with stinking, nauseating waste, Ade pulled out the draft rota. 'Can we check this together? Maybe we can change it a bit then edit later next month?'

Moji stopped and sighed. 'Know what? Let the world not say that Moji has no home training. As this is your first visit have songthing to drink.' Now, a gentleman should bow and make a graceful retreat, shouldn't put herself out, getting late and all that, but as the Fela song goes Ade was not a gentleman like that. Not tonight. With guilty pleasure he tiptoed after Moji through the side door, down an unlit corridor crammed with crates, bikes, organ-grinders and wicker baskets. Hens and fluffy chicks broke into a trot to scatter behind an old fridge that doubled as the mount for an organ grinder and an ironing board. By the flickering light from a mobile phone a teenager mouthed to herself, perhaps committing some item to memory. Been there, good luck. In Moji's tiny trapezoid room a pear-shaped bulb emitted a dim glow. As Ade squeezed past their eyes met and he wobbled for a moment, dizzy from a puff of her breath before he pivoted away to perch on the edge of the narrow bed that ran along the left wall.

'So this is where you live,' he said, then seeing that he expressed himself with the subtlety of a fired ballistic missile added, 'quite nice, not that far from work. Not that everywhere should have a prison near.' Toes and neck hairs curled. 'Prisons are not clinics or supermarkets. I meant convenient.' His armpits wept.

Moji leaned against the narrower side of the wall beside the door, Moji shifted her weight. 'Do you think I am too dim to understand your problems? Who told you about Cordelia and the business that Controller was doing?'

'You,' said Ade.

'Exactly. But you don't give feedback, nothing but hold others closer than your ears but put me at the end of a queue longer than the Third Mainland Bridge.' She fell silent and rapped the wall with her fingers. Across the corridor, a toilet flushed.

Befuddled by shame, Ade half stood up and made a manual weighing scale gesture to buy time.

'That night you made a trap for Controller did you not think that I would worry? My head was full of roundabout questions, memos and faxes. What of Baba Lawyers? Is he a genuine support or a fake? Does he know Nigeria well and what if the plan gets k-leg what would you do if they sack you? What if they bring guns? Even aunty in the shop outside saw that I was worried.' She scanned Ade's face. 'And nearly five days you did not phone me, then you come here to make peppermint eyes.'

Peppermint eyes? Not heard that one. Ade faked a sneeze to buy time. 'Sorry. You deserve better.'

'Deserve? I don't value that word that says you are gifting me songthing *you* think suits me. Do you know what I want in life? How do you know what I deserve ernh? Deserve is personal. Earn is public. Apologise but don't add extra conditions. Or finish the drink and leave. Go deserve yourself.'

'Sorry. Sorry if I caused offence.'

She made bunny ears in the air, '"caused offence" it is now my fault for not accepting your back pocket gift.'

Trembling like a flightless bird before the last club fell, more confused than a yokel on the first day out on the razzle, and with thighs aching for a new resting place Ade tried to fish the statue out of the knapsack, but to his dismay, the figurine snagged on a zip. He gave up. A prong dug into his right thigh. A discrete shift sideways, failed, and the prong followed for an inch, pinged free and quivered. Moji's droll grin, churned him into greater unease, but she looked away, before embarrassment reached his lips. 'Did you hire this singing chaperone hiding inside your mattress from aunty outside?' said Ade, flushing in horror at his gaffe. Moji smiled and her cheeks bunched into rosy mounds, her dimples enticing whirlpools. A peppery aroma and smoke drifting in from the corridor stung the eyes and in a gesture that brought him closer Moji handed over a piece of tissue paper. 'Sorry, you hear, I didn't want to harass but words just flew out of my big mouth. After everything that happened to you and your Iya. How are you feeling?'

Ade shoved his glasses back. 'What can man do? Trying to bounce back.'

'Bounce from the floor or wall or off the ceiling?'

'Off the ropes,' he said.

Moji peeped from under her moist eyelashes. 'And who will be in your side or corner? The executive?' she said and inspected her nails.

'I hope Allah will be in my corner.'

'Only in your corner? Nobody else's?' she said, then as if to blunt her mordant barb made a strangled noise, like a blocked burp. 'Julius, you must be careful oh with this Controller matter. As a foreigner they can throw you in the lagoon nothing will happen. My dad…'

'Your dad was from abroad?'

She shook her head in playful exasperation. 'No. Believe me where he worked was worse than Kakirikiri.' She said her dad worked for an oil company. 'He used to say that the glass is fuller today because someone saw that it was half empty. Dad loved Nigeria. More than his family we joked. Tried to stop the stealing. I was fourteen when one evening I was watching TV and heard mama screaming. The man did not even bother to hide his face. Papa was on the kitchen floor. I had never seen a dead person before and God forbid never again. Mama's leg was like an elephant sat on it. Like straw and blood. Ricochets said police.' Moji stopped, closed her eyes and sighed.

So that's why those gigantic eyes dimmed. Her dad's heroism shamed Ade and made him feel small and narrow-minded enough to fit inside a chewed biro top. 'They say anything we humans find underground is grounds for killing humans. But who looked after you as a child?'

'Here and there and we managed. I always wanted to be a quantity surveyor and I am still trying…'

He smiled, pleased for her that she recovered her bounce. 'I'm listening.'

'Aunty Beki, father's sister looked after us. My brother is with Aunty Tayo. If not for them who knows where we would have ended up. I don't want what happened to my papa to happen to anybody. That is why I was looking for your people at the cemetery to check that you have support. What can a few old women do for a foreigner in this Lagos I was asking myself?' She dabbed her eye with a knuckle. 'But this trouble you have with Controller is it because of Cordelia?' she said, in a tone inflected with wary anticipation.

Lagos boy strike now or forever remain locked in torment and loneliness. 'Sit. I must tell you something.' With a visual frisson of surprise at his brusqueness Moji planted herself near the foot of the bed with her knees pointing chastely at the door.

'Did you hear Ranti call me Abs at Iya's thing the other day?'

She shook her head. 'Abs is short for Afediyabamba, not so?'

'My name is not Julius. It is Ade.' He paused for a moment but Moji reacted only with a sudden and brightening of her features. 'I was born in Lagos. My mother is called Malomo, Iya was her mother. My surname is Bisoye. That is why Ranti calls me Abs.' Ade heaved in an enormous breath and waited, feeling as vulnerable as a man in a remote and leaking diving bell.

'So all this time you kept this secret, I have been defending you against the likes of Peter and nearly lost my job? Moji, stupid woman, when will you learn?' she said, with a mocking slow handclap. She started back. 'Ha, are you secret police?'

'Do I look like a man with the brains to be a spy?' Moji spoke, but Ade raised a hand. 'Wait. You think I planned for Iya to die because I was pretending to spy? To confuse you?' Ade's heart pounded as if to secede. 'Remember the day they cracked my head, and we went to your house and I did not want you to wash the blood off my foot?' Ade shook off the left shoe and peeled off the sock.

Her hand shot to her mouth. 'You? Ade, the flying paintbrush?'

'It is me. When I was small, I wanted to be like Ed Moses, famous like him. We share the same birthday. Because of Iya I decided on Law to help her and others like her get back their land. I went up north to Ahmadu Bello to study.' But deep down he preferred hurdling to Law. Law was riddled with amendments, qualifications and ambiguities. Not hurdling. The race on the day did not concede to tribe or race or religion or the size and reach of your parent's moneybags, to the clothes you wore, how fast you talked, the jokes you re-hashed, the cases you took on. It did not care that his mother was a drunk, that he was only five foot nine, short body with long legs but with thick thighs and a scarred left foot. Hurdles did not mind that Iya raised him on simple recipes and not on state supplements of dubious provenance. What did the finishing tape care for artistic merit, how he jumped, the set of his eyes or the length of hair, or the way words slipped off his unpolished tongue from under his broad nose? To show that the hungry boy who built his first hurdles from scavenged bits of wood could look the privileged scions in the eye and say I beat you over those barriers fair and square meant the world to him. If he made it and won fame and fortune Iya's worries were over and he imagined them all in a sizeable house helping other villagers repel predatory speculators.

He told Moji what happened in Zaria, the quarrel with the bullying Microchip the Dean of Law, suspension from the course, the hopes that he could succeed through Athletics and the despair when he did not get on the team and lost the chance to run in the lucrative Diamond League.

Moji gave his wrist a consoling squeeze. Ade was the sort of man her father admired. A man who makes his own prints, does not follow others. 'What about your foot? Did you have an operation?'

Fearing that Moji might think less of him and his family he did not tell her about Malomo and that he would rather his mother stayed out of his life.

'Cousin Abi talked about you all the time,' said Moji and bent over for a better look at Ade's wizened foot 'That day I brought you here to wash your head I did not sleep, I was asking myself what was wrong with cleaning a simple dirty shoe.' Moji passed her fingers over the ridge of waxen brown skin running diagonally down Ade's instep as if she was reading a poignant tale in braille. 'Go on.' Her earnest expression reassured Ade. 'But to win with that foot and you are not that tall,' she said, in awe. 'But, but, oga Julius, Ade, something is not correct. So this fight with Controller. Is there more than meets the eye?'

Ade's recoiled. 'I signed something valuable to Controller, and he is using it to blackmail me, it is a long story. But I am innocent. Trust me.'

She nodded and tapped him on the wrist. 'But why is Controller so wicked? Only for the sake of money palaver?'

'Yes, money but for what he wants more money I don't know. He has plenty.'

'Maybe he does not know why he wants more money. Greed you may say, but why is he greedy?'

'It is in our nature. Every action is a reason trying to get out. Iya used to say that,' said an Ade relieved that

Moji did not ask for more details about what happened in Zaria. 'Iya meant that even when we think or know we know what we are doing we rarely know why.'

'Maybe that is why failure to get what or who you want can be good for us?'

'Not present company I hope?' said Ade, alarmed at the idea that he may fail to clear his name. What purpose would that serve but to signal oblivion?

Moji must have sensed Ade's disquiet. 'I did not mean to say aim to fail but if you fail, it gives you time to find out why you wanted what you failed at in the first place and if it is worth it and where you went wrong. Am I making sense? But when Controller made trouble for you why didn't you run away?' Moji paused, concern registered on her face.

'I'll explain one day. Bottom line is I could not leave Iya, and I wanted Ranti back but now it is you I want.' Ade heaved a breath. 'Because I love you,' he said and steadied himself against a teetering feeling as he stood before Moji, his heart rocking and slithering as he waited for the desired response.

'Since the day you helped me with my trolley, I liked you that first day.'

'A whole first day? What was wrong with me in the first minute?' he said, still perturbed that he had not told Moji the complete story.

'Be serious.' Moji prodded him in the ribs, then tapped his wrist.

Ade loved the feel of her hand. 'True, when I hear that Mariah Carey song I think of you. And when I see a tall woman in the street walking fast leaning forward.'

'Like antelope? You are calling me antelope?' she said in a querulous tone. 'Ah, got you. You should have seen your face. You said you like to run. Personally I prefer basketball.'

Tweaked by apprehension Ade said, 'is that because they are tall and strong?'

Moji's smile could power a small town. 'See. I got you again. Only joking. You are not a basketball player but you dunk into my head all the time. When I see men painting a wall, I will think of you.' Moji took Ade's wrist in one hand and made a light scrubbing gesture with the other. Their eyes locked, hers suffused with a devotion that disposed of his insecurities. 'But,' she said, with an ominous frown and half turned away.

'What is it?' Ade said, shot through once again with icy foreboding.

'Wife and executive. Plus me? How can three become one?'

The moment to decide and declare had come, as inexorable as a tropical storm. Now Ade saw that just as Archimedes could not relive his euphoria, the eureka eureka moment, by leaping back into that famous bath, Ade, the flying paintbrush, could not recapture his romantic fantasies by getting back with Ranti - except as a sham or safe choice. He'd fought his feelings, tried to avoid her, picked quarrels with her, acted the cool and aloof superior but it was Moji he loved. Loved her for the lobs of gentle insights, oddball sense of humour that gave him hope of rekindling the lightness of being he thought he'd lost forever and he loved her for all the reasons he could not carve into words or thoughts.

'Moji. Listen. I will talk to Ranti.' As he took her hand it was as obvious as a beached whale that his heart beat only to her rhythms and moods. And even his bilious liver warmed to the carnival.

Twenty-seven

When Ranti saw Ade outside the reinforced steel door Cleopatra could not have looked more delighted if, as she got ready for another lonely night, Anthony vaulted in through the window proud and unbowed. Beaming, hopping on the spot, in a pink gown and a red headscarf she rattled open the padlocks and hugged Ade as though he was a returning war hero. Surprised and daunted by her enthusiasm, shamed by the joy in her eyes Ade reciprocated with thespian ardour, sensing the inadequacy of his prepared speech.

'Abs, isn't the mind wonderful, must be telepathy. Ask D. Only a minute ago we put your name down on the list of invitees. What's wrong? Are you not well?' said Ranti and hustled Ade through the bright lobby into a dining room cluttered with bales of cloth stacked ceiling high. With a loud chuckle she pulled him a chair and Ade sat beside her, their backs to the door. On the opposing wall Ranti's diplomas flanked her parents' wedding photograph. From the adjacent kitchen wafted the welcome smell of brewing coffee, fresh bread and a hint of pepper and citrus fruits. 'D will bring another plate. Try the special, courtesy of Ranti, the *moinmoin elemi meje* you love. Iya said if anything serious happened to you, God forbid, they should bring moinmoin to revive you on ITU. Yes or no?'

'Madam Shogun of P and J cook moinmoin? No way,' said Ade, with forced cheer.

'Ask D. As God is my witness. The number one chef in moinmoin in the whole of Surulere and environs.' She bowed. 'Ladies and gentlemen, I present Ranti.'

191

'Only since this last month madam is practising every night as if she knew you will come here today, sir,' said D, leaning through the service hatch. Ranti chucked a limp-wristed wave at D. 'D, mouth bigger than backside,' she said hovering the pot of coffee over an empty cup. 'D, I will deal with you later, telling strangers my secrets,' she said, winking at D and chuckling to herself, her pupils as wide as wedding rings. 'Just because I bought fresh beans from the market last week she puts two and two together…and gets foreplay.'

'Wash that mouth with Omo,' said Ade. Ranti bent double with laughter whilst Ade sat stewing and wished she was not so jolly. As D bustled in to lay two extra places, he glanced at his watch. Five minutes and nine seconds to nine. 'Are they at a party, your parents?' Ade said, to the tug of trepidation. The prospect of meeting Coach, in particular, chilled his bones. 'No I don't want coffee.' He flapped his hands in the air. 'Look at them, shaking because I have never taken them to the house of a big woman TV executive. Stop them before they fly away.'

'Nonsense,' said Ranti with a shake of a head so vigorous she spilt her drink. 'Have a cup of Ovaltine, Bovril or ordinary breakfast tea. Or are you afraid of my love potion?' she said and put her cup on its saucer. 'Read this.' Peeling a short typewritten letter off the table, she handed it to Ade. 'I'm taking Yobe with me. She passed English and Maths. She will shadow my PA. Mum wants you to come to the party they are throwing for me.'

His right heel bounced nineteen to a dozen as if in time with his marching unease, angry for losing control of the agenda. Ranti's mother changed position faster than a second hand, and he never knew where he stood. 'Promotion? So you have decided to go to Ibadan? Well. Only up the Lagos to Ibadan expressway,' he said, out of politeness, then sorry for implying a future between them.

'Come on, please drink something,' she said. Just one cup to mark this most august visit.' She turned to the hatch. 'D, bring hot water and Bournvita. Or do you want Ovaltine, Pronto? Let oga choose.'

'No, no seriously, ok, just a glass of water.'

'But you will come to the party? Please come. Still not annoyed? Are you? I see it in your hard jaw and in your eyes behind those fake glasses.' She tossed a poppadom into the air and tried to catch one in her mouth. She missed. It landed in her cleavage. 'Remember our game? Pervert please snort my poppadum. Or was it snort my poppadum? Without the polite *please*?'

Pickled by stage fright, Ade rushed in headlong. 'Ranti? I'm not sure whether we can go back there, to where we were before, this and, er, my accident,' he said. He felt dreadful.

'Telepathy again between us. I was just going to say that myself, that you need time because of Iya.' She rubbed his back, in quick circular motions as if burping a child. 'Idia went through similar when her grandmother died.'

Why was Ranti making this so cracking agonising and difficult? Was she blind, deaf? 'No. It's, er, more than that. Moji and me at Kakirikiri...'

Ranti's shoulders sagged. 'Should have known.' She rolled a trembling fingertip over the edge of the table. 'So why the chocolates and the carving? To bribe your conscience? Stupid shogun even put the ragged thing on my desk.' She bit her top lip, closed her eyes and shook her head as if to empty it of the latest contents. Last in first out. 'Did I not beg you not to do this again? Dragging hearts through barbed wire. Is it a hobby or are you just a wicked man? What have I done to deserve this? All the time I thought you were writing on my heart in permanent ink, it was but only chalk. Abs I am afraid to say that you are a tragic specimen of a man and I wish we had never met.' Puckered lips trembled.

Ade shot a hand out, but the cup smashed to the floor. He was having one of those days, the day starts with an ironed hole in your favourite shirt and nothing goes right - stride pattern, cadence, warm up, warm down, nothing. 'So we do agree on that.'

'What are you saying?'

'Said it yourself. I am not the man for you.'

'You can't tell that I was angry? Everybody says stupid things in the heat of the moment except perfect robotic man of steel the inflexible Abs, flying paintbrush. This Abs strain of love is worse than Ebola. Thank God it is rare.'

'Arants. Believe me. I wanted us back together. Dreamed of nothing else since we broke up in Zaria. And always you will be special. Anytime anywhere call.'

'How is Moji?' Ranti's stare rocked Ade back in the chair. 'Abs, no answer? Cleaner? Was it proximity, novelty, availability to slip into the vacuum left with prison machinery in the broom cupboard for extra powerful suction?'

'Not like that.' Ade paused whilst D scurried in to flick the last few plates on to a bulging tray. She fled as if from an inferno.

'Why didn't you say you wanted a child?' said Ranti.

'Did I say anything about a child?'

'Hey, everybody come and listen to this logic. The man is married but does not want a child.' She stopped. 'Sorry you first.'

'No, you,' Ade said, broiling with guilt. He twirled a coaster. 'Your help with Iya will always be special to me,' he said cringing at the vapidity of the words but he could hardly download a soaring soliloquy.

'Julius. That was your bogus name wasn't it? Julius Caesar? Julius sees her, hooks, likes and sinks her?' Ranti shot a peremptory hand into the air. 'Abs, look in the mirror not at that belly button and admit that you used me.' Her gaze sharpened, face narrowed. 'But now you are free again I am not on a pedestal anymore. Just an ordinary Ranti, an ordinary woman with moods and sweaty armpits and headaches and pet projects, money worries family ties, one of many million women. That man, erm, I forget the name, in the international newspapers when they kidnapped him in Lebanon, or one of those biblical places, the love for his girlfriend sustained him but six months later married someone else. So don't blame yourself as you will not be the first or the last. That's life.'

Ranti's woebegone demeanour soused Ade in guilt. Was she right? Had he used her memory as a lever, sought her for snobbish, nostalgic reasons - for status and the approbation of Lagos society? But as she dabbed at a sniffle and Ade leaned forward to comfort her the metal front door clanged open and into the dining room strode Coach and his wife.

Egg-bald, with coppery orange skin, the six-foot-tall, twenty stone Coach, with arms as thick as most thighs sticking out of his purple dashiki, towered over his petite wife. His frame blocked the doorway, sweat gleaming on his atavistic Neanderthal brow and his knuckle hairs. 'Rants I smelled coffee and thought you were working late again.' Coach whipped off his glasses. 'Who is this man?'

Ade scrambled to his feet, and tried to free one heel from the weave of the rug. A scratchy noise from the chair drowned his greeting.

Ranti's mother dropped her bale of damask. 'Eh, eh, Jesus in heaven. Is this him? Ade?' She was wearing a commemorative green *buba* and *iro*. Coach turned to her. 'Alaba, so you know this grasshopper runner?'

'Kola, take it calm, remember what doctor said about your BP,' she said, bending over to retrieve the cloth.

'Mister man if you have upset my daughter I will tear your head from your throat with your own hands, hear me?'

'Abs has been working hard since he returned from abroad and we were just talking about old times,' said Ranti.

Ade turned on the most charming smile, but her cold shoulder felt like a stalactite jabbed through his heart. 'Sorry to take your time, er, at this late time and I will go, if you allow me to explain.' This is cracked up. As long as they don't call Commissioner or Controller it is a result.

'And your permission to address came from where?' said Coach. 'What kind of man dissolves away for months then crawls around in the middle of the night like a robber? A black mamba in the shade? Snake is too good a description. Common earthworm.' Coach leaned

196

towards Ranti and eyed Ade askance through narrowed eyes, as a cashier would a suspect currency note. 'God help us, oh in this Lagos town. Can anyone imagine Mr Falaiye's son behaving in this fashion? Distinguished professor on high. Mr Banwo's son? Fantastic incomparable unconquerable lawyer on high. But you, earthworm where were you when she was fighting tooth and nail to get where she is today on P and J TV, enh? Gallivanting, just as a fly does over a pile of shit, compiling the dictionary of excuses for useless and feckless people?'

Ade somehow remained standing but so scared of provoking Coach and arrest that he barely drew breath. Ranti kneeled before her dad to beg him not to call Commissioner. Supplications and placations went on for five suspenseful minutes, both women taking turns to implore the master of the house. 'Thank your lucky stars,' Coach said at last. 'If not for Ranti and her mother I had set my mind on calling Commissioner.'

'Thank you, sir, sorry for all this,' said Ade and staggered from their presence. Ranti saw him to the door. 'I'm really sorry Arants. Thank you for begging Coach. I'll call you when -'

'Don't,' Ranti said.

Twenty-eight

Ade ripped off Bola's eviction notice and nudged Iya's front door open. Niari was waiting in the back room with a cassette player. Through the window dappled sunlight swiped the floor.

'Look at your shoes,' Niari said, pointing at Ade's muddy boots. 'Where you be? Sit, let me finish this bread, then I will give you Abake's things,' she said and tucked into a three-tiered chicken, fish and pepper sandwich. In her fifties and five foot five inches tall, Niari had a long bony face, hooded twinkly eyes, and plucked brows. Photos of her younger self on the bright orange gown showed how little time had rubbed off on her.

'I can still smell her strong camphor and soap in here. Last night I dreamed she walked into my shed with a bowl of amala and ewedu,' said Ade flopping, exhausted, on to the foot of the bed. Rattled by the other night at Ranti's, compelled by a need to be alone he got out of the car and shuffled the ten miles from Oshodi in the unforgiving heat. He told Niari of the recurrent dream in which Iya played Ayo against Chief. If Iya won Martins refused to accept the result but when Chief won, he said fortune favours the haves and seized Iya's land and livestock. Was it a bad sign?

Niari patted him on the chin. 'Son, that is how the mind works when you are bereaved. But you cannot blame yourself. Abake did not want an operation.'

'Operation? What operation? Did you know that Iya was not well?'

Niari nodded. 'Heart. Erotic stenosis.'

Ade could not resist a wry smile. 'Aunty Niari it is called aortic stenosis. Aortic valve in the heart.' Did Iya refuse a procedure because she could not afford to live, or because she did not want to live without her family? Gripped by a shrivelling surge of remorse for dragging Iya around Lagos in her condition, he closed his eyes tight.

'Don't overthink it or you will make yourself sick. An aeroplane has a black box but we cannot know what the dead were thinking except to guess their intentions from what they did when alive. Come at least we know she wanted you to have all this.' Niari switched on the battered cassette player, patted him on the shoulder and handed him an earphone. 'I will play the oriki that I recorded from what Abake wrote out. She said she used to sing it to you.' Iya left Ade a few artefacts, the wooden frame or mattress, old photos and files from court proceedings. If Niari was right, Ade wanted to use the oriki to undermine Bola's negotiations with developers, then force the Martins to intercede with Controller. Plan B did not exist.

'Are you listening?' Niari waved a prayer bead in his face.

'Sorry.' Ade had been daydreaming. 'Does Iya know what the *jambodi* talk at the end of the oriki means?'

'Are you ok my child? I've just asked you the same question.'

'So you do not know either. Why didn't she tell you?' Then to his irritation, Niari spent an age looking for the jack on the player. She found it at last and placed a grey bud in her right ear, handed the other to Ade and they snuggled up with their heads together in wavering candlelight. After a brief crackly song in honour of his great-great-grandfather Jinadu, they wound forward to

199

the rap-like second section of the oriki, the bit Ade called the jambodi part. Again it had the rhythm and prosody of a foreign language and sounded in parts elegiac, devotional, belligerent, exhorting or inspiring, but it still made no sense.

Fighting back his angry disappointment he lit another candle, rolled its base in the dying flame of the old stub and stuck it to the saucer. 'Again,' he said. Niari slapped the rewind button, her look intense, tip of tongue poking out of the corner of her mouth, but the coda again perplexed.

Ade wrenched his earbud away. 'Aunty Niari, if your friend learned it from her grandfather why didn't she explain it to me? I kept asking her, and asking, and she kept postponing. What can man do now?'

'Maybe she wanted you to find out yourself. Or maybe she didn't know what it meant, or she had forgotten.'

'Eh.' He started forward.

'What is it?'

Ade clasped a hand to his head. 'Hey something happened, ah it's gone. Just now I had an idea on the tip of the back of my brain, but it's gone again. It's not the first time. Once a day it will come like that then fly away as if it is annoyed or wants to punish me for letting Iya die,' he said, bowing his head between clenched fists. 'Ah. It could be this.'

'What?'

'Maybe the problem is that the way Iya talks is different from your transcription. I mean how you wrote out what you heard from Iya,' he said.

Niari made a brusque facial gesture. 'I have been doing this since long before you were born. I will give it to you to read for yourself and you can ask someone else to sing it for you.' She thrust two sheets of typed paper into his hand. 'This is the one Abake gave me. This one I sing from,' she said.

Ade apologised. What he meant to say was that in making transcribed copies of old documents mistakes could mount over the years and result in something different from the original, yet still make sense.

'I can only sing what I see in front of me now.' Niari fished a biro and notepaper out of her bag. She was only doing this for Abake's sake. 'Take this to my friend,' she said handing him a note, then she stretched out and in the fidgety candlelight, her gigantified shadow spread across the room, redolent of the empire of a great and enlightening power.

Twenty-nine

Ade turned left on to the concrete path to find Professor Aloja eating a biscuit in front of a weather-beaten cabin beside the lagoon. She was wearing a magnolia ankle-length gown. Curls of thick grey hair peeked from under her yellow headgear. 'A country that does not value its past is a ship without a compass,' said the board above her head. Someone had crossed out *ship* and replaced it with *sheep*.

'From where?' she said.

Ade bowed and turned his head a fraction away as he handed her the note he got from Niari's friend. A nervous jab at his glasses caught the tip of his nose. 'I brought this for the professor. A friend of my late grandmother sent me. Name, Niari and she records oriki for Lagos families.'

'Niari? The singer?' she said with lashings of teasing disdain. She took another bite out of her biscuit. 'Forgive me my stomach has the temperament of a neonate,' she said, in a costly accent not dissimilar to Bola's.

Ade cleared his throat and imparted the correct level of gravitas to his tone. 'Where can I find the prof please because I am trying to claim ancestral land?' Nervousness and a gust of tangy air made him sneeze.

'We've met,' she said, with a suspicious stare.
'I am not sure that is so, ma.'
'Don't act innocent. We've met.'

Ade puffed his cheeks. Had she recognised him as the callow man, the foreigner who rebuked her for rudeness at Chief's party months earlier in June? She eyed him that night with an air of bemusement, as though he was a monkey playing a Beethoven Sonata then asked her friend, in Yoruba, what Yeni was doing with this foreigner instead of one of their *omoluwabis*. Wound up to his gluteals with such comments Ade retorted in perfect Yoruba that they have amiable boys where he came from too. The professor's mouth dropped open. 'Didn't know, did not mean, I did not mean to offend.'

'Didn't mean what you said, or didn't mean me to get it?' he said and wheeled away from the stammering professor, faded into the crowds and avoided her for the rest of the evening.

'Have we met or not?' The professor broke another biscuit and clasped Ade in her powerful gaze.

'Ah, forgive me ma, you are correct in your conclusion that we have met but I cannot recall.'

Professor Aloja's aggressive grunt disconcerted Ade further. She held the note at arm's length with her fingertips, slicing Ade with her eyes at intervals as she read, then as she folded the paper once more her face glowed in a continental smile. 'Ah, why didn't you say that you are from Lai, instead of trembling as though you are a bald gorilla stowaway in Antarctica? Lai and I are like sisters, studied here in this same Akoka.'

'So you *are* the prof of history?' said Ade, with ostentatious astonishment.

'Me indeed and my second Ph.D. Thesis was on amputating male expectations,' she said and with amazing agility slipped her wide feet into a pair of black rubber slippers, swung back then heaved on to her feet.

Ade picked up her glass and hurried indoors after the prof. The smell of her office reminded him of Obe the cobbler's hut - leathery and earthy. 'Careful,' she said and leaned a raffia shield back inside the doorjamb, ducked around a pirogue, under a bunch of manacles to reappear beside stacked shelves. 'Sit, but I cannot take more than an hour of the heat in this room,' she said, fanning her face. 'Your request appears to fall under land tenure in precolonial Lagos. A lot of scallywags write a heap of gross but not engaging domestic product on that topic, that should be closer to the w.c. than the www but you tell me if there is much to choose between the two echoing chambers,' she said, picking up a bronze bust of a girl reading a book.

'Iya, my late grandmother claims that her grandfather's estate was misappropriated or misallocated.' Ade sat on a rickety stool beside a pile of stirrups.

'Misallocated? Why the euphemisms? Stealing is stealing. Facts outlive myths. Passions fade. But the truth is simple beneath the florid obfuscations. But I thought you were from Zimbabwe.'

'I am and I am not but it was easier to go along with perceptions,' he said to galloping foreboding.

'Dangerous and confusing game, lying, especially to yourself. But now you mention it, self-deception is the cousin of self-belief. They both help us survive?' She grinned. 'My boy, stop me stop me before I lose myself in digressions.' She waved a figurine at Ade's satchel. 'What have you got there?'

Ade dipped into his satchel for the broken photo of Jinadu, Iya's grandfather. 'I have an old Ayo board as well. The mat is at home, made of commemorative slats I believe.'

The professor inspected the photograph and placed it on the table in front of her. 'This is of titillating interest. Wait.' She grunted out of the chair, swung into an adjacent office and returned a few minutes later with a stack of old ledgers. 'Most of these footnotes I made in my psychopathic handwriting, sitting outside that inspiring door with the lagoon in my ears.' She pointed at the door just before the wind slammed it shut. Ade got up to wedge the front door open.

'Inheritance is a bomb field. Or is it a minefield?' She chomped on a biscuit. 'Are you paying by the minute or by word count?'

Ade rubbed the ache in his gut. 'Err, in what language?'

She cocked her head to the right and folded her right wrist over the other, just as Iya did. 'Only joking. Go on.'

'Iya, my grandmother lived near Oremi village. According to Iya, her grandfather was called Jinadu. They captured him in battle as a boy or his family driven out during a war. He became a slave to an Idejo family but was so talented that his master helped him set up in business. Jinadu thrived. But after he died Iya and her mother, Jinadu's first wife, got nothing.' Ade swallowed the lump in his throat.

'So who got the property?'

'I am married into the Martins family that won the case. They have papers establishing the root of title from their grandparents Akakambo who used to work for Jinadu.'

'So Akakambo was to Jinadu as Jinadu was to *his* master in a way, though not as master and slave. Akakambo took everything? It is an unusual case, fighting your in-laws for land from under the same roof. Anyway, that is not for now, as far as I am concerned just because they go to court may make it correct procedure and legal but it does not make it right. Many examples in history to back me up, but stop me stop me before I lose myself in digression…'

'That is what I thought,' said Ade, his mind racing back to his confrontation with Microchip, the Dean.

Professor shot an angry look at him for interrupting. 'We know that before your g-squared grandfather's days power shifted to a great extent from the founder Idejo white cap families to the *oba.*' Professor Aloja frowned and stroked her chin. 'Confusion started after the British wafted gun barrels at Dosunmu in 1861, told him to swallow his bile, gall bladder, duct and stones with only what saliva remained behind his tremulous lips, sign their Treaty or accept the constipation of his liver with lead shot. He signed, and the British said ownership of Lagos land passed to their Crown.'

Ade shook his head. 'But what did the Idejo families do?' said Ade to humour the professor. He knew the answer.

'Foul, foul, ole, thief, *iro*, lies they cried. They said the *oba* should not have given their land to foreigners, that even before 1472 when that Portuguese sailor Sequeira came across these wetlands and islands and renamed the place Lagos de Curamo, then Lagos, the Yoruba people continued to call it by their name, "Eko or Onim." Professor stopped to catch her breath. 'His flexuous backbone reinforced in a fashion by indigenous dissent Dosunmu bounced around and said he didn't grasp the implications of what he signed. Now in the interest of balance, I must say that the British will claim that they gave him freedom of choice, the gunship was only to hurry him up, catalyse him in his interest.'

The analogy recalled Controller to mind. 'The gun served as a pinch of a rare metal does in an inevitable and profitable reaction?' said Ade.

'Without nuclear weapons, and I blame our Ifa priests for this, where were they when others were splitting atoms, what choice did Dosunmu have? Fight, flight, suicide, feign madness, intoxication, prayer, juju?' said the professor, counting off the options on her fingers. She laughed. 'Maybe the gods of political retribution are showing the British how it feels to sign something they later find they do not fancy. And at Maastricht nobody held a gun to their head. Now, they cannot bully fellow industrial Europeans with gunpowder or opium.' She crumpled a biscuit wrapping in her hand. 'If you are weak weep and sign because you have to, but never forget,' she said in a wistful tone. 'But to return to the matter at hand, here in Lagos excrement defaced those pristine white colonial fans when the savvy, the freed slaves from Brazil and Sierra Leone petitioned. In response, the colonial officials came up Ordnance no 9 of 1863. Three officers sat once a week for a year to look into claims. They asked the administrator to issue -'

'Crown grants,' said Ade. 'Did that solve the problem?' he said.

Her features darkened at the interruption. She popped a biscuit into her mouth and followed it with a sip of her drink. 'How old are you?' she said.

'Twenty four.'

She brightened. 'Ah, a year younger than my son, that's why you think you know it all,' she said with a chortle. 'Ok, what do you think happened?' she said and folded her arms.

A sudden funk of scalding hatred for this professor's son, a man he had never met, for having such an accomplished mother, engulfed Ade. Unwilling to sound a brat or *penke*, he let her repeat the question. 'What happened? I am not so sure, ma. They did not have enough grants?'

She nodded and tapped crumbs off her lips. 'Glover, the chief administrator, encouraged his clients to apply and of course they got preferential treatment.'

'Is it not only natural?' said Ade, to provoke another entertaining digression.

'A large number got grants because they had squatted in a place without disturbance for three years. But wait a minute said the chiefs. Why did they have to apply for ownership of their land? They will be asking us to apply to look out of our own two eyes, to open our mouths to eat, or when to connect our lower bowels to the world. Even Sango the god of Iron did not ask that of us. Many locals ignored the colonial officers and continued to grant land in their own right. We call them *omo oniles*, owner-managers of the soil, or land.'

'Was that good?' said Ade.

She shook her head and tapped crumbs from her lips. 'It poured mud on a thick morass, especially when those who got land as worthy immigrants or former servants or slaves sold land they did not register.' Professor Aloja beamed. 'So Martins may have won their case but as far as I am concerned, is it still not based on the word of man and I mean man and the size and depth and extent of his networks?' She rocked from side to side. 'And natural artefacts can be more reliable. They don't kill each other or lie for example they used-'

'Was that why Iya insisted on keeping the wooden mattress?'

'Have you come to learn or to lecture?' she said.

'Sorry, ma.'

'Who dictates history? And who records it? Often the same people. Powerful people. Never forget that.' Professor Aloja leaned over to read the spines of the books. 'This one, early 20th century is a good start,' she said, pulling a black album out of the middle of the pile. Sheets of paper cascaded to the floor. Ade held his breath for as long as he could. In her enthusiasm Professor didn't notice the dust. 'We collect and keep everything here, certificates, newspaper cuttings, stamps, postage, and official, but be careful, the paper is as delicate as my ego in the morning mirror.'

Ade pulled the stool up to the desk and leafed through the flimsy pages of the album. Professor Aloja hovered over him like a mother over her baby in the hands of a tipsy relative. 'What's he doing on a white horse?' said Ade. The photo of his great-great-grandfather on that splendid horse swelled his heart with wistful pride.

Professor Aloja tapped his wrists. 'Don't do that. Lie it flat,' she said. 'Sorry, fire away. Ah, that is ceremonial, the helmet and plumes and feathers. Your g-squared g-father must have known the officials. From what I've seen and what you told me, not a man to die intestate.'

'But people change their minds.'

'And sometimes they don't.' She gave Ade a malty biscuit. 'Aren't you going to compliment me? Baked them myself.' She lifted the pieces of Iya's precious photograph out of the padding. 'It's broken. You didn't do this I hope?' she said, in a condemnatory tone.

'My grandmother dropped it during an emergency. You cannot imagine how sad she was when she found it like this,' said Ade, struggling to keep his composure.

'Hey, what is this, oh?' she said and teased open the folds of a card that fell from the back of the photograph. 'Interesting, very interesting indeed, and I have to say that could be one of the understatements of my career. Can I keep this for a few days?'

On the lagoon a slim woman canoed downstream, bare breasts swinging back and forth like accessory paddles with her languid strokes.

Thirty

A plane buzzed, drowning conversation, its contrails called to mind an unravelling barrister's wig. Professor Kosimbe slowed to avoid the bare-chested men carrying bags of rice up the gangway. 'Sheki is greatly disappointed in you,' he said and kissed Tewomo on his arm goodbye. She patted Prof Kosimbe on the bottom and teetered off on blue stilettoes.

'Disappointment is mutual but its implications unequal, sir,' Ade said. Inspired by his meeting with Professor Aloja, he'd dashed straight across town from Akoka to Apapa to drive a wedge between Controller and his friend, and buy time.

'Julius, please don't insult my intelligence. Sheki can be brutally blunt, I agree, but he is honest and good at maintaining law and order, just what this country needs,' said the don, in a clipped tone, angry no doubt because Ade interrupted his fun with stiletto woman. They turned left at the top of the bouncy gangplank, and ducked into a sultry cabin. A pale stripe ran along the wall where a bunk used to hang. As he pulled a chair to sit across the table, the image of Iya sitting beside him, one hand over the other the last time they came to Apapa, choked him with sorrow.

Professor Kosimbe combed his side-burns. 'Sorry to hear about mama,' he said and paused as the ship rumbled to the electric generator.

'Professor, it was out of respect for your relationship with Controller that I did not want to provoke trouble between you, but I am forced to speak out as you would in my position. What do I have to lose now? Controller is a blackmailer. And it is not the first time. If you don't believe me, ask him. Why do you think Iya risked her life to help me, knowing that she had aortic stenosis?'

Professor straightened his bowtie. 'Young man I don't know what you are getting at but Sheki is my right-hand man and I will not sit here listening to insulting -'

'And as they say on those molue buses, the right hand is the most common cause of self-inflicted wounds.'

'I have never seen that on any bus. My advice is count your blessings and drop the calumny. You said it yourself. Your Iya died of natural causes.'

'By that token all death is natural, head crushed by elephant stampede, Trotsky's ice-pick in the head,' said Ade, at once regretting his retort. Lagos boy cool it, you've come to fan the man's egos not probe and provoke. 'Sir, did you know that Controller owns properties registered to his wife and sons? Plus children studying abroad. On his salary?'

Professor made a dismissive gesture. 'Go find another host for your lies and innuendo. Sheki comes from an established Lagos family. Of course he has wide interests, and he maintains properties in trust to stop the more profligate family members tossing the whole thing away. Paying salaries out of his own pocket. Is that what you call shady? I am sure these rumours started in their parlours.'

'Your right-hand man is using the Roadsweepers to collect girls for shady transactions in Kakirikiri and KIYO to silence detractors?' said Ade.

'If you come here to foul the day, then shovel yourself off and ah, he is here.'

The door flung open and Ade's heart stood on end as Controller Sheki Gbagba appeared in the doorway. 'Wonders will never cease. This man has the *ogboju* to show his foggy face here?' Controller was wearing a well-ironed and starched police uniform. One pleat reminded Ade of a shark's fin.

'Sheki, don't vex, it was my fault allowing the man back here. I thought the original plan sounded promising but…'

Controller kicked the door shut. 'Promising? As promising as the sound of a cracked whip, or a broken country and western disc? The man is a walking pack of lies.'

'By the way how was mama? For her spasms I went to see her two days ago. Tomorrow I will go to check her BP again,' said the professor.

Controller's face fell. 'No change. What more can I do?' he said, and biting his lower lip he leaned against the door.

Professor Kosimbe turned to Ade. 'Young man, that mama has suffered. Strokes. Diabetes. Right arm has not straightened for ten years. No speech and she is almost blind. Yet people like you spread rumours and want to kill Sheki too with lies.'

Ade reeled to the absurdity of a lecture on ethics from this pair. Yet he envied Controller's bond with his mother. Was that why Allah let him get away with everything? 'I came to apologise. Put it down to my naïveté and inexperience. I am begging you for some time to work a way out once I finish with probate at the registry. Please, sir.'

'That is not what you said just now.'

'The man is talking absolute rubbish. Seinde, do you know that this Julius wanted me to take girls from the Agidi initiation ceremony for his precious Iya?' said Controller and he pushed past Ade, smelling of nicotine and lime soap.

'Is that true? You are into rituals? And you come here talking as if angels bow at your feet?' said the don.

'Not at all. Not true, sir,' said Ade, his stomach tightening with anger.

Controller chuckled. 'It is late for wrongful indignation my friend. Seinde, I saw through them right from the start, but I was biding my time. As they say, small, small na in dem dey take catch monkey, or thief for that matter. Now he complains. Rightfully so in my generous opinion he has come to beg.' He tapped his shirt pocket for a cigarette.

'I am useless to you in prison, but since Iya died, I found another opportunity for cooperation,' Ade said, relieved to see a brighter sheen of greed flicker across the police thief's face.

Professor Kosimbe fiddled with his bowtie. 'Sheki, you carry on, I have to debrief the emergency operations committee. Commissioners for Health will be attending.'

'I am also tiring of his nonsense,' said Controller. 'When I return from my meeting up in Abuja I will dispose of these loose ends.'

'Abuja still harassing you?' said Professor Kosimbe.

Ade wiped his sweaty hands on the back of his trousers. 'I came here to beg for bygones to be bygones. But these files,' Ade said, swinging his pleading gaze between the men, 'can we not agree on a fair way forward? Then-'

'What files?' said the professor.

Controller chuckle-cleared his throat. 'Don't listen to Julius geyser. The man's head is in clouds of his own steamy farts.' He tapped his shirt pocket and turned again to Ade. 'My friend. Why did you have to disturb Seinde? I have said that -'

Ade threw in the kitchen sink. 'But sir, after the last payment, where will I find you yet another fifty thousand dollars? It will take me more than three lifetimes and Iya my provider is no more.'

Professor Kosimbe shot forward. 'How many dollars?'

Thirty-one

Ade knocked on the enormous steel door of the immensely rich and powerful Church of the Everlasting Saviour, the great rival to the Redeemed Church in Nigeria. Whoever designed the tower, its stained glass windows, the golden steeple in the shape of a Madonna, a dozen steel buttresses swooping to the ground to represent the apostles and the ring of trees and shrubs simulating the back blow from a space rocket, had done so to awe, or terrify.

Two eager youthful men in white shirts, ties, black suits and dark glasses slid open a pocket door, and ran a strip thermometer along Ade's forehead to screen for Ebola. Ade waited, begging for the right result. At last the young men ushered him into a glass pod and so fast was the lift that Ade's stomach plummeted to his boots. He stepped out on hollow legs.

Dominated by a glittering oak table in the shape of a Latin cross, the meeting room tapered to a far wall on which hung a giant white cross. A clock on one side-wall had hands the shape of burning candles. Ade was in such awe of the opulent fittings that he remained standing. At twenty-nine minutes past eleven the dark-suited board members, nine men and three women swept in, led by Isaac. The woman tottering in after them, steered by her fruit trolley, reminded him of Moji. Was she in yet another quarrel with *her* wonky trolley wheel? Ade popped an antacid and stuffed the wrapping into a trouser pocket.

Isaac, a slender man, aged forty, with wise eyes and short hair, stood at the head of the glittering oak table.

When the room swayed a fearful Ade grabbed the table. 'Just the wind from the angels' wings blessing your presence. Nothing untoward will happen to you here my brother. Please be seated brothers and sisters,' said Isaac, in a singsong voice. The man to his right, in a suit most silky, strafed Ade with puffy eyes, the corner of his nose rising as though a rotten egg rested on his lips. Ade sank into a luxurious leather chair.

'John, wait your turn will come,' said Isaac, with a tiny bow. Isaac had a way of swinging the turret he made with his middle fingers round to the person he addressed. 'We know that we are to acquire by the Grace of our Lord the last step towards the campus we want to build to His glory. But Sister Florence introduced Julius to me, after service last weekend. Mr Julius here has something that may be of interest and though it is of course only his opinion we as a famous international educational and religious organisation, must be fair and do nothing to tarnish our good name. Brothers and sisters we pray for an excellent outcome to our deliberations, in Jesus's name we pray.'

'Amen,' said the members.

'Amen,' said Ade, a beat later. Sensing the smouldering irritation with him for dragging them there when they could be hiding from Ebola or tending to their growing flock of shopping bills, Ade got out of his chair, and bowed in an exaggerated show of respect, and also to make his blue shirt ride up his back to scratch a nervous itch.

Isaac smiled. 'The matter at hand, if you will excuse me, is akin to the flow of a river or the passing of water. It looks easy, but not simple and is why I brought it to council's attention. Brother Julius, you mentioned a late grandmother,' said Isaac, in a sympathetic voice designed to elicit support for Ade. Ade blushed, bowed and shifted his beaten up rucksack out from between his feet.

'She is not here,' said John.

Neither was Saint John himself, or Luke or Matthew. But Ade kept that retort to himself. Cool it, Lagos boy, lose the room and you may end up in a Black Maria. 'It pleased God to take my grandmother, the mother of my mother, only a few weeks ago my brothers and sisters. I beg you to consider my humble petitory claim. Anyone who met my late grandmother will understand why I am here to defend her claim to land you earmarked for the administrative campus.' Ade unfurled Iya's wooden mat and opened up the three-hinged Ayo board he brought from her hut. 'This is one of the pieces of evidence I am presenting.'

'Nothing but charred trash. Brother Isaac. This is why we will never make progress in this country. Acting Chairman Isaac,' John said, bouncing to his feet and placing the emphasis on "acting." 'This is a shovel ready project, a shovel ready project and we are nearly ready to sign. After meeting upon meeting, paying for security, for police, for the magistrate, swearing affidavits and the codicils are more plentiful than the hairs on my head. Treasurer, *abi* I lie?' He sat to nods, murmurs and swishes of assent. The woman sitting next to John looked as if she could have done with an umbrella against his spray of saliva. Oblivious or indifferent to that, John smoothed his wispy moustache and picked up a thick manual. In his other hand he held a thick bible. Clearing his voice he puffed his chest with comical self-importance. 'Don't get me wrong, I have nothing against old women. My best friends have them as mothers, but not myself. These two books in my hands, one constitution and governance and the other the word of God are enough to guide us, not wishful thinking. So we should tell headquarters that we are now playing tom-tom drums, singing and dancing with illiterates who enjoy nothing better than to spread old stories?'

From Ade's right came a cheer. Her support earned a nod from John but the woman sitting opposite Ade did not look impressed.

'Brothers and sisters. Brother John has made many wonderful points in his own unique and powerful way. Now have you had time to go through the transcript that our friend Julius sent?' said Isaac and glided over to pat Ade on the shoulder. 'Brother Julius, you have more than this?' He sounded both concerned for Ade and apologetic to the rest of the room.

Ade nodded, but conviction was fast deserting him, and he feared exposure as the flying paintbrush. He took a deep breath, as he used to just before a big race. 'I will give you specific details.' He put his hand in his satchel.

'Mr whatever your name, we have oriki where I come from,' growled a woman to Ade's far left. She spoke with one of those thick Yoruba accents exaggerated for dramatic or comical effect on TV. John turned to the door. 'Ah, good, here he is. I asked the lawyer to attend in the interest of justice,' and Bola swaggered in wearing a blue suit, white shirt.

Ade groaned in fearful dismay. He'd swap Bola for testicular torsion any day. John handed Bola a copy of Ade's manuscript then sat with interlocked hands on the table, radiating the smugness of a jackpot winner. Isaac polished the table then cracked his fingers. Ade fretted, his stomach eaten away by fear.

'You know what you can do with this ill-conceived aboriginal claim?' said Bola, crumpling up the paper and bouncing it across the table at Ade. A hiss of disapproval came from one or two quarters. Bola hurried. 'What of the human rights of genuine worshippers?' he said. He frowned at the chug from the phone in front of him. An aide leapt up to grab the offending device and rush out juggling it as if it were hot charcoal. 'My brothers and sisters his claim has no merit. I was prepared to accommodate his wish to keep his grandmother in the manner to which she had become accustomed, nugatory contributions here and there, but events disposed of the necessity for such arrangements. What we have here is a set of bush artefacts, rehashed oral history - a fox that modern law shot dead a long time ago.' Bola opened a black ring binder. 'Martins can trace our root of title way back,' said Bola, his face as bright as the famous lights on Victoria Island at Christmas. 'I quote from the judgement in Akpan Awo vs Cookey Garm 2 Nigerian Land Report pages 100-101.' He paused to catch his breath and survey the room with the demeanour of one dispensing rare pearls before swine. 'The court will not allow a party to call in aid principles of native law, and least of all principles, which, as in this case were developed in and are applicable to a state of a society vastly different from that now existing merely for the purpose of bolstering a stale claim,' said Bola to louder murmurs of assent from the room. 'I repeat. A stale claim. If you take this one simple point away today, I will rest easy.'

'Stale claim, do you hear that, our brother Julius?' said John, cupping his ear.

Allah, please if only he could for a few moments bend English to his will he'd have the whole world to prod and kick around, even when he was wrong or guilty. Ade wrapped his hands around his glass to still them. Catastrophe loomed.

'Time for a show of hands,' said Isaac, waving the copy of Ade's oriki in his hand. Are we satisfied that we do not have enough to delay our transaction with the Martins family?'

Isaac abstained, out of Christian charity or pity. The vote went against Ade. Unanimous. The members piled the papers in the middle of the table for disposal and triumphant, Bola flicked a silver pen from his pocket and with elaborate flourishes, began to sign the sheets John handed him.

'My son, you try well but maybe if your mama agba was here it will be another result,' said the woman with the strong Yoruba accent. As Ade acknowledged her with a tiny bow, a spark flicked to mind. 'Excuse me, I want to congratulate my in-law on a brilliant defence and for confirming that Akakambo a returnee from Freetown in Sierra Leone passed these lands to his family.'

Bola puffed his chest out in that magisterial manner that so got up Ade's nose. 'Glad you are seeing sense at last. It is indeed the case that Akakambo acquired and gifted the land to his children.'

'To discredit Iya, you omit the native record from the provenance of your grandfather's land. Yet, he based his claim on the native, traditional modes of transmission. Iya's claim is not spurious as you state.'

Bola did not look up from his document. 'This is not the set of a pretentious art-house movie where you just throw words up into the ether in the hope that someone will give them a sympathetic fashionably politically correct rearrangement and interpretation.'

'Just bear with me then. Others here who know Lagos history will have personal experience of what I tried to describe or know someone with similar problems. For the record, my great-great maternal grandfather, Jinadu of Lagos was a trader. They captured him in battle and enslaved, rose to make a name as a trader in whisky, in millet, in buying and selling and what you call native medicine. You may know of Jinadu. Famous on Lagos Island for his white horse,' said Ade, with a pointed glance at John. 'Jinadu had one daughter. That is the mother of my grandmother. I will not take your time as I have discussed this with the acting

Chairman.' Ade paused, took a deep breath to compose himself. John rolled his eyes to the ceiling and picked an orange. Ade smiled to wind him up. 'In those days the girls used to have the cut. After she had my grandmother Iya, she had complications that we now call a vvf, vesicovaginal fistula. Bola, your so-called root of title derives from that unfortunate accident.'

'Nonsense, people just cannot move on. Wallowing daily in their degrading and sorry past, spending their miserable lives searching for excuses and complaints - a fragment of a folk song that may have disturbed the eardrum of a grandfather, the drops of acid rain from the campfire of their master that may have fallen on their hapless great grandmother. And only then will they get what they call closure. We progressives jettisoned that a long time ago,' said Bola and slipped out of his jacket. 'You may be married to my sister, but today you have overreached yourself.' His lips curled up, exposing his beetroot-red gums.

Ade's heart hammered a frantic beat. 'Bola, call me what you want. But let me finish. Jinadu's right-hand man was called Akakambo, the man from whom in this very same room minutes ago you agreed that you derived your family's root of title,' said Ade. 'I, through Iya, therefore have a prior claim to this land. As a lawyer without peer in this country you should know that.'

'We've been here. Where are you now going with this?' said Isaac.

'Nerves cuffed my tongue, the immensity of this place and this occasion, the high stakes and I did not see through to the core of the oriki until my learned lady friend here jolted something at the back of my mind.'

'Go on,' said Isaac.

Ade explained how her grandfather's foreman or right-hand man and his new wife duped Iya of her inheritance. 'Maybe Jinadu should have been more careful, but he was not to know.'

Bola leapt to his feet but with a face now contoured by shadows of doubt. 'Chairman, don't listen to this bunkum, the man is patently deranged and trying to get back at me because I refused him a loan. You may not know but he and my sister have been trying for a child whilst my efforts have been more productive. It is envy, and it sinks him below the contempt of any decent person.'

Ade sensed a huff of disapproval from one corner of the room. 'Oga Bola ah, ah, wait make we hear what Mr Julius is saying, o jare. Are you the only lawyer in this Lagos who get pickin?' said the apple-loving woman sitting opposite Ade.

Ade slid Niari's tape into the player with timorous hope. It had to be, had to be, or he'd sell for less than a teaspoon of dried manure.

'Come on man, 21st century, you don't have DVD?' said Bola, his baritone voice soaring to a shriek.

Emboldened by Bola's disquiet, Ade wound the tape to the start of Niari's recording. 'I will slow this down. When you listen again and look at the paper version, the transcription, you will see as I did that we are looking at a Will, in English of the time, maybe he recited to Iya, to copy or memorise, or maybe he was teaching her how to read, or maybe she found it and tried to memorise it herself. Who knows?' He paused, his heart flapping as if buffeted in a storm.

'I don't think this man is well up there,' said John, looking around the room for support.

'You are right. Utter poppycock,' said Bola.

The woman who loved apples stopped chewing and spat at Bola an angry stare.

Ade pressed the button on the recorder to play the coda of his oriki. 'Naked lawyer, burying your head in the mud will not cure your myopia,' said Ade. 'Ladies and gentlemen, brothers and sisters, I believe this was drafted in English but read out by someone for whom it was not the first language. The arcane legalese of the late 19th and early 20th century, the "easements" and "whereases" and "hereinafters" and "beneficiaries", have been Yorubanised over time but once you get used to the rhythm and beat it begins to make sense so I beg you please, listen with open minds.' He pressed the rewind button. 'Now listen again. *Whereas* she pronounces Harasi, instead of *I give and bequeath* she says Aigi and Biki. There are many other examples. You hear other Yorubanised words Kofiyasi for conveyance and proper place names *Apongbon* and *Idumagbo* and I convinced you that this document, the oriki is part of an agreement, an oral will,' said Ade. 'Maybe Iya memorised it and when she wrote it, or others did the same they introduced mistakes. These added up over the years until it sounds different from the original. As you know my fathers and mothers, brothers and sisters, small changes can add up so much so that the result can look as if it was made that way right from the start as if it was designed to be that way, just as we resemble our parents and their parents but we are not the same,' said Ade, straight from Dr Opa's school of mumbo jumbo but he hoped he made sense.

'I think na true the man talk, oh,' said the woman who loved apples, to Ade's eternal gratitude.

Bola flicked a crumb across the table. 'Chairman, we won the case of cases. I recognise four or five of you from the court,' he added, with a confident air, but the ambience in the room shifted from hostile scepticism to cautious sympathy for Ade.

'You won because your great grandfather Akakambo passed himself off as sole male heir, and registered the Lagos Island and mainland parts of the estate under his name,' said Ade.

John hopped out of his seat. 'Lawyer, this elaborate conjuring trick proves nothing. We've seen it before from other 419ers. The cheques are here ready to sign. When we open our university, we will do proper research based on the holy Gospel, not on these floor shows and myths.'

They call their indigenous word of record myth but the imported from overseas they take as gospel. But not a sentiment to express in church or in the mosque for that matter, Lagos boy. Remember what happened between you and Microchip the Dean?

They heard a loud knock on the great door and in bustled Professor Aloja in a pale tunic over a baggy pair of dark trousers and white heeled sandals.

'Prof, you made it through the go-slow,' said Ade.

'Obviously,' said John.

'Who is this woman?' said Bola.

Beaming, almost tripping over with excitement, a thick grey root dropped from under her dark headscarf as Professor Aloja rushed up to heave a large leather rucksack on to the table. 'I am Professor Aloja of the University of Lagos, personal chair in the history of precolonial Eko or Lagos if you prefer the Portuguese name. Now, in the course of recent research I found a brittle folded note in the back of our young man's photo of his g squared grandfather. I promised to come along to help or clarify,' she said. She turned to Ade. 'After you left I sent my research assistant to the archives and he found to his eternal credit, this digitised version of an original recorded in the anteroom of the Governor's office. Lucky for you the photo had a date on it. They took it in the governor's office. If what you have been debating we take as the starter what I have here is a deeply satisfying main course. Those who can, enjoy, Those who cannot, be happy for those who can. Those who cannot be happy, go practice your frowns because you will be needing them.'

Bola's voluminous Adam's apple sprung up like a hot-air balloon. 'This is preposterous. How did this so-called beer merchant or trader get a recorder in the Governor's office?'

'We can only speculate, but we have found one or two other similar recordings, from the Saros, returnees from Freetown. Others were found by Nigerian scholars, Dike, Ajayi, Biobaku, Babalola, Olusanya.'

Ade nodded. 'I've read a few. Met one or two, but when they were older.'

'Not read my collaborations with Kristin Mann or Ms Alonge?' said the professor with an arched brow. 'This is the recording that Jinadu made. Maybe he went there because he did not trust Akakambo, or they were testing the equipment. I knew he did not sound the sort of person to die intestate. This is his will in his voice.' She tapped the laptop.

'I Jinadu Arokiawu, to Akakambo my devoted servant till his death, this estate. On his death, my daughter Musebi and granddaughter Abake, half of my

228

estate, including all the land at and near Oremi. Should she predecease him, then the half to my granddaughter, Abake witness my hand at Lagos the day and year first above written. It then went on to a much clearer version of the coda part Iya used to sing to Ade and detailed the size and numbers of plots. When Ade heard his great-great-grandfather's grainy Yoruba-accented English, he fell back into his chair, exhausted and elated. He wished Iya was here.

The woman who loved apples clapped her hands. 'Jesus is great, oh. If not for this brother we could have built our college on sand.'

Ade opened his eyes and smiled at her. You changed your tune. And your fruit.

'This mountain of consistent and confounding historical data is too much to ignore. Though I cannot in conscience conclude that they resolve this matter one way or the other I regret to say that in the circumstances we cannot proceed with our transaction in its present form. Not without further-'

'You have no mandate. No no,' Bola said, screaming, his neck bulging, his eyes on fire, as if he dropped his birthday cake into the gutter. 'And as for you, you wait and see.' He pumped a fist across the table at Ade then turned to Professor Aloja. 'Call yourself an academic but cannot spot a wanted man?'

Ade floated to his feet. 'Naked lawyer, if true why let me marry your sister? We will meet at Chief's house over this matter I am sure.' He bowed low. 'Excuse me, ladies and gentlemen. I need a short break,' he said, and, with a complicit nod at the professor, he left his papers and satchel behind on the table to suggest his imminent return but fled the church and called the well-connected socialist banker, Durosote, to tell him the news so he could pass on the news to Bola's creditors, with punitive interest.

Thirty-two

It was five minutes and six seconds past six in the evening when Ade arrived at Chief's family house, thrumming inside from adrenaline, like a leaf caught in a spoke. Save for the toilets, the smallest room in the house, and the size of four table tennis tables, the meeting room gave on to a veranda through a set of French windows and had eight red sofas, four on each side. Scattered across the room and etched with the name Martins in red ink sat cachepots housing wilting bonsai trees. A life-sized bronze bust of Iya's stepmother stood in one corner.

Ade's foot sank into a red rug deep enough to hide a golf ball. Yeni dressed all in red and sat on the same side as Bola and Chief facing Ade. Blinded by the sun, Ade swallowed an antacid, his apprehension reinforced by Moji's warning that whatever happened here, Controller might still hold the best cards. Didn't he always?

Chief dismissed the servants. He started proceedings by slamming his flagon on to the coffee table, blasting into another rant, a louder version of an earlier one delivered to Ade over the phone. 'Today we stop this nonsense. We've done much for this man and shown him better ways of life. I gave him property and a job and introduced him to the pastor is this how this vandal, bushman repays us?' He went on in a similar vein for several minutes, waving a red biro in the air, letting rip with such force that Ade feared for the vessels in the VIP's head. 'Julius or whatever you call yourself sign this thing so that we can settle this matter before month-end, then let's go *o jare*.' Chief held a blue biro out to Ade, as if offering nibbles to a pet.

'Can you not tell the church that you will reconsider the matter?' said Yeni. 'We guarantee that the villagers will not suffer if that is your main concern so that...'

Yeni turned to the jangle of approaching bangles. Princess A floated into the room, her face sharing her daughter's scornful expression. 'Is that him?' she said. Her sparse eyebrows curving like sporty handlebars, she pointed at Ade with one golden arm of her glasses. She paused to give Ade a dirty look then, ignoring her husband's timid nod, glided over to plant herself a yard from him on the sofa.

'Mama, I do not know why we are even giving this man a hearing,' said Bola. 'Let him sue. Is it not in this same Lagos they will hear the case?' He got up to sit between his parents.

'I am surprised to see the naked brief here when he should be trying for a lucrative seat in the Senate,' said Ade.

Bola shot to his feet, saw the stern look on his father's face, shook his head, for a moment hovered over his seat before he landed with a squeak from the leather sofa.

'Bola, I want you to keep mouth shut. You caused this with your reckless spending,' said Chief.

'And you have no blame in the matter?' said Princess A. 'Right from day one, I knew that this whatever you call this person here will piss into our pot. As for this one,' she said, referring to Yeni. 'Sees bed goes and lies under flyover. What was wrong with Dayo Prentice, ernh? Despite everything he was prepared to take you.'

'He had a lucky escape. He told me to my face at the club last week,' said Bola.

'And you think your wife is perfect?' said Yeni.

The arrogance and hypertrophied narcissism incensed Ade. 'Chief. I am sure you did not invite me here for a comparative marital study,' said Ade 'Just give me the files so that I can put the last year behind me.'

'Files? Yeni, Bola what is he saying?' said Chief.

Bola and Yeni exchanged sullen glances.

Chief smacked the table. 'Someone padlocked your mouths?' he said.

'Why don't we hand this bogus man and his wahala over to Sheki,' said Princess A. 'If they ask we should say that we just found out he was the man they were looking for, but we did not know until yesterday.'

'Aduke, you knew and didn't tell me?' Chief said, with a sharp turn to his wife.

Yeni waved her hand in the air. 'Let me talk.' She told them how Ade agreed to take the rap for Bola after the accident. 'That is how Bola is, every time I get rice on my plate he will go and find a way to spoil it with sand.' She sniffed and brushed a tear from her eye.

'Your tears impress me not,' said Ade, 'Chief, I should have told them both to go and boil their necks. But no, I said to myself they are the Martins proper and important people, it will be ok. She said you will help me with the Dean, but it was a barge of lies. What was I thinking? I played a stupid joke to get back at that Olabo girl and said I was in the car with her.'

'Why?' said Chief.

'To make her angry because she does not consider anyone not in her circle human beings. My joke backfired. On me.'

'He *is* guilty,' said Princess A.

'What else have you not told me?' said Chief, his eyes bulging from their sockets. 'Why this wahala over old files?'

'It is because Yinka died,' said Yeni.

Chief rocked backward as if punched. 'What? Did you say lied, or hide or died?'

'You didn't know. At the time you were on that committee, er, for economic development and power,' said Yeni.

Chief sucked his teeth. 'If she didn't die from the accident in Bola's car, she may have died from another thing. So I ask again one last time before I show you my true colours, why the pandemonium?'

Princess made a brusque sucking sound and smacked her lips. 'Ah, Baba Bola, stop playing Solomon for us here. You caused this when you gave this yeye man mouth to talk to the likes of us. Buying him house, taking him as a son. Do you not know that will affect Bola ernh? If we cannot get Bola out of this problem God forbid, what will they say when we have to pack up to that house in Ikoyi. What will people say when *jaguda* come to take water from our swimming pool? When goats climb up the steps and eat these wonderful imported flowers.' She looked as if she would die at the prospect of this most dreadful humiliation, a six-bedroomed house in upmarket Ikoyi.

Yeni made one of her disdainful sizzling tooth sucking sounds. 'Mama, why are you making mende-mende mouth when it was your precious Bola who went to buy billion naira chicken from Togo to start a farm? Now he knows that not every Tom Dick and naked lawyer can run a business,' said Yeni, sneering at her brother. Bola leapt out of his chair. His mum dragged him back. 'Not one of his chickens remain. Is that not a fact, then when that did not pay you, you ran to borrow money to buy shares,' said Yeni. She said the shares collapsed when the head of the Federal Reserve in the US, she's forgotten his name, Berekan (Bernancke) or something hinted at a rise in interest rates. 'Is that not the fact of the case? If I lie let God punish me now,' she said, looking to the heavens.

'Aduke, I warned you that your boy is misguided,' said Chief.

Princess A pulled an apologetic face. 'Today is not for that. If we stand as one family good can still come of it.'

Ade erupted. 'Misguided? Good can come of this? Bola knew the girl was dead, and I in hospital oblivious to his wickedness and cowardice and like a fool I was prepared to believe Yeni when she said she did not know. But who knows what to believe from the assembly tongues of Martins and company?' He turned from Chief to Princess A. 'Mama, you say good can come of it. For you or me? None of you care what happens to anybody else as long as good comes out of it for you. If someone rapes Bola's daughter, Ronke, and she becomes a senator, will you say oh good has come of it, let us leave another girl outside the man's door, no, to be truly sure why not leave her inside his bedroom, no naked first, leg tied to each post and give her hormonal supplements? Who knows, the next batch, triplets could produce an entire cabinet, for export to other continents, ernh? Ade heaved a deep breath and sat there, fizzing. This was what Durosote the banker meant. These people truly believe themselves to be the warders of the world, and that though chance may favour the brave, they have a sole right to dole it out. Then they buy the media and the institutions of learning and security and the rest and use them to tell lies to raise to universal aspirations, the selfish pursuit and acquisition of the greatest profit by any means. Perhaps the pursuit of greed as an end in itself is their real aim. 'Enough, I just want you out of my life, now, out. I need the files and I will sign you the land you need for liquidity. Yeni, you and I have business to discuss because you knew what Bola was doing. I won't forget that.'

Princess A jabbed a fist at Bola. 'Bola, after your book learning overseas how did you allow this to happen?'

Bola scratched his chin, and Ade sensed that his brother-in-law always knew the history of the land. 'You knew and yet terrorised those innocent villagers, you are a disgrace to your profession.'

'You expect me to deliver it to parasites on a silver platter do you?' said Bola. 'And before you ask we did not plan this. Dropped at our feet by a fortuitous coincidence and your sad limitations I'm afraid.'

'Yeni, any dutiful sister would help Bola, not sit there adding fire and -'

Yeni leapt off the arm of Ade's chair. 'Mama. After my disgrace in front of everybody at the party?' She flopped back, jerking her head from side to side, resembling a skittish monocular hen. She slid to the edge of her seat to launch a squawking parody of her mother, 'Bola is going to be president one day, as for Yeni, by your age don finished with carrying children.' Yeni sucked her tongue and turned to Chief. 'Do you want to hear what mama mother said when I saw my period last month? That Yeni will be the only one in the maternity ward with grey hairs there. Can you imagine a woman saying that to her child? And she calls herself my mother. That is when she wants contracts for hair cream.' Yeni dabbed tears and cursed under her breath. 'Millions naira spent bailing Bola out in the UK, but on top of that no respect for me as firstborn. Chief is called Baba Bola, not Baba Yeni. Am I dead? Even if I am dead am I still not his child? Or you have another secret father for me? Or is this because I am a woman? Then you sit there and ask me to take what I earned with blood and sweat and give it away to a waster? No, no, never, *lai lai*. Please don't insult my intellectuals again or everybody will know the Martins story in this Lagos.' Snatching a glass off a stool Yeni sank against the back of the chair, churning knees, the extension beads clanking with her angry titubation.

'Bola, before Yeni scalpulates herself go and get the file from the black safe between the Italian and French section of bags,' said Princess A.

'The file is here?' said Ade. This gets better.

'Let me go with him before he goes and gambles the whole thing away on breastless chickens, oh.' Yeni hurried, barefooted ahead of Bola to return minutes later with a slim brown file which she dropped on the stool in front of her mother. Princess A promptly shoved it across the room at Ade. 'But it's only a copy,' he said, sinking into oppressive despair. He tossed the file at Yeni.

'I knew they were copies,' said Yeni. 'But what if we get Controller to give you the originals? Will you help Bola out of this cash flow palaver by talking to the church people again? Then we close the matter and the two of us will be straight again.'

Ade's mind rotated as though a hemiplegic worm. He'd gone to hell only for photocopies? His phone sang. Professor Kosimbe sounded most put out and suggested an urgent meeting. What now? Ade closed the call with a wistful sigh. Once upon a time he had a simple life in a village with Iya until he blew it on those who did not care whether he breathed or not. 'Yeni, why don't you ask Controller for the files whilst I am here? Then we can discuss.'

'Controller is in Abuja,' said Yeni.

'I am not asking you to walk there,' said Ade.

'Talking to that man may aggravate him,' said a subdued Bola.

They went quiet again. A second hand kissed its way once round the clock face. 'What else are you hiding?' said Ade.

Princess A sighed, dropped her shoulders and mouth in weighty resignation. 'Sheki is the son of Chief and Ladun,' she said in a tone that suggested a long-held grudge.

Yeni turned to Ade. 'Controller has not forgiven Chief for what happened to his mother.'

Bola ignored Chief's hostile frown. 'One night not long ago we were having a quiet drink at the Sheraton when Sheki blew up big time,' said Bola. 'Do you think I have forgotten the state of my mama when your Chief finished using her as a rag he said. I was only a boy myself he said, feeding her and cleaning her because I am still standing you think everything is ok? His exact words, give or take a letter and expletive or two.' Bola turned to Yeni. 'I am sure that it was he who sabotaged my chicken business at the wharf.'

'Not the entrepreneur you claimed to be are you? I will give you the liquidity you need on one condition. You tell the Olabos the truth,' said Ade.

Chief sucked hard. Bola looked pensive.

'You swear on your grandmother's grave?' said Princess A.

'I swear,' said Ade. Anything to sort this steaming mess.

Chief sat forward. 'But I will not be able to-'

'Sit down Bola. Shut up both of you,' said Princess A. 'Bola, draw up the agreement.'

'You know that if Controller finds out that we are talking to the Olabos behind him he will not be happy. What will stop him using the original statement from Julius to destroy us? He will turn it on us and accuse us of deceiving the police. Your campaign, my business, our name, everything will collapse to ashes,' said Yeni.

Ade tried to think. Yeni was right. Controller held that powerful card, the original statement. 'I agree,' said Ade. He needed time to regroup.

'Agree what?' said Princess A.

'That you should not tell the Olabos.'

'Make up your mind, little man,' said Bola.

'But you will allow Bola the credit?' said Princess A.

Ade nodded. 'I will talk to my advisers tomorrow.' Durosote could draw up one of those illusions, packed with contranyms and hidden fees, that passes for a sound financial agreement. 'But you know what this means?'

'What?' said Chief.

'That we are on the same side. Against Sheki, Controller.'

Princess A clucked her begrudged agreement.

'Give me this file,' said Ade.

'It is only a copy. What can you do with it?' said Yeni.

'Lie?' he said.

Thirty-three

The agreement bought Ade breathing space, but he could not shake the gloomy impression that apart from a tenuous hold on Iya's land not much had changed. Home late after a long shift, with a volcanic headache and in a mood courtesy of a tiff with Moji over nothing he could remember, he planned to crash into bed without supper. But Yeni met him inside the front door in one of the pink gowns in which Ade once found her seductive. 'Where have you been? Yagging in town with cunts 'r' us?'

Ade closed his stinging eyes. Where did she grow this harvest of obsessive jealousy? 'Confusion at work without Controller,' he said. Please North Korea. Mount Yeni as a symbol of belligerent defiance on one of your test missiles.

'Listen, I know you are vexed and tired and your head is not straight but why spoil everything with stubbornness? Leave things as they are, please. Ok, I get that you want to go to the Ministry and say I used to be Julius of Zimbabwe married to Martins but now Lagos boy Ade. But what do you think will happen? Salute and a new passport that afternoon? Never. This is Nigeria. And what will cunts 'r' us say if you changed your name back in the middle of that stupid follow-up investigation into Zaki's…problem? Lie low as you are and let us have an enjoyable life. No more people poking noses into our problems.'

Ade prised off her arm. 'Why did you phone P and J to say Ranti was trying to steal your husband? She almost lost her job.'

'The way cunts 'r' us was looking and talking to you that day I began to suspect that she came to make a fool of me. In my own house for that matter. Insult to my

241

intellectuals. Why should I accept that?' She cocked her head in a sympathetic gesture. 'But well done the other day with Bola. Now you and me are working together we will make a strong team. Invisible. Come, sit here with me.' Yeni patted the space on the sofa beside her and gave him a coquettish tap on the inside of his thigh. 'Will you come to Mama Ibeji's party on Saturday?'

Ade wished he was invisible. He sat beside Yeni from the force of habit and because he lacked the strength to fight. 'Wait until this palaver with Bola settles.' Another anodyne response. What was Moji doing now? Fears whipped through his veins - fears of losing her, of declining in her estimation now she'd had time to consider his many wrong turns. Yeni poked his rib. He snapped back. 'What is it?'

Yeni placed her palm over her heart, her gaze imploring. She would call off a feud with Bola. What did she need the Senate for when she had Ade? Bola could have what he wanted as long as Ade relented and let her look after him. 'We *will* be okay in Jesus's name,' she said and made a sign of the cross over her chest. As Ade made to get up, she gasped and gripped her belly and colour crashed from her face. 'Sheeoh,' she said, with a noisy suck of her teeth. She lurched, bent double and panted out loud. 'Ah, ah, that woman Lamilabo has killed me with her fried crayfish, oh.' She shook her head, her face scrunched by agony. Then her eyes rolled up, and she flopped sideways into Ade, as limp and as pale and sweaty as Iya did on that fateful night.

***

Ade never saw such shiny chrome fittings, even on a brand new SUV. Were it not for the light aroma of antiseptic and the prints on the wall, the room could pass for a suite in a 7-star hotel. Above the bed hung a nil-by-mouth sign and a whiteboard on which went the name of the assigned consultant. Yeni's omnipresent red bag looked forlorn on the bedside cabinet, as though it knew that of its mistress's predicament.

Yearning for any form of distraction, Ade sent Moji another text. He wondered what Controller was doing and hoped the police thief was choking on the taste of his own medicine, virtual reality food, and water and space. Ordinary justice was just too good for some. The senior nurse, in a dark blue frock, drew the curtains, flicked a switch on the remote control to reduce the air-conditioned blast from the wall vents. After another quick last look round the room, she smiled to herself with a satisfied air and told Ade to expect Yeni within ten minutes.

Five minutes later they wheeled Yeni her back in, on a trolley. She was wearing a blue cotton hospital gown designed for a much more ample diva. She must be ill not to protest. 'What did they find?' Ade said.

'Armies were fighting inside my stomach, yeah, if not for the injection I don't know, oh, it was hell.' She clucked and poured one of her self-pitying looks over Ade. 'They sent for Dr Opa,' she said.

His heart skipped. 'Dr Opa? I thought you said it was shellfish poisoning?'

'They did X-rays and that thing that makes krun, krun as if a dog is barking.' Yeni clucked in light-hearted self-reproach. 'I don't know what I was thinking. Dr Opa showed me this small thing. It was like a watch spring, tick-ticking but faster,' she said clenching and unclenching her fist in simulation. 'Dr says he sees it as a heartbeat. Are you ok? You are making Sule of Akure face. The Alhaji who ate fried pork by mistake. Don't worry. Many men that is how they react when they hear the news. Congratulations. God has answered our prayers. And I know you will be a hundred percent a good papa to this one and many others.'

Ade's mind flicked back to the night when in his grief, Yeni caught him when he craved the hug and company of even a leprous cobra. Lagos boy, what have you done? Copulated with your coffin. And it must have been during danger week. Gongs went off in his head and horrified, he flopped on to the corner of Yeni's bed seconds before Dr Opa charged in high on amphetamines or adrenaline, minimum. In his slipstream staggered a boyish man pushing an enormous ultrasound machine.

'Hey my friend, fresh life has reached your scalp as well,' said the doctor, pointing at the growth of tight-curled hair on Ade's head. 'Let me show you the fruit of your endeavours.' Grinning with an air of mischief the doctor tapped a keyboard, and the machine clicked into a creamy whine. 'That is where the brain will be forming, that is for heart valves.' Dr Opa said embryos across the group of animals with spinal cords were much of a muchness in the beginning until they diverged and came out looking different at the end of gestation. 'Does that not give you wondrous food for thought?'

Wonder? Terror is the correct diagnosis. Ade did not much care for the crash lesson in comparative embryology and stared at the screen, his innards twisted by shock and trepidation, and in his out-of-body state watched the embryonic dot on the screen flash da-ddy, da-ddy, da-ddy to him - reeling him in.

Thirty-four

At the Ayo benches it was as dark as the inside of a hangman's hood. Soon, candles went up in windows, a vigil to kidnapped megawatts the politicians promised to release, but didn't. Tailor got up and wriggled his sinuous hips in Ade's face in celebration. 'Sore loser, your friend, innit. Cuppa of tea innit? Can you smell rain over the dusty stench of his abject defeat, innit?'

Baba Lawyers laughed. 'Mis-discrimination, misdiscrimation, arrest him for discrimination.' He clapped his hands in glee. 'Tailor, you sound like a pig with a poker sizzling up its trotter,' he said and chop-clapped his hands as if to shake off the stain of defeat. 'Cufffingers, let's go. Can't talk here. That bloody music braying in my ear for hours did for me.' 'Thanks for arranging the transfer,' he said, fumbling with the seatbelt of the black SUV.

Ade muttered a banality and started the engine. 'The rapid turnover of lives at the other place was too fast for my liking so it had to be Expresscare,' he said.

'You're not sleeping well, you said. Problemsomnia, I know it well,' said Baba Lawyers.

Ade killed the engine. He felt trapped, like an escapee handcuffed to another inmate caught in the powerful searchlights. Grieving, fatigue and anxiety had cluttered his brain, and he needed another head, a form of outsourcing, which is why he retold Baba Lawyers his story. He skated over his sorry childhood until Iya's rescue, his drunkard of a mother, missing sister, Saro then came to the nub - Yeni and the baby. 'I don't want to lose this child.' But when he as much as contemplates life without Moji, a horse rears up in his chest, neighs and thumps fear through him.

'Cufffingers, freakish indigestible. Who writes your scripts?' said Baba Lawyers.

'Ade the flying paintbrush. That is why it is so messy.'

Baba Lawyers pointed through the windscreen. 'Drive on for this is a three flyover problem. By the way, Durosote sends the happiest regards. He said he'd never enjoyed himself more than cutting Bola's credit lines. But he wants to hear the complete story from your eminence.'

'I'll oblige if I get out of this latest three flyover tangle.' Ade eased the car on to the dim street. The image of his child's oscillating heart beating on the ultrasound screen swung to mind, and he felt yet another frightening, inexplicable, agonizing stirring of parental affection for this helpless and innocent child he invited into a topsy-turvy world.

Baba Lawyers pointed at the dashboard. 'Cufffingers, please turn on the air-con thingy. But genesis before exodus, going back to your problem, do I understand that the reason you are tying yourself in knots is that you wanted this ideal storybook family and now you are not so sure? So once did I, but I can tell you for the price of a used condom that you shouldn't lay much store by these fairy stories. What is the subtext? Goldilocks as a lying thieving immigrant claiming benefits or a rapacious capitalist digging where she did not sow? Sorry I digress. Any road, bringing a child up under the same roof as both parents is it an overrated administrative convenience?'

Ade's hands gripped the steering wheel so hard his arms ached. 'So your point is what?' He'd chosen to confide in Baba Lawyers because he thought him

246

unlikely out of rivalrous envy or a sense of moral superiority, to judge or shame him, but this cheery dissection, with diversions and digressions, was beginning to grate. 'It takes talent to be this coherent without saying much,' said Ade, angry for making a hash of what he wanted to say. 'Just because-'

Baba Lawyers made an indistinct sound. 'Just because I fucked up my kids who am I?' he said and looked out of the window. 'Take me back to Tailor's, if it's not too much trouble,' he said, with punishing frostiness.

'So you think you know what I was going to say?' In revenge, Ade turned off the air-conditioning and drove on in gut-wringing silence, past the National Theatre, called *fila* Gowon, because it resembled an army officer's cap, came off the flyover at Iganmu and headed north. 'Sorry. I did not mean it, what you think I meant,' he said, feeling dreadful for giving even given the slightest hint that he thought that his friend bore responsibility for what happened to the children.

'Cufffingers, you know your problem? Your mind's sprayed and peppered with poor impressions of yourself. I hope not indelible. And inside that bonce of yours is your real and most lethal enemy, your mind-brain industrial complex, feasting, habituated, addicted to history. It may give you a perverse masochistic kick or rush to keep going back there to feed it, but if you don't kick the habit, I am afraid it could be the end of you.'

Ade slapped the car into third gear. 'Past? I gave up Ranti didn't I? That wasn't easy. And signed land over for Bola's cash flow to get closure, peace of mind and to buy time,' he said, leaning into a right-hand bend.

'That was so the Martins could continue to live in the manner to which they had become accustomed. It is the same sign of a colonised brain, Cufffingers. Have you not become so used to Martins being up there and you below, that you could not bring yourself to rip and claw them off the rotten pedestal? Sorry Cufffingers another example of I'll be blunt, a slave mentality. And whilst I'm at it I'll tell you this for the price of a used bottle top that back home, gorgeous wife falls at knees of a former tenant in her silky designer gown and with a new watch or shirt for you and you will say I am too much hassle for Moji, this one is a bird in the hand and she loves me, my alcoholic mother didn't and she's promised to be good and she is the mother of my only child and I may not have another child and I could do worse, if I behave myself and a child will do good as a glue to cement us together or whatever.

'You are off on a tangent but-'

'Sorry to interrupt but let me tell a story of a case I handled as a police officer. Alao a law student hanged, suicide, in his room. Left a note saying that he should never have been born, but his parents used him as a marital cello-tape and when the tape lost stickiness, used him as a football and when he sprung a leak and didn't bounce as high anymore, abandoned him. In his suicide note he said that a child should be a precious jewel not the marital pillar or plasterboard.' Baba Lawyers sighed. 'Cufffingers do you want your child to end up a statistic? Or in a parable?'

'You think I haven't thought of that? Insha Allah it will not happen.'

'The fucked up didn't pray?' said Baba Lawyers and let out a vast sigh. 'Did Iya die for a vow her grandson made as a seven-year-old when he knew little but the cane, hunger, and a few doctored fairy tales? I could go on, but your hooked brain has your mind in its pocket. Or, putting it another way, you've got the mind you deserved. How? Difficult to say because you are not lazy or lacking in imagination. Maybe it is inertia, the way many of us never change our banks.'

'Where should I drop you off,' said Ade, self-recognition basting and turning his guts on a spit.

'Just there.' As Baba Lawyers got out of the car he turned to Ade and said, 'look at me Cufffingers, I am begging you, begging you, for once in your bloody life, think not as a prisoner but as a prince.'

Thirty-five

Mugged by mosquitoes, a fluorescent bulb flickered halfway along the deserted corridor. Ade, elbows on a desk, chewed on his last antacid, but the pain in his belly persisted. He peered into the carton containing the brand new laptop he meant to give Moji and closed it again to keep in the fresh smell. A van chugged past, its solitary headlamp shivering under the bonnet in the drizzle. Swallowing the pain in his throat he squeezed his eyes closed, shaking his head in sad contemplation. Tonight, whilst she admired the laptop, he could slip in Yeni's news and end it between them. For composure he downed the beer he'd decanted into a can of lemonade.

'What happened?'

A burp escaped and in his leap off the chair Ade knocked over the table, but Moji snatched her hand away. 'I thought you were better than this,' she said and sat kneading her great forehead. The film of sweat on her upper lip twinkled in the moonlight. Moji had her hair cut, number one or shorter, and her bushy samurai eyebrows added menace to her frown. Ade retreated into apprehensive hope as he nudged the laptop box towards her. 'Take this. Just a small thing, for everything you've done.'

Moji did not have to speak. Ade had not seen her look so angry since a disagreement over the rota. 'To give a present is now a crime?' he said.

Moji shoved the laptop back across the table and waved her fingers in the air. 'Can I not write with these and with a pencil and paper? Free because it costs me nothing, at worst only a few naira, not dignity.' Dropping her voice into a minatory growl she said, 'so when were you going to tell me? Is that why I have not seen you? Talk please. Is that mouth on strike or are you owing the sole supplier for the last consignment of just-in-time lies?' Moji shrugged. 'I have a blessing, or maybe I can call it a curse, that I hear things that I do not want to hear. I was sitting *jeje* in one corner when the sister of a friend who works in Apari spare parts shop who does business with your misses said they closed her shop for two days because she was in Expresscare. So take your stupid laptop before I break it on your head.'

Ade leaned back as though to give him more reaction time to face the ferocious barrage. Baba Lawyers was right. With your woman no insult is too small to cause a cataclysmic eruption. 'Sorry, I didn't know,' he said, leaning over the laptop to take Moji's hand but caught hold of a little finger.

Moji picked Ade's hand up by the middle finger and placed it on the table with ironic care. 'Annoyed? Never? Does not even warrant disappointment. Only grateful.' In a sardonic show of relief she looked up to the sky. 'Not two minutes and you've grown two heads. Do you want to marry one as Ade the Yorumuslim, one as Julius Roman Catholic?' she said then folded her lips in and stared at the floor.

Ade's self-worth crashed the harder because Moji was right. For a minute he swung in a painful limbo until Moji got up, ambled away to the corridor wall, half-turned to Ade, changed her mind and disappeared round a bend. A terrifying impulse whipped Ade to his feet, and he caught up round the back of the block.

'Long time no see,' Moji said and sat on a step. Leaden-headed, Ade hovered until, after a lifetime, she beckoned him down beside her. 'Everything I said is the truth, I love you,' Ade said and sat down a foot away.

251

'So you say but your feelings are a special variety, like shadows, one day sharp and clean the next day you need special instruments to see, or it is like a breeze on the cheek.' Tears polished her eyes. Moji squeezed them shut as though trying to compose what next to say and Ade sat paralysed, inches away from the love of his life, in awe of her eerie aura in the soft moonlight. So much did he want her that his heart bulged as though stuffed with that infamous elephant in the room. But how could he burden her with the guilt he would feel if he broke his promise not to abandon his child? 'Moji, you know that I love you…'

'But your child, ernh?' she said and her hands slipped off him and left a cool and naked band around his back. 'How I love you is too gigantic to come out of my mouth but for your sake and the sake of the child, because I don't want to think of you suffering and unhappy, even if you go back to executive it is better. If you love me do this for me no Lekki, please, no...'

Back at his desk his laptop had walked. Well, something was going right for someone. In the car, Michael Jackson segued into Bobby Womack's "California dreaming" and Ade wallowed in the heart-sucking melancholy stirred up by the heavenly harmonies. When Bobby's gravelly voice got to the words, "getting on knees and pretending to pray," tears clawed his eyes and he must have twitched or made a sound because Rashidi glanced in the rear-view mirror. As long and ghostly shadows wafted over the car, in a well-meant gesture designed to spare both their blushes, but conveyed with such apologetic reverence that it gave the game away - which only irked and shamed Ade the more - Rashidi claimed that his eyes watered from an allergy to this car's leather at this time of the day. Then he sniffed and glanced in the mirror, in his eyes an annoying expression of pity for this so-called big man who married a wicked woman for money.

Thirty-six

Yeni had only a small bump but refined an ostentatious full-fronted waddle. As they passed the ice-cream kiosk outside Dr Opa's clinic, she stiffened and pulled Ade back. 'Look. Is that not the bus of cunts 'r' us?' she said and wrinkled her nose at the blue and white van of The Extra Mile Television Company chugging beside an artificial waterfall.

Ade's heart quickened. 'Quick, let us go to the car, Rashidi will be waiting,' he said as Ranti swaggered towards him, as composed and unhurried as an egg timer.

Tinu, Ranti's friend with the shoulder-length thick hair, bustled up to Yeni. 'Sista Yeni, long time. Is he your man? Adele told me. Congrats,' said Tinu, combing her hair with her hand. Ade nodded and backed away towards the revolving doors of the clinic and pretended to make a phone call.

'We are just out from a check-up,' said Yeni.

'We interviewed the Health Minister, what of Bola? Not in the newspapers nowadays and what of that his handsome friend?' said Tinu. She was wearing the same design beige blouse as Ranti's. Her dark overlong hair reminded Ade of burned toast.

'Everyone looks handsome beside Bola. He has new chambers near Zenith, opposite GT Bank. I forget the name of the street, very fine building, near the headquarters of that insurance company,' Yeni said, pointing back over her shoulder. A phone tweeted in a handbag.

Ade scoffed to himself. In return for the line of credit, the arrogant bastard, Bola, had to sell his house and moved in with Chief. He worked for Durosote's

254

Workers' Freedom Party on Mondays. Promoted again by the Minister after a brief course abroad, that he did not attend, Controller was unstoppable. To Ade, he was a slagheap in his way.

'Ah, ah, Ade, now you are going to be baba you don't want to greet us?' said Ranti and shuffled up to stand next to Yeni, on the diagonal opposite Ade.

Ade's hand jerked to his nose. 'Erh. I was on a call to the village.' He sniffed the familiar musky notes of a perfume he bought her. Did she wear it to remember him by or only for work or to use it up? He'd called Ranti to put the record straight after his decisive meeting with the Martins and they spoke a few times, mainly to swap platitudes. After a few weeks, he stopped, thinking it safer to wait until she restored amatory parity with a recent boyfriend or returned to Bambo again. Ranti always denied they were an item. 'What of Ibadan?' he said, squeezing his drenched tissue paper into a ball. His stomach burned, and he'd run out of antacids. The doctors found nothing wrong.

'Bambo did not want me to go to Ibadan. He said-'

'But such a fantastic opportunity,' said Tinu. Ranti's glare silenced her. Not long ago, news of Ranti and Bambo disembowelled him with envy. Instead, a vague weight he had not acknowledged lifted from him and he smiled to himself.

Ranti turned to him again. 'I am starting that production company. How is it going at your place?'

'Oh, we are reviewing the cases,' said Ade. 'They falsely imprisoned many to raise money for Controller to pay warders, the complex internal market in there not everybody gained from but the physical state of that place is a disgrace.' When he wiped his face tissue paper snagged on his bristles. He was getting used to shaving again.

'I met Dr Wale Oloyede, former head of the medical directorate. He initiated many of the reforms that Controller reversed,' said Ranti. 'But he is on the case again in a big way and is writing a book. He gives me hope for this country.' She was going to pick fluff off Ade's face, retreated, scratched her head and patted her hair back into shape. 'Glad everything is working out well for you. You need it,' said Ranti, with another knowing glance at Yeni's bump.

'Ranti, who was that man talking to you and looking at you *one kind*,' said Tinu with a wink.

'His name is Julius. Helps me with my electronics,' said Ranti, with a shrug in her voice.

'Is that what they call it now?' said Tinu. 'Where did you find him so that I can rush in my sockets for application? Now now, oh,' she said, affecting to scribble on her palm.

'Julius enh? Is that code? Ade, are you roonicating with this one?' said Yeni.

To roonicate was to play away while your partner was pregnant. 'Yeni, we are just talking, joking,' he said, with a furtive glance round to see if anyone was listening. Yeni's breaths came faster. Ade readied himself to lie her on the left if she fainted as advised by the doctor.

'Is she always vexed or is it her condition?' said Tinu, sotto voce.

Ade ground his teeth at Tinu's impudence. 'Maybe because she gets bored with nosy experts.' He made to leave.

'Did you not hear me?' said Yeni. 'I said go get me an ice-cream. Now,' she said as if speaking to an obtuse schoolboy.

Ranti's lips curled up in a cruel smile of schadenfreude, amplifying Ade's humiliation several-fold.

***

Ade and Yeni quarrelled to the car. Roadside, fubsy men in huge white *agbada*s banged steel drums and danced in passable impressions of the famous Eyo masquerades. Naked children frolicked in the rainbowed spray of a broken water pipe and couples sauntered into glitzy shopping malls. A boyish man ran over to salute. The shiny black limo or the invisible occupants? If only the man knew that theirs was one of many expensive hearses carrying living corpses. How he longed for a tiny ray of that silvery pink late afternoon sunshine for his bruised heart.

Yeni smelled of woody perfume and the leather jacket. She nudged Ade again. 'Because of cunts 'r' us is that why your face is twisted like Picasso drawing?' She wrinkled her nose and gestured over her shoulder in the direction of Dr Opa's clinic. 'So you want me to just *tanda* and let them make eyes at you? You think I do not know their ways?' she said with another smug pat of her belly. 'Forget the TV woman. She gave you her thing to rent, now another man has paid a deposit.' Her mocking tap on the shoulder scorched through his skin. How in Allah's name could so much shit come out of a mouth so well-bred and fed? But it was not Yeni's fault. It's the way she was made and why should she change when she got away with everything? Zaki, back home from hospital only a fortnight when she boxed his ears again.

For dropping a handbag Yeni stamped so hard on Komole's foot the girl lost a toe. As a distraction he scrolled through his text messages. His hackles rose. He told her that he did not want a phone mast on his land.

'We had a family meeting.'

'You voted on my land without me?'

'We will give you your fair share,' she said.

'Give me my share? The Martins do believe that the sun shines out of their jewelled shitholes? The family property you stole from me? Why don't you pluck my eyes out and throw me an eyelash in compensation? What were you smoking? Abacha's uniform? If I see your car aerial let alone a mast on my property, I will not be responsible for the result...'

Rashidi looked worried and applied the brakes. 'Rashidi, face your front before I vex,' said Yeni, and she slapped the dividing window shut. 'Julius, we will help you to look after the land because you do not have the experience. Look what happened to the one on Tokunbo Street. Forgotten? But you are never satisfied and take everything we do and turn it round in your suspicious mind. That is how you people are.'

A metallic taste rose to his mouth. 'Meaning what and stop calling me Julius. And before it escapes me no way is that pastor choosing a name for my child. Iya has given me a selection and depending on the day of birth and other factors I will choose from Iya's list. Martins are not the only family with traditions. No, no, no. I will not agree,' he said, in delicious fury. 'Iya's photo in the bigger sitting room. You said no. In the dining room. Same answer. Baba Agba Jinadu's papers saddened the Martins so I keep them in the shed. Now this. Over my dead body.' Rashidi gave a secret nod. Seething, Ade looked out of the window. Hadn't it come to a pass when the driver expresses justifiable pity for your predicament?

'After the marvellous news from Dr Opa you want to fight. Every day is palaver. Pastor John is going to choose the right name for the baby whether you like it or not. Go and report me to Iya if you can find her.'

Ade reeled in shock. 'Yeni. Please stop. Have you not gone far enough for one day?' Sick for taking their Roman prison name, sick of the Martins and Peters and Controllers of this world, he shook a trembling fist in an emphatic no to Yeni's attempted reply. Was that another annoying nod from driver Rashidi? Ade churned inside and roused by the earlier irritation and embarrassment with Ranti he almost lost his temper, but a tiny voice urged restraint. Think of the child. Keep calm and regroup, get through this day then the next and the one after that until the end. What nobler task could a man choose than to sacrifice happiness and the chance of genuine love for his child? 'I want the name Iya chose and I will get Niari to compose an oriki.' Last word. Point made. Ade closed his eyes to let his mind drift.

'You know what?' said Yeni, right in Ade's ear. 'Don't insult my intellectuals. If this baby is causing you stress, you know where you can go because a woman in my condition does not need some amateur lawyer barking in her ear day and night. So you made a kobo and a half from land that the Martins family kept for you these past years and now you think you are Dangote. Enough is enough. I want you to go. Yes. Pack and go.'

'Go?' Ade said, to fibrillations in his solar plexus.

'Ah. You did not think of that ernh when you were exercising your mouth. Don't forget that just because we signed agreement I can still finish you in this Lagos. Go and ask anybody. Read my face. It is my baby and I can do what I want and if you are not careful, you will not even smell this child again.'

Stunned and horrified by Yeni's sudden rejection, beset by indescribable sadness and remorse for breaking his promise to his unborn child, Ade retreated to Iya's house to endure a disconcerting, disorientating freedom. At work Moji avoided him, Iya gone and the promise of fatherhood snatched away. Life looked bleak. One evening as Ade stared at an old photo of Iya, Controller called to demand a share of his land. Ade owed him for various services, he said, not least for not slamming him into Kakirikiri. The oily insouciance, habitual cruelty, and that the police thief had him over a barrel to enslave him for ever, and wouldn't stop until he took everything Iya worked to preserve snapped Ade out of his torpor.

Thirty-seven

Ade waited outside the prison gates in shivering suspense. It was a humid and dusty March day. Several Dangote trailers chugged past, crunching the cracked tarmac and churning up dense smoke from roof exhausts. Ade checked his phone for the fifth time in a minute. Nothing yet from Controller. Another trap? Blinking gritty sweat from his eyes Ade put the phone back in the pocket of his favourite blue shirt and watched a hunchbacked man heave a pushcart laden with plantains out of a huge pothole. Well done. If you don't succeed, don't fail again the same way.

The phone rang. Ade whipped it out so hard it landed on the rim of an open drain. 'I thought you were off to meet him?' said Baba Lawyers.

'Change of plan. Car's picking *me* up instead,' said Ade, trying to sound calm, but bulls locked horns in his head.

'Change of plan? That smells like a rat.'

'On that at least we agree, but our votes don't count.' Ade looked at his watch. Eleven fifty-five and twelve seconds. A black hatchback with darkened windows stopped behind a refuse lorry. 'This must be them,' said Ade. Two grim men wearing dark glasses got out of the car. Ade grunted a feeble greeting to Baba Lawyers just before one man snatched the phone, pushed him into the back seat of the air-conditioned car. Blindfolded, as the car joined the traffic Ade hoped this was a well-oiled routine, and they didn't quench his arse by accident. Cause of death: unintended end. Another hole in his plan occurred to him. Controller's thugs had his phone. The fight in his head reached a new intensity, but it was too late to turn tail now. If he believed in spirits, he never needed Iya's more.

After an eternity spent rocking and wheezing over potholes at impressive speed with the siren doing its impersonation of an amplified sheep the car slowed, cut off the din and with a long toot on the horn, rocked to a halt. 'Ok, oya let us go.' The men shoved the phone back in his pocket, tore off the blindfold and Ade squinted out of the window on to a typical Lagos street, noisy, smoggy, with slivers of tar and eager and higgledy-piggedly motor and pedestrian traffic darting helter-skelter in syrupy heat. Blinded by the coruscating sunlight and with serpentine floaters in his eyes, Ade staggered under a railed first-floor balcony then up a bare flight of concrete stairs.

Controller, in police uniform and pressed epaulettes was sitting at a bare table in a room three strides square its walls light blue. Ade smelt fresh paint. Was that in the plan? Controller swept his teeth with his tongue and tapped the brown briefcase lying open on the table. *'Na wa o* this matter between you and your in-laws,' he said.

Ade shot an imploring look at the rusty ceiling fan. The fan's switch box leaned against an old P and T rotary dial telephone behind Controller's right heel.

'The thing does not work,' said Controller, rolling his handheld battery-powered over his face and with the other hand waving Ade into a chair. 'Not something you see every day on a guided tour, blindfolding and an escort,' he said and chuckle-cleared his throat.

Ade shrugged. 'Understood sir. Privacy is not to be flaunted in public,' he said, to a troubling premonition. 'But I brought the draft memorandum of understanding as you said.' Ade unzipped a leather briefcase to give

Controller a tantalising view of the fat brown envelopes. 'Thank Allah that this thing between us is going to be settled at last.' He handed over the smallest envelope. 'Peace of mind surpasses all its other configurations. Sir,' he said, in his most imploring tone, 'but as they say in Lagos, a boy who does not learn from one failure is bound to repeat the course in excruciating slo-mo. There is one final issue that has troubled me since meeting Chief and the rest of the Martins the other week.'

'Julius, what stamina you have for circumbendibus? After this I will enter you for the tour of mouths. You will win the yellow gum-shield at each stage. Anyway talk because I have to meet Chief Fabu at the mosque after jumat,' Controller said, tapping his watch.

Ade wiped his sweaty palms on the briefcase. 'The thing is sir that I want to see my file before I hand over the deeds and memorandum,' said Ade. 'The legal adviser said I signed the original statement in blue to tell the original from a photocopy or scanned copy. If she is right, then the one you have is not the original, and the original is with my in-laws, as they claim. How can I pay twice for the same thing?'

Controller's face turned the colour of a bruised banana. 'Julius fever. Go and tell this fake lawyer and your Martins people that I have the originals.'

'So why did Chief promise the original in exchange for the share of land to cover their cash flow problem? What have I been paying Controller for all this time I ask myself. I don't mean disrespect sir but you see my problem.'

'Julius talker I don't know what you are drinking but if you do not sign this memorandum, virtual reality rice in Kakirikiri by six this evening.' Controller tapped his shirt pocket, for a phone or cigarette.

'If I sign off this land without seeing the original file Iya will haunt me forever.' Sweat swept from Ade's armpits as he handed over a thick brown envelope. 'This is all I am prepared to give you. The money you asked for and the September advance as agreed, in good faith.' Ade handed over another envelope. 'The land? Not yet.' He shook his head with solemn conviction.

'The original is not in this room.'

'Didn't think so. Then we will adjourn, sir. Can I have the money back?'

'Julius Joker get out of here before I lose patience.'

Ade whipped out his phone and tried to make a call.

Controller chuckled. 'Did they drop you on your head in the labour ward? You never learn. The thing is disabled. Are you trying to call that fool, Tony Ware? He won't find you here. I saw through to that transparent piece of his mind at once. Your lanky cleaner friend, Moji, could not keep her mouth shut when Peter turned his charm on her you will be glad to hear, or not. From the dead donkey look on your face I suspect the latter.' He tapped the envelope, tucked it away in a hip pocket and stretched his hand out for more. 'Hand over what is left and for wasting my time I will add a surcharge. Ten million naira. Not much. Only the monthly salary of a retired state governor. And I am worth ten times one of them.'

Ade looked at his phone, pressed the button again but the screen remained dead. He dropped to his knees. 'Sorry sir, I was desperate. But you see my problem? How can I sign my property away for something I have not seen? Maybe we can find another way, through negotiation with them, the Martins again?' Ade handed over a large white envelope and remained on one knee in terrifying apprehension. 'This is what I have left. An advance from the bank but if I don't secure this land how will I pay it back?' he said, his mind strafed by images of a beckoning abyss.

Controller beaming face recalled that of a dreamy teenager after a first kiss. He licked his finger and began to count the dollar notes. When he finished, he flicked them into a bespoke pouch or pocket and eyed Ade with high-grade disdain. A phone appeared in his hand. 'Are you there Daro? O ya, let's go. Bring the van and take this man to the guard room. Good, ok, come now. I am nearly ready.' He turned to Ade. 'Julius, the emperor of evaporating vanities the fat lady is going to piss all over your shredded toga.'

'But we can-'

Controller struck a match but as he raised it to his cigarette, two officers knocked and marched into the room. One, taller, with golden front teeth, wore a beret and wielded two pairs of chipped handcuffs. They saluted Controller, and he replied with alacrity. A bewildered Ade tingled from head to heel, paralysed.

'Are you Julius, alias Bisoye or Afediyabamba?' said the one with the golden teeth. Failing to receive a reply his stout companion gave Ade a painful tap right on the tip of the shoulder with a pistol. Ade raised his flaccid hands to the handcuffs. Was history going to repeat itself and his family left in the gutter whilst Controller and his kin thrived?

'Seinde, you can come in now,' said the senior officer and in stepped Professor Kosimbe, wearing a new jazzy bowtie.

'Wrong man,' said Professor Kosimbe.

'Ah, prof we enjoy our decoys too,' said the man with the pistol. Controller spat out the cigarette and leapt off the chair. 'What are *you* doing here? You? Seinde? Why? After what we've been since childhood?

Professor was wearing a pin-striped charcoal grey suit, blue and white striped shirt and a green bowtie. 'Sheki, when I heard how much you wanted from this man I did not believe it. But when DIG cancelled my permit to campaign unless I showed him that you were a suitable person to run my party I agreed to this test and you let me down, deluded me. Destroyed my faith in-'

'Don't be stupid if you had doubts why didn't you ask me?'

'Call me a naïve fool but I had to know and wanted to say to supporters that enemies put you under the microscope but found nothing. Sadly you are the nidus of the rampant virus killing this country. Roadsweepers, paying the officers out of your pocket, the houses, the girls in the prison, even the business with the young man here. I am ashamed to call you my friend.' Prof blew his nose as if to expunge the corrupting aroma of his childhood friend.

The man with the golden teeth clapped Controller in handcuffs and retrieved a couple of white envelopes with the marked notes from Controller's trousers. 'Ah, must not forget,' he said and leapt across to retrieve the old rotary dial telephone in the corner. 'Controller, you know the rest, rights and procedures. Everything you said to our young friend here is inside this old P and T phone and DIG Kafu will be so very happy to replay the contents,' said the man with the golden dentals. With a sharp nod, he ordered Ade's release.

'Can't you see what DIG Kafu is using you to put his people in charge of Lagos?' said Controller.

'How original? The tribal card. Sorry, we are not playing that game today,' said Ade.

***

An exultant Ade sent a text to thank the banker Durosote for his help, called Moji to tell her the news, then skipped off to play Ayo. In the fading light the washerwoman still hung up a huge load of dripping laundry. The uncivil servant, Chelsea replica shirt man, mouthy Manchester United fanatic, Tailor and rest of the gang were there, eager to hear from Ade.

'I'm feeling public-spirited and need to wipe the floor with someone. Cufffingers. You'll have to do,' said Baba Lawyers as he clattered the seeds into the pockets, 'I'd tunnel through from New Zealand with a fork and a matchbox to see that man's greedy face fall without grace. But Cufffingers, you are one multiloculated discombobulating bastard. Sent me hot legging it to Apapa when you were in Idi-Araba all along. The other officers are back at base wondering what happened. DIG Kafu's lot will be taking the mickey for as long as water flows in the Nile. You should be in Nollywood man. Brilliant.'

'I was not acting,' said Ade.

'My point exactly,' said Baba Lawyers.

'I know a joke, but it escapes me,' said Ade with a tired smile.

'The way you tell them I don't blame the joke. So this Professor Kosimbe, what was his beef?' He sipped from a can of beer.

'Conscience. I think the Ebola thing, how everyone pulled together to control it and how that doctor

267

Adadevoh gave her life to stop the spread of the disease without protective equipment impressed him.'

'Cufffingers, you must come out of the garden of fetching naiveté. Good common or garden envy drove the man. Controller has this power and money and property and prof has what? A few custard-stained rainbow neck-ties and fifteen minutes of fame over Ebola.'

'Such endearing cynicism. I'm surprised your feet trust one another,' said Ade, resenting the condescension.

'They don't. That's why one dogs the other's footsteps.'

Ade's phone buzzed to a missed call from Moji. 'It's Moji,' said Ade.

'Was she the one who dropped the worn hints to Peter? I thought you were not speaking,' said Baba Lawyers.

'Moji is bright.' Which may explain why we are not speaking. Ade suppressed a sense of impending anti-climax.

'So the creep thought he had us.' Baba Lawyers swept four seeds up from Ade's side. A generator fired into action. Baba Lawyers raised his voice. 'When Controller got wind that I might be after him again did he not smell a rat? Mustn't think that much of me then.'

'Cheer up Baba Lawyers. The plan worked. Sorry it put your nose out of joint. Yes? Prof arranged for Controller to meet at that house before they went to his friend's mum.'

'So we were a step ahead of the greedy pig, or do you prefer me to say greedy cow?'

'Porcism and bovism in one sentence, enough to turn one vegetarian,' said Ade. 'You wonder why prof agreed to the plan? DIG Kafu can be vicious when stirred. An old girlfriend of prof's had some gist on an exam cover up in the 1990s. Sex in the mix. Is that how you say it? Sexamgate scandal. No evidence of prof's anatomic involvement but DIG Kafu whisked that little whiff into a threatening tornado,' said Ade, and leapt off the bench before Baba Lawyers' tipped him off the other end.

'Cufffingers. Now you've got the blinking file what next?'

'Who knows? Write a story for the grandchildren?'

'Riveting then,' said Baba Lawyers.

'Liberating,' said Ade and in the long wan shadow of the green mosque watched the sun's last shimmers of the day fade.

Thirty-eight

Ade wanted to surprise Moji to tell her his wonderful news in person whilst she could smell his stink of battle and victory, see beads of sweat glistening on his crown, taste excitement on his lips. A chance to prove himself again was what he craved. After a frantic but fruitless search for his favourite blue shirt, he pulled on a compromise white shirt in suppressed haste, but Beatrice called. 'They say, incident in KIYO.'

That phrase "they say" covered a myriad of lies and half-truths, innuendo, hints, manholes and trapdoors. 'Why are you calling me?' he said. 'When I was just going to look for your friend to thank her for everything,' he added, in a more genial tone. At work, since Moji left, Beatrice treated him like a paedophile and serial murderer, beneath her contempt. 'But I am not one of the officers...'

'Hunh, they say I should tell you they are short. That is all.'

Beset by a chafing sense of anti-climax and indignation Ade dragged himself to Kakirikiri. There, the beam from a 1000-watt beam, one of Controller's less egregious buys, swept the angry sky, accompanied by the thready sound of a colonial-era siren. For a change, Titus, a rotund young man with an oily face "shakytitis," they called him because his hands trembled like a hairspring, opened the gates without dropping the bunch of keys. Ade's ears pricked up to the odd falsetto whoop and fearful murmuring in the distance. Was that Cordelia? Apprehension frying his lungs, Ade exploded into the whitewashed block and charged round the corner. In the middle of a wider section of the aisle a woman with the number tag missing from the back of her shirt straddled a prone Peter. The fifty or so inmates in the cells loved it, 'fuck the baton sucker, give him front and back,' said one edentulous girl, jabbing a finger through the bars.

'If not for God who put us here you no fit touch the elastic from my pants,' the woman said, whipped Peter again with a belt and bounced hard on his back. Peter whimpered, trousers low enough to show an inch of a buttock crack. 'Shut up,' she said.

'Stop now, now,' said Ade. The prisoner's head jerked up and Ade went snow-white blind because the woman sitting on top of Peter was his half-sister, Saro, Buraimoh's daughter. 'What is going on?' he said, his agitated confusion ramped up by Team Leader Ojo and little Vv charging up barking into walkie-talkies. Unfazed, Saro slammed Peter's chin back on to the floor. 'Ogas, why ask stupid questions when you know the answers and gave this oily thing the keys and licence to disturb us here. Cordelia warned us, but for her who knows how many of these girls they wanted to take tonight...' Peter wriggled free and pulled up his trousers whilst Vv and Ojo dragged him away.

'Let him come, he said if I agree for him to fuck me he will not transfer me to Sokoto. Since yesterday they are worse than rabbit. How many inspections in one night, hunh? *Abi*, I lie?' Saro acknowledged the timid murmurs of assent from the cells with a curt nod. 'And if you want to take blood why inside that place?' she said and gestured with a toss of the head at the room at the far end of the corridor. Ade had always thought it a broom cupboard but the contents of a medicine box, syringes, vials, tourniquet and condoms lay strewn on the floor. Saro leapt to her feet and turned to her mates. 'They take you to hospital for check then they sell your pickin to big madams. And are you not one of the ringleaders? Is it fringe benefits you want?' she said, wagging her finger in Peter's face. A commotion started in a cell. Cordelia went limp but the other inmates braced her. As Ade turned to the sickening woman, he heard the thwack of a baton on bone. Saro cried out and Peter hit her again. The lump the size of an egg that came up over her left eye reminded Ade of his mother crouching under a volley of his dad's blows. Furious, he launched himself at Peter, the impact of his fist on the ribcage, pleasing, effective, and perfect - reminiscent of the impact of a foot or bat on the sweet spot of a ball - gave him greater satisfaction than he ever imagined possible between those Kakirikiri walls. He rocked Peter with another, less satisfying but still delicious, jab, and cocked his fist ready for a repeat.

'Lekki Bulawayo boy. I will beat you even your mama will not know you,' said Peter and, staggering to within a foot of Ade, he swung his truncheon. Ade ducked. Peter missed and little Vv burrowed between them. 'Why this? Because of one woman?' he said, flailing his short arms. He smelled of tobacco and bootleg alcohol.

Ade pushed Vv away for a better view of his assailant but a sudden movement from Saro caught his eye. Peter seized his chance, catching him with a blow to the temple. Ade tottered against the bars, dazed, his legs swimming away from him.

Less than a minute later, he wiped the trickling blood from his chin and stumbled into the Sick Bay feeling worse for wear than he expected. The prospect of handing out a beating, let alone to angry men armed with truncheons, retreated before his searing headaches. On a

272

stretcher in the middle of the room lay Saro, moaning, bleeding from a gash on her left cheek, her left arm hanging at an awkward angle. She looked frightened but defiant but spat and managed a blood-stained grin. 'It is true what they say. You are the best of these officers, that is why they punish you.'

'Heh, mister whatever your name is. If you come to make trouble because you are fucking a useless girl then leave this room now,' said the doctor on duty. He inspected Saro's head. 'Peter, too much baton action, I have told you many times that a human head is not a carpet.'

Saro had lost tons of weight, the notch in the base of her neck was deep enough to cup an egg. 'Are you ok?' said Ade, flicking dry blood off his ear.

Saro looked puzzled. 'How for do?' she said.

How for do? The words she learned from him clapped against his eardrums. 'It's me, Ade, flying paintbrush,' he said and when she spoke again, shock and terror, self-disgust rocked him to the marrow as he saw that Saro was the girl who raised the alarm that night on Bar Beach.

'What happened to your King Coal face?' she said.

Embarrassment, cowardice, or fear or sense of self-preservation stopped him asking after Malomo, or why Saro had not fulfilled her ambition as a fashion designer. 'Where did you get here from, I mean have you been in prison for long?' he said, stammering under the curious gazes of the other men.

'I did nothing, but they are collecting junior girls off the street for making business.' Saro sat up and blew her bloodied nose into her gown. As Ade helped swing her shackled feet on to the floor, he glimpsed a narrow band

273

of striated skin below her belly button. Was she pregnant? Had she had a child? Did the belly show that she was one of the girls Controller hired out to rich women or was it just a trick of the light? Not what you ask sister you haven't seen for ten years. 'Have you eaten?' he said and shuffled into the space at the foot of the trolley.

'Hey, you this man. Stop. Who gave you clearance to come inside here?' said Team Leader Ojo.

'She is my sister.'

Ojo and Peter and the doctor could not have looked more shocked if Barack and Michelle Obama and Donald Trump waltzed in wearing pointy white hats. 'No way,' said Ojo, with a hollow laugh.

'Flying paintbrush?' said Saro.

'No way. Who gave this Bulawayo man leg to jump?' said Peter.

'Okay, okay,' said Ojo, in self-mocking extenuation. 'No wonder the man is always wearing boots even when the sun is hot and I suspect him but as he is on recommendation from Chief, did not want to cause trouble, oh.'

'Ojo never fails to quote from his epic poem, the prisoner of hindsight,' said Peter who turned to Ade. 'So you caused wahala for the Controller last week?' he said, wincing and rubbing his ribs, a sight as uplifting to Ade as the thought of Controller yearning for clean water in prison.

'Doctor, how long to finish stitching?' Ade said.

The doctor leaned over Saro with a battered pair of forceps. 'As she is your sister, I will find a fresh packet of stitches from the store. These have passed the expiry date.'

Ade picked up the packet. Expiry date July 2011. Only three years expired. How for do, it could be worse. 'Team Leader Ojo, if you don't want to fry in DIG Kafu's pan review the arrests made by Roadsweepers, starting with Cordelia. This woman here my sister is no longer your concern,' said Ade, with thunderous pride.

***

Saro answered Ade's anodyne questions with quick snorts. When he refused her a cigarette she shrugged and sulked. Ade spent the night by her trolley in a damp candle-lit hospital room relieved that she did not have hepatitis, a broken leg, worst, Ebola. To think he used to rock this girl to sleep singing *Papadon Bridge*, instead of *papa don't preach* by Madonna. How, why, had she gone from his greatest cheerleader who came to watch him run, to the wilful girl who, instead of doing her housework or homework, threw tantrums and picked endless quarrels with Iya, from innocence to Bar Beach and Kakirikiri? Allah forbid, he could have chosen her instead of Cordelia that night on Bar Beach. Ade shuddered at the abomination. Had the same ugly thought marked Saro's mind as well? Was that why she took her hand out of his and turned to the wall and they both pretended that she was asleep? Or, was he making too much of her simple exhaustion? As Baba Lawyers said, she was shattered or was it slaughtered?

That week Ade released Cordelia and scores of emaciated abductees to their grateful families. Moji popped in, scanned the busy room, hovered for a while and backed out, pulling the heavy door shut after her. At the end of the shift, to his pole-axing dismay he learned that she'd quit.

Thirty-nine

Saro re-awakened Ade's suppressed fear that they were both cursed, as if Malomo's womb still held them in walls soaked in alcohol. A few weeks after Ade found Saro somewhere to live she left the house and did not leave a contact. Whether the elders pushed her no one confessed, but Saro attracted more male visitors than the rest of the suburb put together was the word on the ground. Weeks later she turned up at Kakirikiri, gaunt, collarbones as thin as straws, dishevelled, and covered in a florid rash. She asked for an advance on her share of the estate. Ade held nose and obliged, rebuking himself later for patronising her. Who was to say that Saro couldn't turn her share into billions and win the UNESCO prize for outstanding service to an international charity? Meanwhile, he had a more important and elusive fish to find and net, for both their sakes.

'Good evening ma, is she in today?' Ade said, raising his voice above the din of the late evening traffic. The shopkeeper frowned through her straggly brown braids and pointed at her forehead. 'Dem write gateman for my head? Please commot make I see road,' she said. She licked her middle finger, prised open a polythene bag and peered over Ade's shoulder to make a grand show of leaning first one way then the other to greet a recent arrival, an elderly man in a threadbare blue buba.

'Papa, the man is asking for Moji. As if by force ah, ah,' she said.

'Oga move make madam see road, keh,' said the old man in a hectoring tone. 'Who are you sef?'

'Julius, call me Ade, a co-worker. Moji and I work at Kakirikiri. See, this is our uniform.'

'Hunh, if she no want to do can you not leave her?' said the man.

'Baba, *e jo*, let me buy you that Stout,' said Ade.

The man's jug ears swung out with his big grin. 'Theresa, this young boy is not a hooligan oh. Friend, don't lose hope. A woman is not worth waiting for if she does not keep your worth waiting. Is that not how they say it on the radio?' The old man stared at the bottle of Guinness in awe, as if it were a magical source of his inspiration.

The shopkeeper's lined face cracked into a wry smile. 'Baba Sunday you are wiser than a babalawo's tortoise.' Ade waved his change away. 'God bless,' she sang and disappeared through a back door, sauntered back a minute later looking disappointed. 'Moji no dey.' But she said he could wait there behind a crate if he kicked the rubbish away, and she gave him a stick to fend off the rats. 'I am serious, bigger than a cat many of them.' Half an hour later, with an empathetic wave and smile the shopkeeper rattled the shutters, tossed Ade a packet of biscuits and a bottle of water then sprinted after a molue. Her kind thoughtfulness called Iya to mind and tears knifed to Ade's eyes.

Midnight ticked past without a sign of Moji. Passing cars volleyed long shadows over him with their headlights and lulled him to sleep.

Cheery female laughter, a man's self-satisfied tones and the thunk of a car door yanked him to life. Ade ducked and peered through a hole in the wall, a tortured man, dreading the sight of Moji with this fresh man who loomed perfect in his imagination. A man worthy of her. A man with a vision, wisdom and foresight, with a washboard stomach that rejected offal, a man with

277

Federer's right arm and Nadal's left and a tongue and wit equipped to make women genuflect. In dreamy trepidation Ade saw a tall, slim woman in a white blouse and a grey skirt lean into the car to kiss the man. Ade retched. With an elegant pirouette she waltzed past his hideout, paused in front of the shop, and with a tut of sudden enlightenment turned around to sashay next door. Seconds later, metal bars rattled, that door clattered open, bright light fell out, shot back in and closed the door behind her.

Ade flopped back against the brick wall, spent, but relieved that it was not Moji. Sliding one shivering hand into the satchel for the statuette he carved for Moji, to his horror, he grasped not the pimples representing Moji's short hair but the sharp contours of a Nefertiti haircut. Ade's flopped back in remorseful disbelief. He'd brought the wrong one.

'Just praying,' Ade said that morning when Zaki caught him kneading his temples at breakfast. In a torrid night he dreamt first of Iya playing Ayo, then followed a nightmare - a tragedy involving Moji, Ranti and Yeni. Ade pushed away the steaming plate of moinmoin. Outside the door, Rashidi gave the car horn a respectful tap.

'Zaki, tell Rashidi to wait. Have you finished your homework? Tonight I am going to be late, maybe quite late.' Zaki looked disappointed that Ade had not eaten the moinmoin. 'Oh, your moinmoin is the best in the world but when the heart is empty sadness fills the stomach. Talking of stomach what will you eat tonight?'

'Eba sir,' said Zaki.

'Again?'

'Better pass elubo sir.'

278

'Who told you that?' said Ade.

'Stomach of Zaki, sir.'

Rashidi's toot cut short the burst of laughter. Ade rushed to the car, but in his haste forgot the figurine and Zaki must have brought the larger one.

Ade shoved the statuette back zipped up the bag, stepped into the shadows to hide from the old Guinnessophile swaying back up the road. Ade must have fallen asleep again because his sticky eyes opened to a towering Moji. Wearing a pale tabard over a checked shirt, sleeves rolled above elbow, from a shoulder hung a brown bag with Ade's satchel in the other hand.

'What are you doing here?' Moji sounded both angry and tired, her shoulders hunched and eyes baggy.

'I'll go then, give me space,' Ade said, and scrambled upright in his boldest bluff. 'That bag is mine.'

Moji hopped back and flipped the carving out of the bag. 'Ah,' she said, made a crunchy sound, replaced the carving with ironic caution and shoved the satchel at Ade. 'Go then.'

'No way am I going except taken by earthquake Richter scale 1020. How are you?'

'Been better.'

Better because she was sick? Better than expected? Better without him? Better with someone else? 'That is good,' Ade said and crept forward to narrow the void between them.

'Not good, better.'

Was that irritation, or fatigue in her eyes? Lagos boy, make a move, last chance. Moji did not resist when he guided her past the shop in to her room. They sat side by side in the weak light. Ade caught the silvery tear

279

glowing on her cheek and licked it off his fingertip. 'Now, it will grow inside until I explode, and you'll be arrested for love poisoning.'

'How will they know it was me?'

'Pathologist will report that this corpse's heart tapped out the name, Mo-ji, Mo-ji during the post-mortem. Listen. Three into one is one. It was exactly twelve days and fifteen hours ago that I left Lekki.'

'But what of your baby? You said...'

Ade shook his head. 'Yeni wants to punish me, won't let me see the baby when it comes but I'll fight for that child with all the armed forces in my heart. In one way I owe it this chance with you.' The child, for whom Ade wanted to give his life, in a sense came to save its father from its mother. 'Yeni waited until she was pregnant before she threw me out.' Though grateful for his freedom rejection hurt and recalled the long months spent yearning for his mother to come back for him when he was six years old. When she didn't Ade's heart turned to stone against her.

'That is harsh, but what if...'

'You mean what if she had a miscarriage? Yeni will blame the stars, you, me Iya, her mother, you again, juju, the moon, everybody and everything. Park Yeni to one side. I came here for you.'

'To deploy the same armed forces from your heart?'

Ade raised his hands. 'For you I come unarmed, with love.'

Moji snuggled up and chuckled. 'Ade, without you I will dry up like that imported stockfish.'

'That looks like a mummy?' Drawn by her sunflower eyes and coy smile, he hugged her tight. She put her arms round him and he fizzed in her aroma, and to the sough of her breath, and her kiss, and the urgent press of her softer thigh. As he got as near to making love as made only the cruellest difference, Moji slid away. His hands dropped, and yearning splashed into steamy but not terminal disappointment, because in her eyes he saw flickering, promise.

Forty

Loud banter, rustling of grass brooms sweeping the ground, the plangent calls of street hawkers and a smoke-tinged petrichor wafted through Iya's front door. Ade kneeled on Iya's favourite wooden stool and gazed out of the front window. In the distance, bare-backed, yellow-helmeted workers put the finishing touches to the plumbing in Jinadu Recreational Park on land Ade leased to the State.

He shoved his new Law textbooks under the stool and resumed his restless pacing. Hurry up Moji, hurry up child, daddy waits. Lagos boy, lucky boy so soon a father again and dampness rose to his eyes. Weeks earlier, ready to drop, Yeni came to the village to order then beg Ade to come back, but on sighting Moji in the front room she exploded into a colossal jealous rage. 'Only two minutes you leave Lekki and you find another woman, a prisoner for that matter. Is this the best thing you can do? All that money? Sheeoh, typical Lagos man. Cannot last five minutes without a woman. Give him another five minutes and he bounces to another like basketball.' The rant gathered momentum until right there on Iya's threshold with Ade pleading for restraint, Yeni's waters burst. Ade rushed her to Expresscare. The baby boy Ade later called Jinadu, after great-great-grandfather, but Yeni insisted on calling Mowe, because Chief said so, arrived at ten seconds to ten o'clock that Tuesday evening. Yeni refused to let Ade into the labour ward. Distraught, Ade drove home alone in a brewing thunderstorm and wept into his pillow. Weeks later, in an unprecedented U-turn, Yeni brought the little boy to the village - a mark of respect and to bond with his daddy, she said. Ade was not deceived. With Moji pregnant, Yeni brought her son to claim priority to his paternal estate.

Exhausted by a day of wary anticipation, Ade sat back and scratched an itch in his close-cropped hair - he'd long shaved his beard and discarded the skin-lightening cream but not the thick-rimmed glasses. This baby had better hurry. Had it not put its mother through enough? The doctors said apart from Moji's narrow birth canal they foresaw no problems. What if they were wrong, and she developed complications? What if the baby rushed out too fast or put on a neonatal impression of an incumbent politician and stayed *kampe*, refusing to disentangle itself from profitable attachments, or because it has the foresight to anticipate painful teething and potty training, teenage heartbreak and external exams, and immolating clashes between conflicting emotions, to a future with parents who pretend to know what they are doing when they don't and the baby said no thank you I get everything I want in here fresh and delivered to my doorstep - why start again at the bottom on a crowded polluted planet?

Ade's phone startled him. He'd forgotten he left it on the window-sill behind him.

'Any progress?' said Baba Lawyers. 'This suspense is stretching my struts.'

'Hey baby you stretch my struts. I'll teach my boy that line one day, when he's ten. Start early that's where I went wrong.' Ade's boy with Yeni was three months old.

'And the girl will slap his cheeks off his face,' said Baba Lawyers. 'Keep me posted will you? Must dash. Might get to see my boy. Thanks for the contacts. My boy's agreed to see me, but whether to kiss or bite me, who knows?'

'It's this can-do mentality of yours that will help land grandmothers on Mars,' said Ade. 'I wish you'd told me. We could have found him much earlier if I'd known.'

'I know, before all the brouhaha of the election. What's happening? Buhari made the right noises during the campaign but that was months ago, and we still don't have a working cabinet. Man used to be a soldier. I've seen more dynamism from a botoxed corpse.'

'And that's because you focused on the maggots,' said Ade. In May 2015, with Ebola long defeated, deaths not reaching past three figures - thanks to Dr Adadevoh's sacrifice, and to Prof Kosimbe and his team - Bola's PDP party lost the Presidential election. The victor, APC's Buhari, a former soldier pretending to civility won in the first peaceful transfer of power from one governing party to the other in Nigeria.

'Some say that's because he packed his cabinet with the descendants of the same people foisted on the rest of the country by your vengeful or well-meaning people…'

'Before our reluctant, or, was it, gleeful, retreat?' said Baba Lawyers. 'Depends on which books you read.' 'But getting back to your lot. Did the PDP lot not do the same thing when they were in power? Will anything change? Don't blame us. You've had plenty of practice these last fifty years or so?'

'Fifty years is not long compared to a thousand for some other countries.' Ade swallowed his reflex pique. Sardonic or not, Baba Lawyers was right. Africa is the manufacturing centre for plausible excuses. Exchanged for imported solutions. Would anything change after this election? Yes, for sure the sun will still rise and open its golden eye every day over Lagos without asking a senator or anyone else for a bribe. But will the masses, vendors, doctors, lawyers, engineers, surveyors, PhDs and illiterates, civil servants in white shirts and snaking ties still have to snatch out of whatever little sleep they've had inches away from the snoring generators, to crawl off sweat-soaked mats, to push and shove, curse, and fight to scramble onto bursting buses every day, the toll of promises unrequited etched on sooty faces and, on wizened shoes? Do the leaders not see weary market women struggling to make a crust from nubs of emaciated peanuts? They don't see the cachectic young women staggering under sandwich boards promising visas and fresh visages to everlasting erections or do they not see pot-navelled kids, armed with tattered sponges tapping on car windows, miming hunger and begging to clean windscreens? Do they not see the best-paid legislators in the universe fart in the faces of their people and vote themselves juicier allowances? And by 2020 will bright and cheerful children on their way to school still weave pelotons through the hordes, oblivious to their fate, that they, like generations before, will grow up to support on shiny black backs, grow up only to inhabit, not inherit it, this idea called Nigeria, or, unfed or fed up, yearn it to escape?

'Buhari will do what he likes, appoint friends to the finance and the arms departments, and appoint Cordelia Minister of the Interiors,' said Ade.

'Who is Cordelia?' said Baba Lawyers.

'Old friend.' Ade cringed at the memory of those reckless days. Baba Lawyers' search for his family sent Malomo to mind. What if she marched in to demand the

285

house? Should he hand over the keys or say vamoose? But what if Malomo crept in looking miserable and defeated, jaundiced eyes yellower than tangerine rind and skin as droopy on her arms as the sleeves of a cassock, could he avoid breaking down and giving her a weepy hug, falling at her feet in penitence for starting the whole saga with that big mouth when he was a boy of six? But what if Malomo walked in, as if nothing had happened, as if she had only just popped out for the papers these last eighteen, nineteen years and abducted by alcohol and misfortune and shuffled through the door, arms as stiff as those of a geriatric member of a Soviet Politburo, not swaying, knotted hair bunched into thick clumps, and sat, asked for Saro and Iya and for a glass of goat's milk? What then? Don't judge people said Iya, every action is a reason trying to get out. Maybe he should seize the initiative and look for her before she found him. Was she alive?

Zaki's loud knock shoved Ade's thoughts aside and in charged the boy, shirttail flying fashionably over his shorts. 'Is everything ok? You said you have madam where you want her, sir,' he said.

'Just where did I say I wanted her?' said a bemused Ade.

'In labour, sir.'

Ade chuckled. 'It was my plan yes. And it worked.' Was that a hint of a naughty grin on the boy's face? Ade gave the boy a playful shove on the back. 'Go, I will shout if we want you.' Ade leapt into the back room. Vinyl carpet creaked underfoot, and he smelt disinfectant.

'These must be the real contractions, deep,' Moji said, her face suffused with pain, and with the grace of a

286

listing super tanker she waddled around the bed in a flowery blue maternity gown.

Ade's chest swelled with pride for his adorable Moji, just as desirable as ever. King of kinky from Kakirikiri she called him the other day. Sick with worry he put his arm around her and dabbed her forehead with a towel. 'Are you ok? Should I get a taxi? Maybe I will call Rashidi, or get Baba Ologba to bring his ambulance, the van or the hatchback. Or should we say whichever taxi or van gets here first?'

Moji mooed, grunted, looked at her belly and held her hands out. 'Do I look as if I care how I get there by omolanke or molue as long as this pain goes now, now?'

'Don't make that noise. The baby may drop.' said Ade, fanning her face with his hand.

Moji gingerly lowered herself on to the bed and closed her eyes. 'You must be the special commissioner for the ministry of talking nonsense in labour.' She puffed. 'Of course, I am ok, I just enjoy shouting because I don't have better things to do.' She moaned again. 'Ooh,' she said and closed her eyes. 'I think this time it has come.' Beads of sweat jostled for space on her forehead.

Fear gave his voice a croaky quality. 'Midwife said you should slow the breathing.'

'And what did she tell you to do?'

'Should I call Mama Ibeji?' said Zaki in a worried whisper, poking his head through the door.

Ade clapped his hands hard to emphasise the urgency. 'Call her, call anybody,' he said, as a matted wet furriness appeared between Moji's legs. 'Hey, I see something.' Respect. Even Malomo did this? Iya too?

The cut must have made it so much worse. 'I see something coming.'

Moji growled and waved him away. 'Ade. Just stand far over there, better for us both and Mama Ibeji when she comes, you hear me? Go and read one of your books.' With a long grunt, she pressed a clenched fist into the bed. Tortuous veins gathered on her temples, and her face. Her belly domed, the baby's slimy crown emerged an inch, stopped, as if for a rest, or as if still considering its options.

Where was this Mama Ibeji woman? Ade washed his hands with soap and water in the basin and squeezed into a pair of Mama Ibeji's gloves which were so tight they made his hands look like trowels. He wheeled around just in time to see the baby's peeping crown turn - a slow quarter circle to its mother's left thigh. 'It's coming,' he said and in terrifying excitement he crouched, his hands held out in those small gloves for a catch he dared not drop. Out slid a glistening shoulder, then came a rasp and a glug, imagined or real he could not be sure, and the baby stopped. 'What's happening?' said Moji.

Shit of no nation. The baby's head had turned blue-black, hung limp and its delicate eyelids swelled. Whipped by terror Ade's heart reared up and up in force and rate of beat. Ade tore the gloves off his sweaty hands and called Mama Ibeji. 'Where are you? Where are you? How far?'

'Oga, why are you calling me now at this juncture? Was it not madam who said she will not need me and will go to Expresscare?'

'Madam? Which madam?' he said, then with realisation he exploded into hateful anger. 'It was not my madam here who phoned you. Please help me. It was coming out, then stopped. Please I am begging you. Take a taxi or okada whichever is faster please.'

'Can you see the head?' she said. The experienced midwife sounded muffled, as if she was getting dressed.

'Yes, I see the head but no movement.'

'Tell madam to raise her legs.'

'Moji darling, can you put your legs up, now, please Mama Ibeji is nearly here.' He wiped sweat and tears from his eyes.

'Mama, nothing is happening,' said Ade, his voice a sob and a squeak, his baby a foot away, dying, its face bloated and ugly.

'Ok press just under the left hip bone, but gently, oh.'

Gently? How else when he did not have enough strength in his fingers to tap a thread.

'What did she say?' said Moji, her hand came up and crashed back.

Ade had not heard from his love for an eon. Hang on Moji, love, Moji hang in. When he wobbled the mound under the other hip nothing happened. Blood dripped from Moji's swollen tongue. 'Maybe raise your legs against your stomach one inch more darling, now please, if you can manage, don't push. Now I will try shaking here as Mama Ibeji said.' Ade felt a give, a slither and heard a hiss or rasp. Was that real or him again slipping into hapless daydreaming? 'It's coming, truly but I don't want to say too much.' The lower shoulder appeared. 'No, wait, don't help,' he said. The baby's head turned, and the other shoulder followed with a slippery momentum. Fresh air fanned into Ade's baking lungs. 'It is a girl.' Ade grabbed his bloodied goddess in his bare hands, and she opened her sticky eyes, blinked, thrust out her mini-feet and brayed once then one long exhausted but exhilarating cry and little by little her tiny purple fingertips turned dusky pink. In scampered an untidily dressed Mama Ibeji. 'Na wa o, for madam Yeni oh,' she said as she rolled up her sleeves. 'But you did well, very well.' Ade flopped, trembling, on to the bed in delayed shock. How could Yeni do this? Such tremendous stamina for animosity.

Brimming with love and pride, as he clasped his treasure to his chest, this tiny human carved out of love by love for him to love each nano-bit of her he became as one indissoluble whole with an exquisite sonority, a musical harmony lifting from and with his heart, more sumptuous and inspiring than ever he experienced on the track. Ade looked to the sky. Iya, cry for me no more, my dreams, those long shots in the dark through wishful thinking have come true, laugh for me, poke fun at me for crying because, thanks to you, the flying paintbrush is a loser no more.

Glossary

Abi?- is it not so, is it not the case?

Agbada-free flowing outer robe of suit worn in West Africa

Agbako-accident, misfortune

Ajebutter-spoilt child

Amala- a thick dark paste made from yam skin

Apakati-mayhem

Babalawo-traditional herbalist, literally father of the mysteries

Baboosh-destroy, render to zero

Buba- loose shirt that goes halfway down the thighs

Commot- come out, off, away

Craw craw-itchy rash

Dabaru-Spoil, undermine

Dem- they

Dey-does

Eba-pasty staple made from fried grated cassava or gari.

Efor-vegetable dish

Elubo-same as amala, thick paste made from yam skin.

Eyin Iya a da oh- May Iya have a great legacy

Eyo-costumed dancers, or masquerades that come out during the Eyo festival. The Eyo masquerades represent the spirits of the ancestors.

Fufu-dough made from boiled and ground plantain or cassava, used as a staple food in parts of West and central Africa.

Gangan-a lot

Gele-Woman's head wrap

Haba-is a mild expletive like heck

Idejo family- according to tradition the land of Lagos belongs to this family

Iro-wrapper

Jaguda-loutish

Jambodi-rough bodily contact, higgledy-piggledy

Jeje-quietly, minding own business

Jumat- Friday prayers

Kampe-strong, durable

Koni koni girls-loose, fast girls

Ko tan- see what you brought on yourself

Lai lai-never

Mago mago- dodgy, underhand, chicanery

Mende-mende-precious, butter won't melt demeanour

Moinmoin- a form of bean cake

Moinmoin elemi meje-bean cake garnished with seven other ingredients/spices, fish, snails, beef, peppers etc.

Molue- a small bus, with two columns of seats which seats three people on one row and two on the other word believed to come from remould, as in remould the other buses if they get in the way.

Mugun-fool

Mumu-fool

Na wa oh- a term expressing surprise or astonishment

Obe-gravy

Obokun-a type of catfish and gave its name to the 280s Mercedes saloon of the 1970s

Oga-boss or mister

Ogboju-braveheart, effrontery

O jare- a curt dismissive phrase.

Okada-often a motorcycle taxi, named after an airline.

O mase o - what a pity

Omolanke-pushcart

Omoluwabi- is a person of honour or integrity who believes in hard work and respects the rights of others and gives to the community.

Oya-come on, let's go sometimes reinforced with the phrase *o jare*

Oyinbo-white people or pale foreigners in general

Patapata-completely

Penke-prick, alec, know-all

Sabi-understand, know, awareness of

Scalpulates-loses her hair

Shebi- can mean that is it, yes, I agree, don't you agree?

Sisi –Miss

Sokoto-baggy trousers often worn with buba

Sura-chapter or section of the Koran

Tanda-stand there like a plank or oaf

Wahala-trouble

Wallahi tallahi-Arabic term adopted for use in West Africa to indicate an oath

Wetin-what

Yansh-gluteals

Yeye-nonsense, something immaterial, irrelevant, flim flam

ACKNOWLEDGEMENTS

Thank you family and friends for making me laugh out loud, even when my heart was bare. I am grateful to the staff at Epsom and at Marsden Hospitals, and to the NHS front line for not letting life have it all its own way.

Sola Odemuyiwa is a cardiologist in Surrey.
Also by Sola:
Deadly Conception
The Pregnant Mule
The Line in the Sand

Thank you for buying Ade, The Flying Paintbrush. I am grateful and hope my efforts provided a pleasant distraction. Please share the book with friends and family by posting on social media and I hope that you could take some time to post a review on Amazon. Your feedback helps me improve as a writer. You can follow this link: https://amazon.co.uk

Your review is important. Thank you.

Printed in Great Britain
by Amazon